NO WOMEN
WERE HARMED

NO WOMEN WERE HARMED

HEATHER MOTTERSHEAD

SPHERE

SPHERE

First published in Great Britain in 2025 by Sphere

1 3 5 7 9 10 8 6 4 2

A CIP catalogue record for this book
is available from the British Library.

Hardback ISBN 978-1-4087-3093-5
Trade paperback ISBN 978-1-4087-3100-0

Typeset in Garamond by M Rules
Printed and bound in Great Britain by
Clays Ltd, Elcograf S.p.A.

Papers used by Sphere are from well-managed forests
and other responsible sources.

MIX
Paper | Supporting
responsible forestry
FSC® C104740

Sphere
An imprint of
Little, Brown Book Group
Carmelite House
50 Victoria Embankment
London EC4Y 0DZ

The authorised representative
in the EEA is
Hachette Ireland
8 Castlecourt Centre
Dublin 15, D15 XTP3, Ireland
(email: info@hbgi.ie)

An Hachette UK Company
www.hachette.co.uk

www.littlebrown.co.uk

PROLOGUE

And so, I am mad after all. If all the beaks and screws who have had the misfortune to incarcerate me were given a bible, they could all attest to my insanity without fear of eternal repercussions.

The asylum superintendent believes that divine intervention will end our assorted plights: every morning we must endure his turgid preaching and, even if he forgoes the excesses of the Old Testament, he continues to bludgeon us with the Apostles. I fear I can quote Luke chapter and verse, and if 'lunatic, heal thyself' can become the mantra for my salvation, it is not altogether unattributable to that saintly being.

Yet, I cannot heal, it is too late. I knew my course of action was madness and still I took it, never veered from it, even though death was the inexorable outcome. In heat and in anger and, yes, in love, I trod that dreadful course, each painful and wonderful step of it.

The shackles gouge my wrists, disturbing the scars of Strangeways Prison's fetters. But no matter: if I bleed, I will not die. I am already dead.

CHAPTER ONE

I wake bone-cold: a thief has stolen my bedclothes. It is as black as hell in here save for the paltry white glow from the attendants' station. I feel my way down my bed and find the covers wedged between my bed frame and mattress. I drag them up to my chin and swaddle myself as best as I can. The sheets are stiff and offer little comfort, but at least they are clean. Matron is very particular about the cleanliness of her linen, but the blankets, being woollen, invariably smell of second-hand death. On the wall of the laundry, a framed sampler proclaims that 'what cannot be boiled must remain soiled'. Both Matron and the superintendent favour the embroidered adage; Matron leans towards the practical, the superintendent the spiritual. When I have inherited the earth and am in my shroud, it will undoubtedly be starched and laundered.

I stretch my legs and touch another's skin: it is Elise. She has pushed her bed next to mine, but the attendants have chosen to ignore this transgression. Elise is a hopeless case: the best sanatoriums in Europe have failed, force-feeding has failed, and so here she is, at the foot of a lunatic's bed, curled up like an emaciated foetus. Since her committal she has sought only my company, whereas I, in all my years here, have sought none. I think she derives some kinship from my accent, and I cannot deny her that comfort. I put my arm around her and stroke her flame hair, as if she were a child.

Soon daylight will no longer be denied; it creeps from behind the blackout curtains with its false promise of a glittering day. From the infirmary come the renewed sounds of coughing and moaning. In the bowels of the building, screams and rantings are supplanted by a sudden silence. Soon the first bell will sound. Here, we live and die by the bells: bells to get up; bells to pray; bells to eat; bells to work; bells to sleep; and bells to shit.

At the sound of the bell the curtains are drawn back and the ward's gas lights are lit; I shield my eyes from their intrusive glare. The yawning night attendants emerge from the attendants' station and unlock the ward doors, eager to escape to their beds, and two of the day attendants, Rowse and Clarke, enter the ward with their early morning smiles and their soapy bowls and towels ready to give a daily wash and brush-up to those who cannot walk to the washroom. Clarke is only in her twenties but is already a veteran of four asylums, but Rowse is a recent recruit and is too soft for this place and in a few months she will scamper back to the West Country. I can see her, back where she belongs, with her face pressed against the udder of her favourite cow, her nimble fingers teasing out the creamy liquid and squirting it rhythmically into a wooden bucket. She has the red hair and porcelain skin of her Celtic ancestors; age has not yet painted her face with broken veins, and only her hands are marked with the pox scars of her trade.

Two of the old biddies, Queenie and Maggie, pull their sheets over their heads and feign sleep. They should both be in the geriatrics' ward, but Matron, although usually a stickler for rules, is loath to move them from the neurotics' ward, as they have both been here for years, before even the superintendent, and he has been here for ever. They have always had beds opposite each other but are not friends. 'Foul-mouthed harridan,' says Queenie. 'Stuck-up bitch,' Maggie flings back, every day, for years and years, but their mutual animosity and riling up the attendants with their truculence is the only pleasure that they have these days.

'Now, Queenie,' says Rowse, 'I know you are not asleep. Just a quick wash and a look at your nails and skin.'

'It was done yesterday,' says Queenie from beneath the covers.

'Rules say you must have a wash every morning, Queenie. It's for your own good. Cleanliness is next to Godliness. Do you want me to get Miss Clarke to see to you instead?'

Queenie flings away the covers and sits bolt upright, holding out her arms and lifting her face for inspection like a client in one of those new beauty salons I have seen advertised in the *Leeds Mercury*.

'That's my girl,' says Rowse, as if she is addressing one of her cows, and Queenie submits to the ritual without further complaint. She's not a bad old stick really, not like her nemesis, who will snarl and occasionally spit at you and whose mind, they say, has been addled by syphilis. Nobody knows why she is called Queenie, but I suspect it is because of the way she crooks her little finger when she drinks her tea or how she holds her shoulders back and looks down her nose at you, which is remarkable considering she is five foot nothing. Rowse, who should know better and will be reprimanded if Matron finds out, has confided that Queenie was diagnosed with melancholia way back in the sixties. They say she lost her love or her child or both and now she has wailed and bled and dried up without offspring.

At half-past seven the second bell rings and I walk with the rest of the able-bodied patients to the refectory for a quick sermon and a blessing for the food on our plates for which we must be truly thankful. Breakfast is as regulated as our lives – five ounces of bread, half an ounce of butter and a pint of coffee, not a drop more or an ounce less – but it is much more than I sometimes had in the lean times. At half-past eight, a bell summons us back to the ward until another at nine o'clock sends us to the airing courts for our morning constitutional. When we return, the attendants are leaving the ward with their dusters and dirty mops and, as it is a Tuesday, the dirty bed linen from fifty beds has been deposited in a large basket in the corner of the ward ready to be wheeled to the laundry; the combined odours of sweat and vomit reach my nose before I see it. Elise and the other bedridden patients, excused the airing courts, are sitting up in their clean bed linen eating a cold breakfast, oblivious to the smell that is emanating from the corner of the room. They say that smell is the first sense that you lose in your dotage. Perhaps it is the same for those who have no sense at all.

'Say goodbye to your friends,' says Rowse to them; they wave to us, although I am by no means certain that they know who we are.

It is my fifth year of toil in the laundry and ironing rooms; but one day soon I shall be free of it all. I tell myself that every day, for I am as sane as the next woman, although in here, unfortunately, the next woman is probably mad. But, for now, I am one of the seven in ten female patients who labour with swollen hands and red, dripping faces in the steam and the filth, boiling napery, sheets and, worst of all, nightshirts and drawers soiled with every shade of God knows what. It is like being back in the prison laundry and I sometimes feel like an inmate rather than a patient. Work, sleep, work, but this time with added prayers and the shit of the incontinent, although without the everyday threat of violence, both from inmates and jailers. Every day I scoop everything into the coppers, where it boils merrily for hours, and then I haul it all back out and feed it through the mangle, where it has the life squeezed out of it. Then everything is rinsed and then back through a mangle before it is out on the line to dry and then back in, stiff as boards from the starch, for ironing. Week after week, month after month, I feed my copper the same filthy laundry. In winter, the laundry will not dry outside and must be brought inside to be draped over lines until we are all nearly blinded by the steam, but nonetheless grateful for the warmth of the room. But in summer, the sheets flap on the line like clipper sails and by the time I peg them all out the first sheets are nearly dry. On those days I take my time pegging out the washing, as back inside the laundry I will once again sweat like an old sow; on those days I imagine being in my own home, pegging out only two embroidered sheets instead of hundreds with *Property of Sunnyside Asylum* stamped upon them, until I am summoned inside by an attendant who has been sent in search of me. But it is Superintendent Sharp's edict that working in this inferno will double a female patient's penance and hasten a cure, and, as he is an esteemed medical man and oversees the whole asylum, who am I to doubt that?

It has been rumoured that we laundresses have become so efficient in our work that the asylum, to boost its coffers, is to take in washing from local hotels. I am unsure how their patrons will feel about their tablecloths having been washed in the same coppers as some lunatic's undergarments. After all, patronage of the afflicted is all well and good as long as it is kept at arm's length.

The male patients are spared laundry work and get to work in the fresh air or in the asylum bakery. But, except for a twice-daily airing, the female patients are kept inside; it is almost as if we cannot be shown to the world and should be doubly ashamed of our madness and our deviance from the female ideal. From the laundry window I can see the men in the gardens, mowing and digging and soaking in the rays of the spring sunshine; and even in the winter, when the ground is as hard as bell-iron and their spades bounce off the unforgiving earth, their bodies muffled against the cold – even then I envy them their outdoor freedom. But look is all any of us can do, since male and female patients inhabit separate wings of the asylum. We never get within touching distance of each other lest we are overcome with passion, apart from in church, where we are separated by the aisle, or at the Christmas and New Year shindigs, where we must behave or be threatened with being banned from future entertainments.

There are some new patients in the laundry today, sent to the asylum for a few months by their doctors or more likely their families, who either cannot or will not pay for a private sanatorium.

They huddle together, some of them holding hands, until the attendants tell them to step away from each other. They have a variety of afflictions to which women seem to be particularly susceptible: they may be frigid or too lascivious, or too timid or too outspoken, or be grieving to excess for the loss of a child or a husband. There is a long, long list, but if the latter were a barometer for a diagnosis of melancholia then our dear old Queen should have been committed years ago. Instead she gets to live in luxury and rule an empire. That's life for you.

The newcomers hang around the boiling coppers awaiting instructions and vowing, if they ever escape, to behave in the way that society expects and never again be sent to this hellish place. I suspect it is a ploy by the superintendent to shock these new delinquents into conformity before commencing any other treatment; I would say it works very well.

One of the long-term patients holds up a sheet to her nose and breathes in the impregnated sweat. 'Smells just like my first husband Fred,' she says. 'Takes me back to when we were first wed, when we couldn't keep our hands off each other. Had loads of washing to do then, didn't need any starch afterwards on his nightshirts. Or was it the butcher when we couldn't pay the meat bill? I forget. It must have been nearly every fortnight I didn't have enough money for the butcher.' Her cronies laugh and follow her as she walks over and elbows me in the ribs and says, 'How about you, Lily? What about your lovers? Or did you kill them all off?'

I ignore her and start to put another load into the copper. It did not take long for word of my conviction to spread around; at least it means my reputation has gone before me and most of the patients who work in here avoid me. The woman's statement is truer than she can know, of course, but as far as anyone knows I am here to serve out my sentence for grievous bodily harm against one man, and that is more than I ever intended anyone to find out. But the other thing, the mention of lovers, has set me thinking about feelings that I thought long buried. Titus has always been there of course, in a small box in the corner of my mind, threatening to sneak out. They say you never forget your first love and I will never forget Titus, but I am never going to share him with these women, to pull apart and sully with their lewd thoughts.

'I hear you slit his throat from ear to ear,' she says, making a motion around her throat with the laundry tongs.

She seems determined to have her two penn'orth, so I say, 'I was convicted of wounding but I am entirely innocent.'

She laughs and says, 'That's what they all say in here. Just as they say they are not mad.'

'Well, then, perhaps you had better watch your back – the conviction was with intent. What are you in for, anyway? I expect you are not just a regular lunatic. I would say perhaps you master-minded a robbery, but you are too slow to catch a cold. The only thing that is not idle is your tongue.'

'You want to watch I don't shove you into that copper with all the other shitty stuff,' she says.

I put down my load of dirty linen and, arms folded, take a step towards her so that we are barely two feet apart and I can hear her quick breaths. Her cronies, one by one, step back from her until she is left standing on her own, like a shepherd without a flock.

'And just how do you plan to shove me in there?' I say. 'Your entourage seem to have deserted you.'

The newcomers hide behind the ironing boards in the ironing room and start to whimper. Two attendants who have been gossiping by the laundry door rush over and set their bodies between us. 'Get back to work,' says one of them. 'It's too hot in here for you lot to be starting something.'

The woman shuffles back to her copper and makes a hand gesture towards me behind the retreating attendants. One of the regulars from the ironing room walks over and says, 'Are you all right? That Polly is a right piece of work, rough as a bear's arse. Just ignore her. Let me help you with those filthy sheets. You'll do yourself a mischief lifting all that into that copper on your own. You need to let somebody else help you sometimes.'

I thank her but confirm that I will be perfectly fine on my own. And I *am* on my own. I have no family and no friends. I have acquaintances – Elise, Queenie, and even Maggie – but they are not friends, even if they may wish to be. She shrugs her shoulders and walks back to the ironing room, and I shove another load of the filthy stuff into the boiling copper.

CHAPTER TWO

It is Sunday, our day of rest, although it is a day as regimented as the rest of the week, otherwise the devil will no doubt take particular interest in the idle hands of the weak-minded. But there is at least no physical labour for the patients: the superintendent is a keen observer of the Sabbath. Except for those who work in the kitchens, for even on a Sunday we must be fed. I have yet to be deployed to the kitchen, although I have requested the move from Matron on several occasions, reasoning that I have been diligent in the laundry. Matron says that the next step up for me would be a move to the sewing room and that there is a long waiting list for kitchen work, what with the prestige of being trusted with food preparation and the titbits that she knows we lunatics steal. But I expect her reticence has something to do with the proximity of kitchen knives.

We and the geriatrics' ward are the first sitting in church, two wards squeezed into the five rows of pews built for sixty people. Queenie, Maggie and Elise have been excused attendance, and will take the sacrament from the vicar, for, as it is a Sunday,

Superintendent Sharp has been replaced by a real vicar, in their beds. It smells like the church of my childhood: polish, musty hymn books and long-dead flowers. If I close my eyes, I am back there, its cool limestone walls permeated by generations of marriages, christenings and funerals, and, outside, the small graveyard with rows of the same surnames on the gravestones: generations of farmers and their offspring given back to the soil. But this church has known only one wealthy family until we, the family of lunatics, a loose gathering of even looser minds, claimed it as our own. The only perk for church attendance is the communion wine, the only drop of alcohol we get, and the vicar often has to prise the chalice from our grasp; there is always a bit of a rush to get to the front of the queue in case the wine should run out. But the patients need not worry: a quarter of the attendees are Catholic and there is no way they will be imbibing the wine of the heretic.

The church is at least two hundred years old, and dates from before the old house was demolished to build the house that became the asylum. The original owner, who owned hundreds of acres of land, had had the church built towards the end of his life. The story goes that it was built as an indulgence, even though he was not of the Catholic faith, but I suppose he reasoned any port in a storm to obtain forgiveness for the youthful sin of having the village that once stood here obliterated to provide hunting grounds for his estate. The grounds are much smaller now of course, only about twenty acres, but enough to keep all us lunatics of every type fenced in and hidden for fear that our madness might offend the sensibilities of decent, normal folk.

I am a hysteric, a term derived from the Greek for uterus: I am an emotional slave to my biology. *Hysteria*, the prison doctor wrote in bold red letters on my transfer papers. Mad as a hatter, they said behind my back. Or that is what they told me afterwards when I was sent to the neurotics' ward, having been in the padded cells at the back of the psychotics' ward for two weeks following my initial confinement in the seclusion cells. It was all a blur at the time: one moment I was in Strangeways at Her Majesty's pleasure with seven years to go until freedom, and next I was in here for God knows how long. I did not know that at first, having assumed I would be released from the asylum at the end of my sentence, just as I would have been from prison. I was all set to be let out the Christmas of '98, counting down the days – six years, ten months and three days, it was – imagining a Christmas tree with presents beneath and mince pies cooking in the oven and maybe even someone for whom I could knit or sew a Christmas present. It was day attendant Clarke who told me; her mouth was and still is as dribbly as those in the geriatrics' ward, despite Matron's insistence on discretion. She said she thought I knew that I had to prove my sanity to be released, thought Matron or Strangeways' governor would have told me, and that she was sorry I had to find out from her, with a smile that told me she was not sorry at all. It is now the January of 1897 and I should have less than two years to serve, but God knows when they will deem me sane enough to be released. I have not been in the seclusion cells for at least three years, and I am doing sterling work in the laundry; just ask Mrs Brown, the overseer. Yes sir, no sir, three laundry bags full, sir. Every month, I have asked Matron about my release date, but she says that I will have to wait and see, and I wonder if any of my good work has been recorded or whether it is only my previous bad behaviour that has found its way to the pages of my asylum notes. I raise my head and look towards the altar and offer God a little prayer for my release, although I doubt that He will pay any attention to the ramblings of a lunatic.

CHAPTER THREE

It has been three useless months since I started pestering Matron daily about my release. Thirteen weeks is sufficient time for a response to my request and I take this as a sign that she will never show any interest in that direction and so I have finally given up and taken to my bed. Not even the prospect of a bed bath or the indignity of having to be turned every day for fear of bed sores will coax me to get out of it. At night, Elise no longer crawls to the bottom of my bed for fear of being kicked on to the floor, and the nurses now sedate her so that she does not disturb the other patients with her wails. The doctors have poked and prodded my body, and the nurses have taken my temperature every day for a week. Dr Roberts has declared me physically well and diagnoses that I must have relapsed into hysteria. I have been prescribed three trips per day to the airing courts, but I refuse to budge, even though I crave fresh air. So, he lets me stay in bed, hoping that the rest will cure whatever ails me.

Nothing ails me that release would not cure. But if despite my efforts I am not to be released, I have decided that I might as well feign a malaise and loll around in bed for years like Elise; I will have my lily-white skin and my memories, at least for the moment, until, with age and medication, even they will disappear. I cannot say I have always been a model patient, I have never tolerated any non-sense from other patients or the attendants, but I could have played up much more than I did. Surely a sane person would rage against their treatment and only one numbed by opiates would yield to it? But placation has never been in my nature, not since I was a child and resented that I, more than any of my sisters, had no other choice than to attempt to diffuse my mother's pendulum moods. And my Titus could be a bit of a mardy bugger but at least he loved me, or I hope he did. And music hall customers always needed handling like children, especially when they were in their cups. I had thought when I was sent here that I was past all that subterfuge.

But I am sane enough to know I cannot carry on with this maudlin stuff for much longer or the doctors will decide to try another so-called cure on me or, worse, write 'incurable' on my medical records and damn me to a life in the institution, until I am as dribbly as the old biddies and life is as dull as the tea they give us. I can see those monochrome years stretching out in front of me, a procession of bells and meals and work and lights out at nine o'clock, until I am pushing up the daisies. I cannot let that happen. When Dr Roberts next does his rounds, I will say that I have considered his advice and am now much rested and wish to start his exercise regime. I will be walking every day with a view to returning to work greatly refreshed in a few weeks. He will scribble some words in my notes and be smug in the knowledge that his diagnosis has been vindicated.

When I have finished my treatment, I will work harder in the laundry and get myself noticed by making myself indispensable, and, since Matron has been of no assistance in pursuit of my release, in a few months I will appeal to a higher authority. Not God, who has, as I suspected, not answered any of my prayers, but Superintendent Sharp, who in this asylum has more powers than any God. In the daylight hours I will carry on with a false smile and a bitten tongue, and at night will try to stop the potential hopelessness of all my endeavours from seeping into my dreams.

CHAPTER FOUR

It has been four weeks since I took to my bed, and as I have adhered diligently to Dr Roberts' exercise schedule, I am now considered cured. I wake ready to embrace the day and the inevitable monotony it will bring.

The first bell has already sounded when Matron strides into the ward and walks over to my bed. Elise, buried under her bedclothes, continues her staccato sleep.

'Patient Day,' she says, turning her head from Elise, 'report to my office after your breakfast and airing.'

'I am due in the laundry,' I say.

'I have told Mrs Brown that you are excused duties for an hour or so. Half-past nine,' she says, with a jerk of her neck. Matron looks like a chick that has fledged too early. She is less than five feet tall and all bone and wire and jet-black hair.

'Of course,' I say to the top of her head.

Matron's office is in the oldest part of the building. It was the morning room in the old days and is situated at the end of a long wood-panelled corridor lined with portraits of the great and good of the asylum; the attendant hurries me along under their manly gaze. But despite the profusion of male portraits this is Matron's domain: on her door is a polished brass plaque with the word 'Matron' engraved on it, as if it is both her profession and her name; perhaps she likes it that way. I feel as if I have been summoned to the office of a stern headmistress without the faintest idea how I have erred, and half-expect there to be a well-worn slipper or cane situated somewhere behind her desk. I can imagine her, slipper in hand, telling the superintendent that the male patients can do as they please under the rule of the head male attendant but that her attendants, and the female charges in all six of her wards, will behave themselves.

We are ten minutes late, because I pretended that I needed to use the privy. We stand outside the door and listen to the hushed female voices within. 'Come in,' says Matron, before the attendant has an opportunity to knock on the door. We enter two abreast and loiter in the doorway until Matron says, 'That will be all, Davies. Come back in fifteen minutes. And next time, be on time.' Davies opens her mouth to protest but instead scowls at me and leaves the room muttering under her breath.

Turning to me, Matron says, 'Now, Miss Day – Lily – please sit,' indicating a chair by the door with her outstretched arm. The room smells of sunshine and beeswax, not the miasma of carbolic that we must endure. She remains seated behind an oak desk that threatens to swallow her; there is no cane or slipper to be seen. The interloper, a girl, stands silhouetted against the window. 'This is Dr Fairchild,' says Matron. 'The superintendent has taken a specific interest in your case, especially as the course of treatment prescribed for you by Dr Roberts has seen you much recovered from your recent episode. The superintendent has requested that you spend time with Dr Fairchild; she is a *psychiatrist.*' She enunciates every consonant, rolling the letters on her tongue to convince me of its import.

The doctor bounds over to my chair and extends her hand. She is a new breed, recently qualified from Durham University, she tells me. She is my age but is unlined and unsullied whereas I, with my death's head skull, have lived a thousand of her lifetimes. I take her hand until she is forced to pull it from my grasp.

'Lily,' says Matron, 'it has been agreed that you will regularly visit Dr Fairchild in a room here at Sunnyside, away from the wards. This is a special privilege. She will ask you to tell her about your life before you came here. It will be your chance to prove your sanity to Miss Fairchild, who will report her findings to the superintendent and the board.' She smiles at the girl, who blushes. 'You will of course be supervised by two attendants at every session.'

'Will that be satisfactory, Lily?' says the good doctor.

'Of course it will, won't it, Lily?' says Matron.

There is no free choice, we all know it: you would have to be mad to refuse such an opportunity. But is that not exactly what they have already declared me to be?

'I will think about it,' I say.

'Excellent,' says Dr Fairchild, clasping her hands together.

Davies knocks on the door and Matron barks at her to enter, declaring our meeting over and telling the attendant to escort me to the laundry. I want to skip down the corridor but there is nothing that looks madder than a grown woman skipping: there are a pair of old biddies from the geriatrics' ward who skip hand in hand around the airing courts, and I fear their regression to childhood is nearly complete. So, instead, I walk to the laundry with my chin on my chest to hide my smile, silently thanking whichever God has given me this opportunity for release, leaving Matron and my bluestocking doctor to concoct their plans for my rehabilitation.

CHAPTER FIVE

Two weeks later, on an afternoon in late March, I am seated, unfettered, in a small sitting room, and spring sunlight is streaming in through the bars of the small, high windows. The gardeners must be working on the lawn by the woods as the scents of pungent ramsons and newly mown grass are wafting in on a warm breeze. The room is painted forest-green, but at the door's edge the paint has cracked and flaked to reveal utilitarian grey, destroying the charade. Two leather upright chairs, old and slightly grubby, are placed in the centre of the room, separated by a small oak coffee table. A meagre fire burns in the cast-iron grate and a grandmother clock ticks away in the corner, announcing her presence every half of an hour.

There is a knock, and an arm pulls aside the damask curtains that have been masking the unlocked French windows and Dr Fairchild stoops under the doorframe and enters the room, her face the colour of beetroot. She takes off her mackintosh and hangs it on the hook by the door, then stands in front of the fire, warming her hands through her calfskin gloves.

'I walked from the station,' she says, by way of unnecessary explanation. She sits in the chair opposite mine, regaining her breath. 'Good afternoon, Miss Day. In these sessions, please call me Pomona. I am named after the Roman goddess of fruitfulness, not the immigrant ship bound for America that went down with over four hundred souls lost before it had barely left the shores of Liverpool. May I call you Lily?'

'Of course,' I say, for once glad I have a name that does not have to be painfully explained to every new acquaintance. She enquires whether I would like tea or coffee, as if we were a tableau of genteel ladies taking afternoon refreshments. I tell her my preference and she remarks that it is hers also. She removes her gloves; she has pale wrists, slim but strong, unmarked by life. Two attendants, neither of whom I have previously encountered but who by the look of them must be required to keep order in the psychotics' ward, sit behind me until Pomona calls for coffee with the flick of her wrist, and one of the attendants leaves the room in search of our refreshments, muttering as she brushes past my chair. A small bird, a wren or a finch, has squeezed though the bars of the far window and sits on the sill, walking from one side of it to the other every few minutes. When the attendant returns with the tray, the other attempts to shoo the bird away, but the window is too high and it remains on the sill, content to watch the proceedings unfold.

'Cream and sugar?' Pomona says, confident that a patient will not decline a rare treat.

'Black,' I reply.

She pours the steaming liquid into two china teacups decorated with red roses. She places the coffee pot on the tray, out of my reach. As she hands me the coffee, there is a slight rattle of the teacup in its saucer. 'I am afraid there are no biscuits. Cook informs me that we are all out,' she says.

'How remiss of her,' I say. She does not rise to the sarcasm.

'Now, Lily,' she says, taking out a gold fountain pen and unscrewing the lid; the nib is swollen with Indian ink, anxious to make its mark on the reams of crisp white paper that she has extracted from her briefcase, 'do you know why you are here?'

'I was transferred here from prison.'

'I mean why you are here in this room?'

'You asked for me to be brought here.'

'Yes, but *why* did I request that you be brought here?' She pushes two stray strands of blonde hair behind her right ear and begins to write on the naked sheets with long, looping strokes.

'It seems you believe that I can be cured of my insanity.'

'And is that what *you* believe?'

'I believe that you believe I can be,' I say.

She writes what looks like a huge question mark on her paper; it is ugly and spoils the lines of her neat handwriting. 'I understand that my predecessor, Dr Ledbetter, saw you on two occasions in the infirmary. Did he never encourage you to work through your feelings, to purge yourself of bad memories?'

I am less confident than my doctor that talking through my feelings will act as an emotional emetic, despite what Herr Breuer theorises. And yet, for a lunatic, one treatment is just as good as any other. I wonder if she is prepared for the deluge that may ensue.

She waits for my answer, screwing and unscrewing the top

of her gold pen. She takes a sip of her coffee. I attempt to drink mine, but, unadulterated by cream, it is still piping hot, and scalds my throat. The clock strikes the half-hour and one of the attendants shifts her weight from one foot to the other and glances at her pocket watch. High on the windowsill, the bird is asleep on its wing.

'I'm afraid Dr Ledbetter and I really didn't see eye to eye,' I say.

'And why was that?'

'Things fell apart when I tried to poke out one of his.'

'Now, Lily, I know that is not true,' she says, scolding me like an errant child. 'I have read all your notes.' But she edges her body to the back of her chair nonetheless. 'If these sessions are to be of any benefit to you, you must start to tell me the truth.'

The truth, the whole truth and nothing but the truth, Your Honour.

'You do wish to continue with your treatment?'

Her cheeks, which have paled since her exertions, have a hint of blush high on the cheekbone, and perspiration, as thin as gossamer, sits above her top lip. She has the demeanour of a schoolboy who, having sneaked a look at his report card, has given the re-sealed envelope to his father with a look of pride and anticipation.

'I was unaware that we had started the treatment,' I say.

'What I propose,' she says, ignoring the caustic nature of my response, 'is that, starting today, every month or so you come to this room. Later, as you become more accustomed to the sessions, we may have them on a more regular basis. We shall take afternoon tea. I will make sure that Cook has our order in advance, and we can talk – as much or as little as you like; we can even drink our tea in silence if you wish. Would you like to do that?'

The bird wakes as if she is aware of the sudden change of dynamic in the room. Her tiny brown body erupts with a strong, sweet song. It is a jenny wren; she remains perched in the window, with all the stubbornness of her breed, until on a whim she flies around the room, makes a reconnaissance of her adopted territory, and then flies out through the open window. My mother always said that the arrival of a bird has a meaning, messages from the beyond and all that rubbish. And for once I hope that she is correct in her superstitions and that this jenny wren will signify change – though whether for good or ill, I cannot foretell.

I have received many proposals, of varying degrees of propriety; this is one of the more acceptable. The promise of afternoon tea and the chance of escape for an hour or so, even to this makeshift sitting room, is more promising than an afternoon in the asylum. Not that a promising proposal will necessarily have a favourable outcome; it is my unfortunate experience that outcome is inversely related to promise. But this girl with her flicking wrists and naked hands has piqued my curiosity. Maybe she will hold the key to my release from this hellhole.

I take a sip of my coffee, but it has grown tepid and unpalatable. I replace the half-empty cup in its saucer with a clatter. I look at my doctor and she returns my gaze, unperturbed by the noisy cup.

'I would very much like to do that,' I say with as much nonchalance as I can muster – she has enough exuberance for both of us. 'Where do I begin?'

'At the start,' she says, with a thin smile, her pen poised, and head cocked. It is an action she must have been trained to do – she is a picture of encouragement. And so, begin I do.

Wenlock Edge, Shropshire, 1871

I was born near the market town of Much Wenlock, into a brood that was already nine strong. 'Strong' may perhaps be an inaccurate adjective to describe my siblings, as my birth only raised our actual number to eight, my twin brothers, born fifteen months before my arrival, having died of diphtheria or some such, while my mother was confined to bed for my imminent arrival. If I seem callous in my description of their demise that is not my intention; it is only that my parents never spoke of them or wept over their passing. Children lived and children died; that is how it was, and most of our neighbours had at some time suffered the same loss. My mother laid flowers on their grave on the anniversary of their death; she did not visit on any other day, even though my father would weed the grass and clean their tiny gravestone every Sunday, after morning service. She placed no wreath at Christmas, no daffodils at Eastertime; not even their birthday was commemorated – it was as if their loss, not their birth, had become a celebration. Sometimes I imagine their poor venerated souls desperately trying to detach themselves from earthly apron strings as they claw their way into the arms of St Peter. And whether because of fate or choice, or out of sadness for the loss of her twins, I was to be her last child. I was christened Lily, that funereal flower, as, according to my father, all the virtuous names had been used up on my elder sisters. But Lily is a good a name as any, and, in the end, perhaps more apt than Patience or Constance or Prudence.

Now I run a little ahead of myself, but going back to my

childhood home – even if only in my mind, the actual path being long barred to me – is at least of some comfort. My father owned a farm, or probably still owns a farm, at Wenlock Edge. The Edge overshadowed the farm, its ancient limestone jutting out like a huge pallid hand, shielding those living beneath its benevolent palm from the extremes of weather. Despite the farm's enviable position, the summers were still hot and the winters were still cold, although occasionally the reverse happened. But a country winter is unlike the biting grey cold of a winter's night in the city slums that freezes the piss in the pots and the bones of the ragged children. For even the chilliest winters, which made us children snuggle three-a-bed under an eiderdown and layers of blankets to garner some degree of warmth, had a purpose: we knew that spring sunshine would soon warm the frozen fields, and frost, nature's own harrow, would split open the earth as it thawed, and the annual cycle of tilling, sowing, growing and reaping could begin again. And in the scorching hot nights of summer, when we could not sleep even with the windows flung wide open, our legs scratched and our muscles aching from the gathering of the grain harvest – even these were happy nights for us. We knew the grain stores were full for winter and soon cooler nights would herald the arrival of autumn and the picking of the apples, damsons and greengages that were busy ripening in the substantial orchard at the rear of the farmhouse.

The farm was much like any other in the Welsh Marches and much like any other anywhere else in the country: some years the yields were good and some years the yields were bad. My father had inherited the farm from his uncle, his father's only brother, who, at the age of forty and imbued with a hitherto unknown religious fervour, had gone off and got himself killed in the Anglo-Persian war. This was rather unfortunate for poor Uncle Herbert, but very fortunate for my father, who inherited Little Meadows Farm and would otherwise have been left penniless by my grandfather who had been steadily gambling away the family home and business.

My father's passion was for growing rather than rearing, and in this pursuit he was most earnest. As I had no surviving brothers, he tried to pass some of his knowledge on to his youngest girls: Mercy, Honesty, Prudence and me. My eldest sisters had only been taught the skills that a farmer's wife would need, as I expect in the early years he was still holding out for a son. I do not think he ever had the heart for livestock, and would secretly hope that the cows would birth heifer calves rather than bull calves who would have to go to market. We did keep chickens, geese and a few pigs, but it was always my mother who would wring the chickens' necks when they were too old to lay. She was always good with her hands—

My doctor holds up her own hand now, its elegance betrayed by the nails which are bitten like a schoolboy's. 'That's a wonderful start,' she says.

She has not noticed that I have rehearsed this speech since our first meeting in Matron's office and have trotted it out by rote, like the timetables I learnt at school. Or perhaps she thinks I speak so eloquently all the time.

'Can you tell me of an event that you remember from childhood? Something that happened to you rather than giving me your background. Not that that is not important.'

This I had not expected but, reaching in the deep recesses of my memory, I launch into an event that I well remember.

Little Meadows Farm, 28 December 1880

It is five o'clock and outside it is already as black as pitch. Honesty and I are in the back kitchen, washing our hands in a bowl of icy water that she has just poured from the jug. We are panting and red-faced, having made a dash from the warmth of the milking shed into the cold of the late afternoon; in the foldyard, the water trough is already an inch thick with ice. My mother is still outside securing the ducks and chickens against Mr Reynard, although I do not think that even he will be venturing out on such a night. Prudence is in the kitchen making a pot of tea. Her tea is habitually awful and has not improved with practice, but at least it is warm, and we walk into the kitchen and wrap our hands around the cup she offers, gulping down its stewed contents.

'Take one up to Father, he's in his study,' says Prudence.

It is my father's habit to go to his study in the late afternoon in winter when all the farm work is done; milking and caring for poultry, which may last well into the evening, is women's work. With a candlestick in one hand and a cup and saucer in the other, I climb the stairs, the cup rattling in its saucer but not a drop spilt, yet knowing that, for all my efforts, it will grow tepid on his desk. He has left the door ajar and as I enter the room he is leaning over Uncle Herbert's walnut desk, the latest books on crop rotation spewed across it. A heel of bread and some cheese and pickled onions, which he often takes with him for his dinner if he does not want to be disturbed, lie uneaten at the table's edge. On the mantelshelf, three candles he had lit earlier are nearly burnt down to their wicks. I put the cup and saucer on his desk, slice off a sliver of cheese and eat it nestled into the armchair by the fireplace. This is my habit: to sit wordlessly, warming myself on the dying embers and breathing in the familiar smells of whisky and Dark Bird's Eye pipe tobacco. After a quarter of an hour, he looks up from his desk, startled anew at my presence, as if my sitting there is not a regular occurrence.

He throws a few more coals on the fire, wipes his hands on his trousers, and takes the opposite fireside seat, a large glass of whisky in his hand.

'Lily, I have great plans for the evolution of this farm. I aim to increase crop rotation, diversify into other food crops, and eventually, if I can twist your mother's arm, I'm going to buy myself one of those new-fangled steam tractors to do the ploughing. It will pay for itself in the end – and don't worry, Samson will be put out to pasture, not sent to the knackers' yard,' he says.

I clap my hands together, caught up in his enthusiasm and grateful for our old shire horse's reprieve, but understanding only a smattering of what he is proposing.

He refills his glass with whisky, the tea long forgotten. 'I have been so blessed to have been given this farm. I wasn't cut out for life as a solicitor, even though I come from a long line of them. I hated the long hours, the clients, and the drab offices in a drab city.'

'But don't you have long hours and demanding clients here on the farm?' I say.

'True. But I shall be eternally grateful for dear Uncle Herbert for rescuing me from that life. And of course, it's here that I met your mother.'

He does not know that I have heard him and my mother whispering about Grandad Day's gambling problem and how grateful we should all be to Uncle Herbert. 'Tell me about how you met,' I say. I have heard it before, but he always seems happy to retell the tale. A watercolour of my mother, painted by my father in some far-off time, stands in a brass frame in the middle of his desk. In it she is laughing up at him as if they are sharing a secret joke, her hair splayed out behind her, her body crushing the poor bluebells on which she lies. The red of my mother's hair bleeds into the blue of the bluebells, leaving her head outlined in a halo of purple. She looks young, beautiful; she cannot have been any more than fourteen years old.

My father takes a tartan blanket from the blanket box, warms it in front of the fire and places it over my legs. There is a draught from the landing whistling through the open study door, buffeting the candle flames and casting dancing shadows onto the walls. He gets up and closes the door, picks up the picture frame from his desk and settles back down into his chair, tracing the outline of my mother's face with his right hand.

'I'd been to Bridgnorth Market with the last of the potatoes,' he says, speaking to the frame. 'As I recall, I'd got a good price for them and was about to go for a glass of ale, it being thirsty work you see, especially with all that soil in the air, when I saw her sitting on my empty cart, her head covered by a scarf, selling her potions and oils and some such. I don't think she had sold many of them; her basket was quite full. I was about to tell her to move on when she turned and smiled up at me. I must admit I was taken aback; I had been expecting to see an old crone, not a young girl.' He hands me the picture frame, as if to confirm the validity of his recollections. 'I said she could stay there until I had finished my ale. When I returned, she was still sitting on my cart. I was bold and asked her where she was staying, and, as it was only a few miles from this house, I offered her a ride home. At first she declined, saying her brother would be picking her up, but it was a bitterly cold day and dusk was starting to fall, so eventually she agreed.'

'And what did you talk about on the way back?' I say, already knowing the answer.

'Your mother wouldn't sit up front with me, I think she thought I might run off with her, so she sat at the back of the cart, her legs dangling, ready for a swift getaway. When we arrived at the camp I asked if I could see her again and she said that I could. I'm not sure your nanny and grandad were very pleased with this stranger turning up with their daughter on the back of his cart, but she was headstrong even then. I think it was about the third time I called on her that Grandad Lovell allowed us to go out for a ride in the trap unchaperoned. She sat up front next to me with her basket of food and my paints wedged between us. It was hot that day, too hot for spring really. We'd had strict instructions from Grandad Lovell not to travel too far away, and he was a big man in those days, a man you wouldn't like to cross.'

I thought of Grandad Lovell, all bent over and blind, picking his way across our yard with his walking stick on Christmas Day; I could not imagine him big and strong.

'We'd just got to Bluebell Wood when she jumped off the trap, flung off her shoes and ran barefoot into it, crushing the poor flowers underfoot. The wood was not new to me, but to your mother it was the most beautiful thing in the world. And because of that I saw it with fresh eyes. She lay down in the bluebells and I fell in love with her then and there. We were married within two months of that painting.'

There is a knock at the door. It must be my mother and as usual she must, like everyone else, wait to be invited inside my father's domain when his study door is closed. Tonight, my father decides to play a game, our game, where we pretend that we are not there, stifling our laughter with our hands so that she will not hear us. She knocks again, this time with more force.

'Come in. I'm sorry we did not hear your knock,' says my father.

I do not think that she is ever fooled, but she plays along. 'I'll ring a cowbell next time. Why are you up so late, Lily? You've missed your dinner so you will go hungry to bed tonight,' she says with what looks like a smirk.

'I have had some of Father's cheese,' I say.

'Still, you ought to be in bed like your sisters. Come morning the cows will not milk themselves,' she says with a voice that I know to be the precursor to a smack.

'I'm training her for the future prosperity of the farm. And who knows, perhaps one day cows *will* milk themselves,' says my father. They laugh together the way adults sometimes do, and then he winks at me, the smack averted, and plants a kiss on my forehead before shooing me off to bed. I run to my bedroom, knowing in my heart that I am his favourite.

*

Pomona does not look at the paper on which she has scribbled my story but continues to look at me; I presume that this false intimacy is important to my progress. After a minute she looks away, ending the game. I knew she would not last long; I was always the winner in staring contests.

'I believe we have made an excellent start,' she says. 'I have a good idea of your background. As these sessions progress, I shall be able to start to formulate some hypotheses. Please give this some thought before our next meeting. I do not expect you to remember everything. Childhood recollections can be piecemeal at best; sometimes they are not even our own memories but fragments of stories, and at other times our minds can work as a shield and withhold our memories from us. Adult recollections can be more useful as they are usually more vivid, but it is still important to record those childhood memories.'

Pomona places the loose sheets of paper into a black leather notebook down whose spine she has written 'Miss L. Day', and bundles it all into her briefcase. She stands and scrapes back her chair; it makes an awkward interruption in the otherwise silent room, like a cough during a funeral service. 'Shall we meet next month?' she says as she puts on her mackintosh; it is a man's, and although it is the correct length, the width drowns her slim figure.

'I look forward to it,' I say.

Rain has started to fall heavily now. Pomona heaves open the French windows, which are still stiff, having remained dormant all winter, and disappears into the deluge.

'Formulate some hippoteas. La di bloody da!' says the taller attendant. 'I'll give you hippoteas.' She stands in front of my chair, grabs my shoulders, and hoists me to my feet.

'Hypotheses is the word you are after - suppositions made as a starting point for further investigation,' I say with a smile that cannot be viewed as anything but condescending.

The shorter attendant walks over and slaps me across the face. 'That's for yer lip,' she says. Pomona, with her back to the asylum and already halfway down the driveway after our first session, will not see this manhandling of her patient.

'Next time order some flapjacks to go with your hippoteas,' says the taller attendant, choosing to ignore my explanation of her misheard word. 'I'm rather partial to a flapjack with a pot of Darjeeling. Had some in a posh tea shop in Harrogate the once. But they do so get in one's teeth,' she adds, and opens her mouth and jabs two grimy fingers between her decayed top teeth, gurning in my face.

The two of them laugh at her wit until the shorter one turns to me and says, 'Not funny enough for you? Don't know why we got landed with this job. We're not a pair of nurserymaids. Give me your normal loony any day, not these flippin' loony convicts. Should be sent back to prison, the lot of 'em. Don't know what they're goin' to do next, you can't trust 'em as far as you can throw 'em.'

'I fear that may be quite a way,' I say.

'What you sayin'?'

'Nothing.'

'Well, make sure it is nothin',' says the taller one. 'It's bad enough havin' to listen to yer bleedin' nonsense when that hoity-toity madam is here. Spoutin' off about yer poor hardworking life on yer poor farm that yer father was bleedin' given. Makes me sick ter me back teeth.'

'If you 'ad any,' says the other, and they start giggling like a pair of schoolchildren until the clock reminds them it is time I was returned to the ward.

The taller one pushes me towards the door and the other locks the French windows and thrusts the key into her apron pocket. She picks up the tea tray from the table and holds open the door to the corridor while the taller one shoves me through it. We play Follow My Leader along the winding corridors, the shorter attendant rattling away at the front, the taller bringing up the rear with one hand on my shoulder and the other pressed hard against the small of my back, which is already bruised from her prodding. I am going to be black and blue if these two continue to take me to my sessions.

As we navigate the corridors, the noise from the wards is louder than usual, and when the attendants open the door of the neurotics' ward we are met by a cacophony of shrieks, and the pungent aroma of old, wet sheepdog. The shower that has just enveloped Pomona has interrupted the patients' afternoon walk; even the airing courts, which occupy a higher position than the lawns, have flooded. Now the patients sit at the end of their beds in their wet clothes, dripping onto their bedding, and tomorrow Matron is going to have a hard time getting them out of their beds for their morning constitutional.

It is barely half-past three, but Maggie is shouting for her afternoon cup of tea and Queenie is shouting at her to be quiet. Some of the other patients follow Maggie's lead and the ward is filled with the stomping of their feet and the chant of 'tea, tea, tea'. Others, upset by the noise, begin to cry or silently wrap their arms around themselves and rock to and fro on their beds. In the middle of the mêlée is Matron, who is flapping around like a malevolent crow.

My attendants thrust me through the doorway of the ward and linger at my shoulders, awaiting Matron's instructions. Matron spies us out of the corner of her eye and shouts, 'Is our patient all safe and sound, Jones?' They both nod their heads and short Jones holds out the key; Matron snatches it from her hand and sends them both back to their own ward. I walk to my bed and hope that Matron has forgotten that I am due in the laundry.

'Look lively, Rowse,' says Matron. 'Get them out of their wet clothes and into their beds or on to a chair and give them their cup of tea. Clarke, take those coats to the cloakroom to dry out or you'll have them all in the infirmary with pneumonia at this rate.'

'But they are not due tea till four o'clock,' says Rowse.

'For goodness' sake, girl, must I do everything? I've got five other wards to cope with. Use some initiative.'

Clarke returns from the cloakroom and Rowse beckons her with her hand, and the two of them begin to supply the patients with cups of tepid tea; a proper cup of scalding tea, that universal panacea, is not allowed for the mentally defective.

'Tea, Lily?' says Rowse.

'Thank you. Make it a strong one,' I say.

'Bad day?'

'So everyone says.'

She raises a smile somewhere between bewilderment and sympathy as my attempt at humour is wasted and she moves the tea urn on to the next lunatic. Matron wanders over and I expect to get my marching orders, but instead she says, 'How was your first session with Dr Fairchild?'

'I fear that I have no previous experience in judging the goodness or otherwise of a meeting with Dr Fairchild,' I say, with the impunity of the mad.

'But she wishes to see you again?'

'Next month.'

'All is not lost, then. I will make the arrangements and will inform the superintendent of your progress.' She strides away, the laundry forgotten, and I am left undisturbed for the remainder of the afternoon, which I spend reading old news in last week's newspapers. I am unsure if Pomona will secure my release, but it is more of a chance than I could ever have hoped for. But I will not be over-eager: telling someone repeatedly that you are not mad means nothing. No, with a little steer in the right direction, I will let Pomona confirm that I am not.

Leeds, 29 March 1897

Pomona Fairchild's notes on Miss Lily Day (Hysteric, Sunnyside Lunatic Asylum)

First meeting. Subject is in neurotics' ward. Imprisoned for GBH but sent to Sunnyside about one year into an eight-year sentence.

I am doubtful of the diagnosis of hysteria that she received in prison – argumentative but no obvious nervousness, insomnia or convulsions.

No hysteria mentioned at trial, only emerged after imprisonment.

Well employed in laundry and soon to move to sewing room.

Has taken a sickly child under her wing which may hinder her progress.

Strategy: Use Freudian talking cure to purge triggering memories. Offer titbits of my life to encourage trust.

Curb excitement that her release depends on my opinion of her mental state.

CHAPTER SIX

We have been sweating away in the sewing room all morning, enjoying the therapeutic benefits of hard work. But this work is a step up from the laundry room, a confirmation of my increasing sanity that I am to be trusted with needles, and I am gladder than I thought I would be to be rid of the stench of soiled sheets. The sewing room is large, about a quarter the size of the ward, and with its high ceiling, stone walls and arched windows it is more akin to a nave in a parish church than a workroom; the April sunshine pours through, illuminating our stitching and our journey to normality. But despite the room's ecclesiastical appearance we work diligently, and, being the best seamstress, I have been charged with overseeing the quality of our work. We sit in front of our new treadle sewing machines, our feet and fingers going nineteen to the dozen. The attendants walk between the rows of machines, monitoring our production and ensuring that we do not sew ourselves to our work.

Today, instead of sheets for the asylum, we have started on a special order for lawn napkins for the Grand Hotel; we have already made three score of the two hundred that have been ordered and should get them all done by the end of next week. There will be a note at the bottom of the hotel menu that will thank the superintendent and endorse our industry. After two hours the bell sounds for luncheon, and we have an hour's respite before the next stint of sewing begins. But this afternoon I have been excused from my work as it will be my second session with Pomona. Daphne, who is a good needlewoman but has a mouth like a fishwife, will supervise our output, so I expect there will be much dissatisfaction to address when I return.

At two o'clock, Jones and Jones lumber into the ward and tell Rowse that they have been sent by Matron to escort me to my next session.

'Matron says Rowse is taking me today,' I say.

'Nice try, Day,' says tall Jones, with a right face on her, confirming that nothing I say will ever be nice. They jostle me along the corridor and into the sitting room where, despite the unseasonal heat, the French windows have remained shut. Matron has decreed that, owing to there having been two absconders in the past few weeks who have yet to be recovered, security must be improved, and the French windows must remain locked until Pomona's arrival.

There is a vase of white magnolias on the side table and their scent fills the airless room until tall Jones opens one of the small windows and the scent starts to dissipate. But I prefer the aroma of the magnolias to the smell of the attendants' perspiration, which, as we settle in our usual seats, wafts every few seconds over my shoulder. While we await Pomona's arrival, the Joneses prattle and waft and poke me in the ribs every few minutes.

There is a rap on the French windows and tall Jones walks over to them, draws back the curtains, turns the key in the lock, and forces them open. Pomona breezes in; a cheeky wind has tugged at her hat, leaving it askew, and beneath it her hair tumbles over her face like a creeper, even though she continues to push it back behind her ears. Her hair is not straight as I had thought but holds a kink, that even a flat iron cannot control against a determined wind. She wears a fitted green jacket with a fur collar. It suits her better than the mannish coat that denies her shape, but it is a choice far too warm for today, and she has a mark around her neck where the fur has chafed.

'Good afternoon, Lily,' she says. 'I hope you are well rested.'

'I haven't lifted a finger all week,' I say.

'Matron informs me that you have performed so well in the laundry that this week she has allowed you to work in the sewing room. How have you found the work?'

'I prefer it to laundry work, and it reminds me of my early days working in a clothing factory in Leeds, although of course I got paid a wage for that.'

'Do you not earn tokens for your work here?'

'So that I can buy a bar of lily-of-the-valley soap or extra food? Forgoing carbolic soap is hardly an incentive to work, is it?'

'But it is meaningful work.'

'That subsidises the running costs of the asylum.'

She scribbles in her notebook and the Joneses chunter in the background until she tells them to be quiet.

'What I would really like to do is work in the vegetable gardens,' I say.

'Even though that also subsidises the asylum's costs?'

'I'm prepared to overlook it.'

'I believe it is the male patients who do most of the cultivating and the heavy outdoor work. Women patients are believed to fare better with inside work, although occasionally they are called upon to weed the gardens or puzzle the potatoes, whatever that entails.'

'You mean riddle,' I say, trying but failing to hide my smile.

'Riddle, puzzle, whatever the word is. Unlike you, I have no farming experience. But I agree it may be of benefit to your recovery. I will have a discussion with Matron, but first we must get you on the road to recovery. Ah, I see our tea is here already.' She glances at her notebook and looks at the attendant to her right. 'Jones, as the saying goes, will you be mother?'

I pity the poor child who will have short Jones for a mother – and the poor sod who will make her one. She jumps up from her chair, takes the tray from the side table and places it between us. She pours the tea, spilling it into the saucers, and hands it to us without enquiring if we require milk.

'I don't think our Miss Jones has a hope of a future in a tea shop,' I say.

Pomona laughs and says, 'Heaven forbid. Now Jones and, er, Jones, before we start, you must understand that you have been given a great honour and responsibility in looking after Miss Day in these sessions, and I was remiss in not telling you at our first session, but it is of the utmost importance that you are at all times discreet.'

Pomona must be a real novice at this not to have told them this earlier; but then we are all new to it. 'I don't think they have the slightest idea what you mean,' I say.

Pomona tries again. 'You must speak of nothing that Miss Day may say during these sessions. Is that clear?'

They grunt and nod and, taking this as a signal of their acquiescence, Pomona turns to me and says, 'Today we are going to make a start on your childhood.'

She picks up the silver sugar tongs – their sharp bevelled edge is surely an oversight by Matron – and adds two cubes of sugar to her cup, stirring it vigorously. I pour milk into mine and, masked by my right sleeve, use my left hand to shove a couple of garibaldis up there for later.

'I think that started years ago,' I say, taking another garibaldi and nibbling the end of it. 'I only vaguely remember it.'

'I am sure that is not true. Look at what you told me at our first session,' she says with a smile that is designed to encourage my revelations. I am a good reader of smiles. 'I suggest you start with something that most of us can recall: your schooldays. Did you attend school?'

'Biscuit?' I say, offering up the plate.

But she will not be waylaid in her questioning. 'No, thank you. Did you attend school, Lily?' she says, this time with pen poised in anticipation of some miraculous revelation.

'I believe it was made compulsory to attend to the age of ten in 1880.'

'I am well aware of the law, Lily. I am asking if you attended.'

'For a year. In my early years my father taught me. And we were lucky to have an extensive library in his study.'

'And how did that make you feel?'

'That I attended school, or that my father taught me, or that we had a library?' She really ought to be more precise with her questions.

'How did you feel about school, at least for now,' she says with a sigh.

'I did not feel anything. It was a matter of government law that I go to school until I was ten. It was annoying that my sisters, being older, didn't have to go. I suppose I could have written a letter of complaint to Mr Gladstone.'

'Do you not think that schooling is important?'

'I didn't need it, but I expect it can be advantageous for some children. I'm sure the attendants sitting behind me must have learned much, although it appears they may have forgotten most of it.'

'So, you learnt nothing?'

'Nothing I couldn't have learned at home. And I learnt about the wages of sin at Sunday school. Could I have another cup of tea?'

'Did you not enjoy your schooling?' she says, refilling my cup.

'I thought the idea was to study, not to enjoy.'

'I would have thought it could be both.'

'Perhaps for you,' I say, draining my cup and eating the last biscuit even though I am full.

The grandmother clock chimes a quarter to the hour and Pomona declares our session over for the day, even though there are fifteen minutes remaining. Tall Jones stands up and reaches into her apron pocket for the key and short Jones, still seated, starts to yawn; I can hear her intake of breath and feel the warm, stale exhale on the back of my neck.

'Keeping you up, are we?' says Pomona.

The girl is at least not stupid enough to reply, but my back and neck suffer for Pomona's barbed comment and the lack of biscuits all the way back to the ward.

Leeds, 30 April 1897

Pomona Fairchild's notes on Miss Lily Day (Hysteric, Sunnyside Lunatic Asylum)

Last session: subject very unforthcoming.

Have suggested to Matron that we swap attendants, the 'bruisers', as I like to call them, for some more genteel girls to bring and collect subject, with whom she may feel more comfortable.

I will henceforth be seeing subject on my own at my own peril!!

Matron remains unconvinced of the wisdom of this decision, suggesting subject be drugged, but I have refused.

CHAPTER SEVEN

The asylum has six wards for female patients. Each ward has fifty beds in two rows of twenty-five with barely two feet between them. The ward in which we lunatics are placed is determined by our deemed brand of lunacy, or, if the asylum is overcrowded, any ward that has a space. Many of the patients will be in the asylum for life and will end their days in the geriatrics' ward, a repository for elderly patients, and by the time they reach there are either completely mad, or drugged up enough to forget which type of lunatic they once were.

The ward is a sea of yellow; it's nearly the end of May but still there are daffodils everywhere: stuck in makeshift vases on windowsills and bedside cabinets and even in the washroom. It is the same every spring: for three months, visitors, as a gesture to the ward's name, bring in bunches of daffodils. All the wards are stuffed with flowers, as they too are named after spring flowers: Superintendent Sharp decided a few years ago that wards should not be known by their medical name but would be given flowery names, to symbolise a *new beginning*, as he foolishly likes to call it. It is all a façade for the visitors, who can say, to anyone nosy enough to ask, that their relative is in Primrose Ward or Daffodil Ward, without having to reveal the mental ailment to which their relative has succumbed. But it gives the recipient of the flowers a chance to nurture something, even though the vases in our ward are taken out at night as they cannot risk us trying to poison someone with daffodil water.

As I am not allowed to work in the gardens, it is nice to see something thriving, rather than just existing, within the confines of the asylum. A few months ago, we did have something else living on the wards. A patient in the dementia ward was given a canary as a present for her seventieth birthday. I have always thought it cruel to keep such a wild creature cooped up, but it is a bit of a fashion now to allow patients in asylums to have the responsibility of caring for a caged bird. We did not see the bird, but we would hear it chirping away in the day and sometimes in the night, even though it had the same bedtime as the rest of us and a leather hood put on its cage at lights-out. Maggie suggested that we call the bird's owner Aunty Mary, although to my knowledge it never went up the leg of her drawers; I expect she was not wearing any half of the time. The attendants used to let it hop around the ward when Matron was not around. Sometimes you would hear a thud as it flew into a windowpane in its quest to escape. It would be put back in its cage and lie dazed on the floor of it for a few minutes before jumping on to its perch and chirping away again, probably lamenting its situation and calling its captor all the names under the sun.

One morning, or so I am told, its owner lifted the leather hood and found it lying on the bottom of its cage, dead as a dodo. The poor old girl kept trying to force food into its mouth and stick it back on its perch, but it fell off again, of course, and one of the attendants had to fetch Matron because the woman was becoming distraught, and the bird was becoming increasingly featherless and clawless. Some idiot suggested that the canary had succumbed to a gas leak like the poor birds sent down the pits to detect methane; another proposed that an intruder had come in the depths of night to dispose of the bird, although as the wards are locked at night this seemed unlikely. There was suspicion that the woman herself or one of the night attendants had killed it, but nothing could be proven, although Matron never did let her have another bird, and our night-times became blessedly free of twittering.

Elise has had a dozen bunches of daffodils from her parents, who, unable to communicate with her even though they doggedly visit every fortnight, have overcompensated by saturating her with flowers. She does not acknowledge the profusion of blooms and so Rowse has placed a bunch in the meagre space by her bed, and shared the remainder between me and Queenie, as neither of us ever receives any visitors. Like me, Queenie has sisters, and they say that in the beginning they visited every week, but I have not seen hide nor hair of them since I have been in here; perhaps they are all dead. My sisters do not visit either, but they do not know I am here; they do not know where I am. Not that they would wish to visit me after what I have done. Like me, Queenie never speaks about her sisters; it is better that way.

*

It is two o'clock, and I am waiting for the gruesome twosome to arrive to take me to my next session with Pomona, when Rowse walks over and sits on the end of my bed.

'I'll be taking you to your sessions with Dr Fairchild today instead of the Joneses,' she says. 'Well, me and another attendant from the infirmary, who should be along in a minute. Matron's orders.' She is wearing a huge smile. I expect that she will be glad of a break from her usual duties for a couple of hours.

'Why is that?' I say, but she shrugs her shoulders.

I suspect the reason is that Pomona has picked up on my antagonism towards the Joneses and my reticence in speaking in their presence, or at least that is what I have portrayed to her; really, it is the prodding I cannot stand. I thought perhaps I had over-egged the pudding, but my plan seems to have worked: she has had them replaced.

A tall, thin girl with a shock of blonde hair walks into the ward and over to my bed; the bumps of a rosary protrude like a growth beneath her blouse. She sticks out her right hand. 'Hello, I'm Agnes O'Neill,' she says.

I take her hand in mine. 'Pleased to meet you, little lamb,' I say, in a voice too reminiscent of the Big Bad Wolf, and she takes a step back from me, surprised that I know the significance of her name and no doubt vowing in future to follow Matron's orders and not wear her rosary at work for fear of strangulation, especially from this stranger whom she has been pressganged into accompanying to see a psychiatrist.

'Oh, don't worry, Agnes,' says Rowse. 'Lily wouldn't hurt a fly, would you?'

'No, of course not.' I laugh.

Squash, obliterate, put it out of its misery maybe; but hurt it?
No. Never.

In my little room, my two girls sit close behind me and giggle
and chatter, but, because I am a lunatic with my back to them,
I cannot hear a thing. I am used to being invisible and at least
they do not prod, and it is a joy to hear the burr of their rural
origins, nurtured on the facing Atlantic coastlines of Cornwall
and County Cork, mercifully not yet sharpened by their current
residence. Sarah Rowse has a young man and they have been
stepping out for two weeks; he is an indentured joiner and works
'ever such long hours', so they must make the most of their Sunday
afternoons. Agnes O'Neill has no time for young men or for going
out, but she attends church every Sunday and sometimes during
the week as well. Every Saturday she sends a long letter and a
three-bob postal order to her mother.

Pomona arrives and sits in her usual chair, fans herself with her
notebook, which has replaced her loose sheets, and proclaims she
is parched from her walk. She pours the tea herself, filling her own
cup and then another, passing it to me across the table. Turning to
the attendants, she says, 'Leave us now and return at half-past three.'

Well, I did not expect that, and neither did Rowse, judging by
the look on her face. When they have left the room, Pomona leans
towards me.

'Lily, I am sure you are wondering why we have had a change of
attendants. At my request, Matron has chosen two new members
of staff to accompany you, country girls with whom she hopes you

will be able to establish a rapport that you clearly did not have with the previous girls. But they will not be in the room for our sessions; from now on you will be seeing me on your own. To begin with, Rowse and O'Neill will accompany you to and from each session, although eventually I hope only one girl will be required. I must take responsibility for your actions; the sessions can only continue if you are able to behave. Can I trust you to do that?'

I object to being spoken to like a child, especially by someone of my own age, but now is not the time to behave like one. 'I will not let you down,' I say, with several confirming nods.

'It is my responsibility to ensure that you do not let *yourself* down – that we work together and get as much out of these sessions as we can. The board is relying on my assessment of your sanity. It will be quite a challenge for me, but I am always eager for a challenge. We can talk as little or as much as you wish, but I did hope for some communication, or you will just have to nod or shake your head when I interrogate you! And that will get us nowhere,' she says.

'Of course,' I say. I decide I will offer Pomona a meaty morsel to chew upon, something that underlines to her how different our lives have been; and if her delicate nature is disturbed or shocked – well, then she will experience the consequences of what she has asked from me.

Little Meadows Farm, July 1883

It is a warm evening in July and I am in the orchard watching a pair of red squirrels chase each other from tree to tree; they swing backwards and forwards like circus acrobats, their eyes bright, their tails fluffed up with the excitement of the pursuit. Mercy calls them rats with tails, which I suppose is a bit unkind, but they did dig up and eat all her tulip bulbs one year. She paid them back the next year though by planting hyacinth bulbs among the tulips. Poor poisoned squirrels lying dead on the floor of the orchard, curled up and bloated like wasp-ridden windfalls. Mercy said that that is what happens to vermin, and that she did not care. But then again, Mercy does not like anyone.

Today, though, I am busy killing rats, not their more beautiful brethren. There are always rats where there is grain and poultry: big black beady-eyed buggers who steal feed, eggs and chicks and even have a go at the hens if they are feeling brave enough. But this year we are overrun with them. I have seen a few of them around during the day, peeping out from between the hay in the far barns, as if on a covert reconnaissance mission for their nocturnal activities. For it is at night that they maraud en masse, whole families from the youngest pipsqueak to the oldest *grandes dames* in their ancient, tattered fur.

You might expect a farmer to loathe foxes more than rats, given their proclivity for happily slaughtering a whole houseful of chickens for the sake of it, leaving in their wake a trail of blood and body parts, a grim discovery for the poor unfortunate whose turn it is to let out the hens and collect the morning eggs.

But whereas foxes raid for a few days and move to another farm, rats are relentless: we get rid of a few every day, but they keep coming back. Two weeks ago my father set up ten rat traps and, when we checked them, we had only two dead rats and eight rats' tails, for a rat will gnaw off its own tail in a bid to escape a trap.

As the traps were ineffectual, my father decided to use something stronger. I went with him to Williams the chemist in Much Wenlock, where a tin of arsenic powder costs tuppence, which seemed to me a small price to pay for murder. My father signed the poison's register and joked with Mr Williams that perhaps he was going to poison my mother. I expect Mr Williams had heard this numerous times from his customers; if anyone had in fact murdered his spouse, it would have been impossible for the poor man to testify which customer had threatened it.

My father kept the arsenic powder in a tin on a high shelf in the implement shed, away from prying fingers. He sprinkled the powder on some cattle feed and left it overnight in the hedgerow that surrounded the hen coop. We found ten rats the next day, all blood and vomit, their limbs contorted, their eyes accusing, and we picked them up by their tails and burnt them in the iron bin in the yard, in case their carcasses should poison the livestock or the water. And my father declared our mission a success – until it killed his beloved sheepdog, Bessie.

I can see him now, cradling poor Bessie in his arms, his eyes filled with tears and her dear head lolling back and forth, her mouth bloody and frothing. She had dragged herself to the drive and lay there panting and spent. My father had found her on his way back from scything the meadow grass. He had howled and we had all run from the orchard and crowded around them. I told Honesty to run to the kitchen to fetch Mother.

She should not have been near the chicken coops; she should not have slipped her chain and gone in search of her charges. My father repeated the words over and over, as if we children could give him absolution. I wished then that I had the Gift, so that I could have told my father that morning to make sure Bessie was safely tied up in the yard. They say Nanny Lovell had it, and, although my mother showed no inclination to the prescient, it was always hoped that one of us girls would discover our talent in that direction.

We buried Bessie in a deep hole in the middle of the field by the mill pond: my father could not cremate his best friend. He made a cross from a branch of the big oak tree and wrote 'Bessie, the best sheepdog ever' on it in Indian ink; when there is heavy rainfall the words trickle huge black droplets onto her grave. Most weeks my father sits by her grave talking to her when he thinks no one is looking.

So tonight, I am out here with a spade and an oil lamp, for it will soon be nightfall, attempting to catch rats. At first I tried to use a shovel to kill them, but it was too heavy and unwieldy, whereas a spade is just the job. Not the flat side, mind – I do not want to squash them – but the sharp side that nearly cuts them in two; and it is quicker than a trap or arsenic. Honesty and Prudence are too squeamish to hunt rats, and Mercy would kill everything that moves, so in the end it is left to me. I have just killed a female, her belly bulging and her nipples pink and erect. I expect there are at least ten babies in there, so it is eleven for the price of one. But there are many more to go, because when you see one rat you know there are ten nearby. That makes eight rats tonight, twenty-odd if you count the babies and a hundred-fold if you count the babies those babies would have had. I throw them into a pile in the bin for my father to burn in the morning, for they are, after all, just as much vermin as Mercy's squirrels. I walk back to the house and take off my shoes before I enter the back kitchen for fear of waking the household. There are splatters of rat blood and guts on them, but I shall not wash them until after I have waved them under the nose of Honesty and Prudence, who will no doubt shriek at the proof of my bloody endeavours. On the kitchen table my mother has left milk covered by a muslin cloth. The milk is a little warm by now, but I am thirsty and drink it down in one. Hopefully this will be my last night as a rat-catcher, as my father has said that tomorrow he will fulfil his promise of last week, and procure half a dozen farm cats.

Pomona's face is impassive and she scribbles something in her notebook; I suspect it is to give herself time to decide how to respond. Her decision seems to be to not respond at all.

'Thank you, Lily,' she says eventually. 'Would you like to talk about your schooling now? We did not get very far on this subject in our last session.'

I smile at the change of tack and decide to play along with it.

'My father felt he could educate me just as well as any school-teacher,' I say, 'and he was probably correct. I was always a quick learner, far better than any of my sisters. I could read as competently as an adult by the time I was seven years old. It amused my father to get me to read aloud the front page of *The Times*, even if it was sometimes yesterday's news by the time we received it. I could write a fair bit early on too.'

'Were you always academic?' says Pomona.

'It always felt that way,' I say.

She purses her lips in a way she will regret when she is older. I drain my teacup and she offers me another.

'You well know that is not what I meant. What I meant is, were you always good at the three Rs, as they say?' She emphasises the word 'they' as if she does not subscribe to the phrase.

'More the two Rs. Reading and writing. I was more than proficient at arithmetic, but reading was always my favourite. In my single year at school our teacher would prevail upon me to help the slower children, even though some were the same age as me.'

'And what did you like to read?'

'Whatever I was given.'

She scratches more lines into her notebook. She will have a novel by the time we are finished. 'Really, Lily,' she says, 'I sometimes cannot tell if you are lying or not. You have the makings of an excellent poker player.'

'Oh, I never gamble,' I lie. '*Aesop's Fables* was my favourite book. My father gave me his copy when I was about six years old. It was dog-eared and tea-stained, and the pages sprang open as if divided by an invisible bookmark; but, because the book was loved by him as a child, I loved it all the more. I used to secrete it in the bony place between the headboard and the bed frame, in the days when we had to share a bedroom. Not that the others would have wanted it, but Honesty or Prudence might have taken it out of malice. When the others were asleep, I would light my candle and read for a few hours without fear of their snitching. I have a copy now of my own; Titus bought it for me.'

Under the hieroglyphics that Pomona now uses – called

'shorthand', so she tells me – she writes *WHO IS TITUS?* in capital letters followed by one of her looping question marks. But she does not ask. The question she should actually ask, as many have, is *where* is Titus? But she will, in time.

'How did your father manage to educate you all? Was he not too busy on the farm?' she says instead.

'He used to try to set aside an hour a day for it. Sometimes in the summer months it was impossible for him to take time away from the farm, and for us as well really, but in the winter months it was much easier. My sisters were not interested in books, but even they learned enough to read a newspaper and check a grocery bill. And of course, I had Father to myself in his study for a few evenings every week as well,' I say.

'And your mother, did she teach you?'

'Not to read; she could barely read or write herself, which was strange because Grandad Lovell was a veritable bookworm before his eyes went. But I learned sewing and cooking and preserving and country remedies from my mother, just as she must have done from Nanny Lovell.'

'And was your Nanny Lovell a strong presence in your life?'

'She died long before I came along, although I know a lot about her from Grandad Lovell. I think he had a bit of a soft spot for me because I look the spit of her, or so he said, and when I was a nipper he would sit me on his lap and read to me and then meander from the book and tell me tales about her. I expect he only recalled the good bits; I suppose that's what happens to your memory when you get old. It was a shame she was not there to teach us.'

'Why is that?'

'I think she would have been a better teacher than my mother, who was not cut out to teach. I think she adhered to the principle that we would learn through some sort of osmosis and she would chastise us when we got things wrong; she always thought we erred out of spite, and, since I was the one who usually complained that I had tried to complete the task correctly, I was always accused of being the ringleader and would receive the punishment for us all. But we all ended up pretty good cooks and needlewomen by the time we were sixteen, so perhaps she had the correct method after all.'

Pomona looks up from her notebook and then closes it with a thud. 'I was not taught how to cook,' she says. 'It was presumed I would always employ a cook in my establishment. I did learn how to plan a menu and to choose the correct pudding and the right sauce to go with a dish.' She throws her head back and laughs. 'And as for sewing, I had needlework lessons from some old maid, and as a project it was decided that I should sew a sampler for my mother's birthday. I kept it secret so that my mother would not see it before the big day. The old spinster was a twice-a-week churchgoer, whereas my father was a staunch agnostic, and my mother went to church only at the holiest of times, out of propriety. The woman, Mrs Ruskin, asked me to choose a line from the Bible to embroider. I had no idea of any such lines, apart from a few Christmas carols, but I was at that time in love with the book *Black Beauty*, so together we chose some words that she felt would be suitable. I worked for months on that sampler, what with the lettering and the illustrations, and, when I had finished, Mrs Ruskin had it framed in ebony, and we wrapped it in brown paper and string. Imagine my mother's surprise when she opened my present on the morning of her birthday to a find a sampler embroidered with the words *The Four Horsemen of the Apocalypse* with relevant illustrations in my own childish hand of my interpretation of death, famine, war and conquest, sewn into each corner, and me looking up, all smiles, for her approval. Looking back, I can see she was torn between praising me for my efforts and thinking where she could put the darned thing without hurting my feelings. In the end she put it in the downstairs water closet that only the men used. It is still there, a resident joke now and an assured conversation-starter.'

We laugh together, proper belly laughs, until she holds up her hand and says, 'I can thank my brother Edward for my formal education, as it was he who insisted upon it, telling my parents that men of this modern age wish their wives to have had a proper education. Whether that was true or whether he just wanted the best for me, I do not know, but my parents would do anything for the golden boy. That is why they were so upset about Oxford . . . But I can hear our girls tramping down the corridor, and I believe we have talked enough for one day.'

My girls knock and enter the room and Pomona bids us goodbye and I can hear her laughing to herself all the way down the path, unaware of how feigning a belly laugh is as easy as pouring a pint of ale.

CHAPTER EIGHT

The asylum, like the rest of the world that is coloured pink on the school atlas, is *en fête*. 1897 marks the Diamond Jubilee of Queen Victoria, Empress of India, the Windsor widow, and the twenty-second of June has been designated a public holiday. God Save the Queen! We are to have a celebration tea, not in the refectory but, as the weather has been declared set fair, in the garden.

Matron has been planning the celebration like a military operation. The lawn has been mown and measured, markers have been placed for the positioning of the trestle tables, and tree branches overhanging the perimeter fence have been pruned for fear that one of us may take advantage of the crowd and celebratory atmosphere to scale a tree and hotfoot it down the road. The perimeter railings and gates too have been inspected for damage for fear of a mass breakout; Matron will leave nothing to chance. Those attendants who will be supervising the festivities have been drilled, and placated with a day and a half off in lieu of the public holiday.

The gardeners have been working since sunrise and now the trees are strung with Union flags and bunting; in preparation for our feast, three long trestle tables have been placed in the middle of the lawn and decorated with red, white and blue paper table-cloths. Last week a typed menu was placed in the refectory to inform us of our coming repast: we will be having an afternoon tea of cake; a choice of ham or cheese sandwiches; fruit; and lots of cups of tea. As a treat, those who smoke will be offered tobacco, with extra fruit for those who do not indulge. But with the pros-pect of celebrations within the confines of the asylum being the only ones I will ever attend, I do not feel like indulging in any-thing unless it is a gallon of mother's ruin.

At five minutes to one, Matron struts into the ward and instructs the attendants to accompany us to the garden. I raise my hand and ask Matron if I may be of any assistance to her; the attendants laugh, but Matron does not follow their lead. Instead, she declines my offer politely and says that she is sure the attendants will be able to cope. We line up in pairs like children and shuffle out of the ward into the blinding sunshine, where the kitchen staff are making the finishing touches to the place settings. Along with the geriatrics' ward, we are to be the first sitting of one hundred guests and there are to be five sittings in all, each lasting last one hour. The female wards are to attend first, the male wards are scheduled to attend from four o'clock, and all sittings will be completed by six o'clock. Not everyone will attend the festivities; the few who have declined have been herded into our ward and chaperoned for the afternoon and those who might have disrupted proceedings have already been straitjacketed off to the cells.

We take our seats around the table and behave like guests at any other party: we ignore everyone not in our clique. By a quarter to two we have progressed to the fruit, except for the old biddies, who are still dribbling their way through their slice of Victoria sandwich cake.

What else could there be on this special day? The tobacco has been decreed to be solely for the male patients. Maggie, who has somehow managed to muster enough strength to attend the celebration, is up out of her seat faster than I have ever seen her move and is complaining to Matron that she would like 'a bit of baccie'. Matron will not be swayed and says that Maggie must make do with extra fruit, which is hardly an alternative: we have apples not pineapples, for goodness' sake! Maggie sits back in her seat, arms folded, chuntering to herself, calling Matron names that would make a sailor blush.

As an apology for my behaviour towards her when I spent weeks in bed, I have swiped an extra slice of fruit cake to tempt Elise, who eats so little of the asylum food that it is a wonder she survives. But she has expressed a liking for dried fruit, and on the rare occasions we are given fruit cake she likes to pick out each sultana and raisin and consume them one by one, like a hedge sparrow.

At ten minutes to two, Matron declares the tea over, and we sing a cock-eyed rendition of 'God Save the Queen'. Not that she will hear our supplications for her health and victories, or those from any of her subjects in her far-flung empire, as she is too arthritic to travel any further than St Paul's in her carriage. But Matron says that there are to be soldiers of every hue from all over her empire leading the royal procession and that it is expected that millions of people will gather in London to witness this spectacle of

Imperial might. The momentous occasion is to be recorded on this new-fangled moving film and shown to her subjects in theatres all over the globe. We will not get to see the film, but Her Majesty has telegraphed a message to bless us and all her subjects, which cheers us up no end. In '58 she did pay a visit to Leeds to open the new town hall with Prince Albert, who declared that what Leeds really needed was a decent theatre to lift it from its cultural mire. Two decades later it was built; too late for poor Albert, though.

Back on the ward, Elise and Queenie, two of the absenters, are sitting together on Queenie's bed, but only in the sense that they inhabit the same space, for they neither talk nor look at each other. Queenie is reading her forty-year-old diary; some of the pages are torn and a few detach themselves as she reads. She places them back, careful not to rip them, smoothing down their edges as best she can. Her head moves back and forth, following each line as she whispers each word, her mouth contorting into smiles and grimaces in equal measure. Deep in her medical records, I expect it says she was subjected to the dreaded cold-water treatment, as, on the rare occasions she leaves her bed, at the hint of a raincloud, she will refuse to go out for an airing, and will wail and shake if a shower catches her unawares. They seem to favour water therapy, these doctors, and it is a wonder that after breakfast they do not have us all jump in the cut. I have had the water treatment, but in my case I was ensconced in a warm bath for three hours, face red, skin turning into a prune; I do not know if it calmed me down, but I was certainly cleansed of something. But the cold-water treatment, when the poor patient is restrained in a chair and an attendant fires ice-cold water at them to either cool their mania or rouse their spirits depending on their condition, has been banned by the superintendent. Queenie is now treated with the current wheeze: good quality food and vigorous exercise; but she can rarely be persuaded to partake of either. She's a fixture here now, but where else would she go? She would be dead within in a year in the workhouse.

Elise, with her back to Queenie, stares at the wall behind the bedhead. I fear Elise has the morbs just as Queenie does, but it is a more acute malady, and she will not survive for thirty-five years as Queenie has. My return to the ward drags Elise out of her stupor and she turns and rises to hug me, and Queenie, encouraged by this show of affection, does the same, as if I draw them like a bellwether for the mentally afflicted; but I will leave the guidance of the flock to the superintendent. I remove their arms from my waist and sit on my bed; I cannot be the mother to one and the daughter to the other that I suspect they crave. In the spirit of ingratiating myself, I suggest that tomorrow morning they might change from their nightclothes into their daywear and we all go out to the airing courts together for half an hour, but they both shake their head vigorously, as if I have suggested that we take a trip to Blackpool and jump off the Tower.

A few days later and I am seated, once more, in my little room. For the first time this year, the French windows have been opened and I am enjoying the freshness it brings. O'Neill is absent today: she has had an upset stomach for the past two days and is vomiting all over the place. Matron has assured her that she could not possibly have food poisoning from the asylum kitchens and that she must stay in the attendants' residence so that she does not infect the patients. Langley, who seems to revel in the gruesome details and has no doubt embellished the story, has been sent in her stead. She is a poor substitute for O'Neill: Langley has straggly grey hair on her head and her chin, and a voice that would grate cheddar. She is not one of 'my girls'; I suspect she has never sunk her feet into a fresh cowpat so that the warm green sludge squelches between your toes, or foraged for field mushrooms on a dewy September morning and marvelled at how so many have erupted from a patch of grass that but yesterday had been as smooth as a calf's hide. I hope O'Neill recovers before our next session.

Pomona is late. Rowse shuffles in her chair and whispers to gangly Langley that she will give the doctor another five minutes and then she will go in search of Matron. Sarah is not her real Christian name. I heard her tell O'Neill that her name is Sorrel, but she does not use it as she was bullied for the name as a child; but I think it suits her. I can imagine her searching for the bitter, lemony leaves in a sun-dappled wood, with the sound of the sea whispering through the trees.

Two minutes later, Pomona hurtles through the door, apologises for her tardiness, and tells us that in future she may take a cab. 'Where would you like to start today?' she says, dismissing the attendants and wedging herself into the chair opposite, pen poised in readiness, cheeks flushed from her exertions.

Little Meadows Farm, 25 October 1887

The last Tuesday in the month is always my father's day to go to Shrewsbury. My mother never accompanies him, but he usually takes his young girls, as he calls us, and we wheedle a few pennies out of him to go to the shops even though we have our own money, having received the six pound notes that my father gives to each of his girls when we reach the exulted age of sixteen or when we are married, whichever comes first. My father usually goes to his bank and to Fleets, his tailor, for a few a few 'odds and sods', as he calls them; his suits and shirts, which will 'last me a lifetime', having been purchased in the days before the farm, at a Savile Row tailor. But today it is just me and him, as Prudence is helping Mother to pickle shallots and Honesty is off to Manor Farm to help with the potato harvest. I have never known Honesty to want to get her hands dirty or to miss the chance to visit the linen shop or the confectioners', but I expect it has something to do with Percy, Old Farmer Frank's only son. Old Farmer Frank was sixty if he was a day when he married Percy's mother, so Percy is quite a catch as soon he will undoubtedly inherit Manor Farm which is well more than two hundred acres. Honesty and Percy could be twins, all fair hair and blue eyes, beautiful really; it must be like looking into a mirror.

Honesty had always been a chubby child – angelic, people said, with her cherubic curls and red lips. She had hated her looks and so of course we had all teased her, the way envious children often do. But she had her revenge: she outgrew the puppy fat, but the golden hair and full lips remained. She has had half the lads in the district sniffing round her at some time or other like flies to a freshly dropped cowpat. But I have never known Honesty chase after any man. Percy is, I expect, used to being chased and caught by the local farmers' daughters, and, although they might be good enough for a roll in the hay, he has not stayed with any of them for more than a fortnight. But I have seen the way he gazes at Honesty when he rides past our farm on his horse and thinks that no one is looking.

Whatever the reason, I am happy to have my father to myself. When we arrive in Shrewsbury, he asks me if I would like to go to his bank with him, as he thinks I am now old enough to find out about banking the farm's takings. My planned trip to Leake and Aduit booksellers, where I would normally spend an hour looking through my favourites and a few of the new titles, is instantly forgotten; he has never invited any of my sisters to go with him to his bank. As we walk up Wyle Cop, several passers-by greet him with a handshake. He stops to talk with a gentleman in a frock coat and top hat – 'My solicitor,' he says, after the man has departed. One man asks my father if he would like to go for a glass of ale, but he says not today, as today he has his daughter with him, and the stranger tips his hat to me. I had not seen any of this before, and it is strange to think of my father as having this other life; that year after year this is his habit; that he is something other than my father the farmer.

My father's bank is on the High Street. It is a large stone edifice with the words *Midland Bank* carved above the oak front door. The inside of the bank is huge and smells of cigars and what I presume must be money. This is a man's domain; even the tellers are men. The men stare at my father with me in tow as if he has brought in a pet monkey on a leash rather than a young woman; it's obviously not the done thing. He ignores their stares, pays in his takings, and then suggests we go for a meal. I think I might burst with happiness; this is the best day of my life. It's a proper restaurant as well, with tablecloths and napkins and waiters queuing up to serve us.

'I've been coming here every month for years. The food is wonderful, much better than your mother's – but don't tell her, it'll be our secret,' he says with a wink. 'How would you like to look at a new seed drill before we return home? I'm going to treat myself to some new implements, since your mother vetoed the idea of a steam tractor. Too expensive, she said.'

'Why not buy a tractor if you have the money? It's your farm and you have wanted one for years,' I say. I have never spoken to my father about money before, but, since he has chosen to take me to his bank, I reason I am old enough to broach the subject.

'And hear about it for months afterwards? You know what she's like.'

I have never heard my father speak about my mother in such a disloyal way, and now twice in one day, even though we both know the revelations to be true. 'Ignore her and do it anyway,' I say.

'There are more people than me at home who might reap the repercussions, though, aren't there? Anyway, if you have finished your milk, let's be on our way,' he says, stifling the conversation, embarrassed that he has dropped below the standards he has always set for himself. My father takes my arm, since at sixteen years old I am little too old to hold his hand, and we walk to the Mitre and collect a rested Gideon and our trap from the stables at the back. A mile out of Shrewsbury we stop at the yard of an agricultural merchant and look at harrows and ploughs and perhaps seed drills; I do not know because I am not paying much attention. I am just itching to be on our way and sitting beside him on the journey home with a grin on my face because I know I have cemented myself in my father's affections and his plans for the farm.

CHAPTER NINE

Today I found Maggie dead in her bed. She had not roused herself after the first bell, which was not unusual as, all summer, she and Queenie have persisted in their game of feigning sleep even though Matron has threatened to take away their evening cocoa or send them to the geriatrics' ward. Queenie was sitting up in bed, shouting across the ward for the old goat to get up, and Rowse asked me to wake Maggie, if only to stop Queenie creating a disturbance among the other patients. I walked over to Maggie's bed; her whole body was buried under her bed sheet. I got down on my haunches beside her and whispered that it was time to get up; there was no movement and so I said the words more forcefully. She did not move, and I thought she was really playing up this time so I grabbed her bed sheet and pulled it down to her shoulders, only to reveal Maggie as white as the sheet under which she was lying, and just as stiff.

It was the syphilis that had changed her brain to mush and her arteries to stone. She had been in remission for years before she was admitted to Sunnyside, but it did for her in the end. I think we all knew it was coming: since the start of September she had started to talk gibberish and had taken swipes at Matron and Rowse, and the spitting had worsened. They say her husband gave it to her and that he is long since dead from it. So too all her children, who survived only a few short hours before being consigned to the ground like thousands of other poor souls afflicted by congenital syphilis, and all their mothers had to show for nine months of hope was a death certificate with a cause not even given the dignity of words: 'FTT', failed to thrive. He had not told her he had caught it, and if she had had a rash she had thought it some skin complaint, a flea bite, or perhaps a bed bug. She had had no reason to suspect he was off every week for a tuppenny quickie behind the Nag's Head. She had not even realised the truth when the babies kept dying; she had found it out much later and by then it was too late to take the mercury and, she told me in one of her more lucid moments, she could not have afforded it anyway.

Queenie is wailing, and has been since Maggie's demise. I will not shed a tear for Maggie. Not that I disliked the old coot, but I have taught myself to control my tears in the presence of others since the days when it seemed to please my mother to make me weep when she smacked me, and I would sit staring defiantly at her outstretched hand, daring her to try harder.

Queenie covers her head with her bed sheet, which is becoming sodden from her tears. I walk over to her bed and put my hand on her shoulder. She shrugs my hand away and says, 'I don't want you. I want Maggie. I want my friend.'

'But, Queenie,' I say, 'I thought you hated Maggie. You didn't have a good word to say about her when she was alive.'

She pulls off the sheet; her eyes are red, and her cheeks are streaked white and shiny with dried tears. 'She was my friend. What do you know about friends? You have no friends or family. No one ever visits you,' she says. It is not the time to say that she too has no visitors. 'You are not here most of the time and it's only me and Maggie and of course your pet Elise and she's away with the fairies most of the time. And now Maggie's gone.' She stares across at Maggie's bed, which has been stripped of its bedding, had a good scrub with carbolic, and is awaiting its next occupant, as if Maggie has never existed. I bet Matron wishes she had let Maggie have her bit of tobacco at the Jubilee celebrations four months ago.

'It's like she was never there,' wails Queenie, mirroring my thoughts.

I need to stem her tears otherwise I expect when I return from my shift in the sewing room I will find that the nurses have carted her off to the infirmary, and that might be the last time any of us sees her.

'I think they poisoned her,' says Queenie between sobs. 'Put something in her cocoa.'

'But we all had cocoa from the same urn,' I say. 'We would all be ill, wouldn't we?' Not that they would be averse to doing such a thing to be rid of a few of us. I hear they lace the male patients' cocoa with something so that they do not commit the sins of Onan underneath the bedcovers.

Queenie continues to weep and rock herself back and forth. I need to try something else.

'She's not in pain now, Queenie. Just think of that.'

'She wasn't *in* pain.'

'Perhaps not physical pain, or perhaps the drugs helped to ease it. But I expect she had mental pain. Who knows what demons have been assailing her these last few weeks. You know she was not her usual self.' I am clutching at straws, and she knows it. I try a final time; perhaps Queenie has embraced religion in her twilight years. 'She has gone to a better place. She will be reunited with all her lost babies.'

Queenie wipes her nose and eyes with the sleeve of her nightdress. 'Yes, she will be, won't she,' she says. She sits up in her bed and submits to her morning wash without complaint, smiling and staring at the bed opposite where her adversary has resided for nigh on fifteen years. When I return that afternoon, Queenie is out of her bed for the first time in months and is sitting at the bottom of Maggie's recently vacated bed. The bed's new occupant is a girl, thin, pale, about twenty years old; she leans against her pillows, listening to Queenie's gabbling and cradling an imaginary baby in her arms.

Pomona has been away studying and has missed our September and October meetings, but Matron says we shall have additional sessions if Dr Fairchild deems it important to my recovery. I am not sure it can be, for, before she went away, both our July and our August sessions were entirely unmemorable; I suspected Pomona was suffering from the heat, or perhaps was focused on her forthcoming trip, and we had both been listless, I merely recounting trivial stories about life on the farm, and she offering fewer comments than usual.

Tomorrow is Guy Fawkes Day, but the superintendent has banned any celebration for fear of disturbing patients of a nervous disposition; that is all of us really. But the ward will still be alive with colour from distant celebrations, despite the blackout curtains, and no doubt the unfiltered noise will have Elise cowering at the bottom of my bed.

I am gazing out of the French windows of my little sitting room at the bare trees beyond. O'Neill has had to wipe a porthole about a foot wide in the misted-up glass so that we may see Pomona arrive, although with the warmth of the fire it is quickly hazing over again. Tendrils of mould cling to the damp wall by the window, threatening to encroach on the curtains.

O'Neill and Rowse both have the night off after this, and will be attending a bonfire that is 'a big one, the biggest ever!' O'Neill hopes they will not burn an effigy of the Pope, or she will be straight back to the asylum on the next omnibus. Rowse has an assignation with her dashing new beau whom she met at the Princess's Theatre, and is hoping for some fireworks of her own. O'Neill does not like dancing or the theatre, and besides has no young man to accompany her, and so instead has been attending Mount St Mary's Church on Wednesdays, Saturdays and twice on Sundays. It is to no avail; the bump is already showing. She is lucky that Matron reserves her hawk eyes for the patients.

Pomona bustles through the door at three o'clock, bringing with her the smells of decaying leaves and fungi, a sure sign that the year is drawing in. She has two new notebooks stuffed into a carpet bag and a new hairstyle that is centre-braided and tied with a generous green velvet bow at the back. She is wearing a new suit; it's not off-the-peg. I've worked in such an establishment long enough to know the difference. The suit is frost grey with leg-o'-mutton sleeves, and, to complement the bow, a silk blouse of eau-de-Nil. It makes her look elegant, older, a woman, not the girl she used to be. I suppose we all must grow up some time.

She dumps her bag on the floor and locks the outside door.

'Look, Lily, they have entrusted me with a key at last,' she says, holding it aloft before bending down and depositing it in a pocket in her bag.

'Wish they would give me one,' I say.

'One day you will not need one.'

'Yes, one way or the other.'

After the girls depart, she leans towards me and says, 'Lily, as you know, I have been away for a conference. I have been at Leeds Medical School, a pioneering establishment at the forefront of psychology, and have been studying the works of the eminent Austrian psychologist Sigmund Freud, a man I greatly admire, who, along with the esteemed psychiatrist Breuer, has novel ideas on your condition.'

She makes me sound as if I am with child, and I make a gesture with my arms to indicate a bulbous belly. Pomona sighs.

'Hysteria, Lily, although I know you know that. Anyway, back to today's session. As it is soon to be Guy Fawkes Day, I wonder if we could talk about a childhood celebration. I will be interested in your choice.'

Little Meadows Farm, May 1888

I love late spring, when the dawn chorus wakes you up at a silly hour but you do not care because there are hours before the cows must be milked and you can throw open your bedroom window to let in the early sunshine and run back to your bed to read the book that weariness, rather than the lack of light, made you abandon the night before. But there is still a nip in the air, and you are for once grateful for your mother's reliance on old sayings, for 'ne'er cast a clout till May be out' has ensured you still have the warmth of your winter eiderdown.

There is a footfall on the landing and my mother opens my bedroom door without knocking and says, 'I've never known a girl read so much when there is plenty of work to be getting on with.'

'But the cows aren't due to be milked for another half an hour,' I protest.

'I'm not talking about the cows,' my mother says. 'In case you have forgotten, it's Honesty's wedding today. The flowers in the barn need checking and the sandwiches need to be started and the cakes put out ready. And the glasses need to be dusted and the wine and cider need checking in the cellar.'

'Can't Honesty help?'

'She's not going to be doing any work today, for goodness' sake! She needs to make herself look beautiful! Not that she is not beautiful already.' Mother looks me over, tuts, grabs the book from my hand and shoves it on my nightstand. 'At least she found someone to marry her. Not stuck with her nose in a book all the time.'

I am tempted to say that at sixteen I can hardly be considered an old maid, but instead I rise and pour water from the jug on the washstand into the bowl and splash my face with it; the water is cold, despite the sun's rays. My mother stands motionless in the doorway like a sentinel, expecting me to dress in front of her. I turn to face her and we stand staring at each other for a minute, until she sighs and leaves the room, slamming the door behind her like a child; it is her only means of resistance, as we are long past the days when, towering over me, she would slap me with impunity.

In the kitchen, Hope is cooking an early breakfast. As it is a special day, there are eggs poaching in the poacher and fat bacon and sausage from one of our pigs, probably Petunia as she always was a prize porker, sizzling in the frying pan. I expect Honesty will not be able to eat any of it in her condition. I feel an unexpected lump in my throat: it will be her last breakfast in her childhood home as a single woman. Tomorrow it will be just me and Hope left to fly the coop. Not that there is any hope of Hope ever leaving. She was already of marriageable age when I was born, but there has never been much interest in that direction, either from her or from any suitors. She is not blessed with looks, but she is a good cook and a hard worker. She is not capable of running a farm like me, but would make a decent farmer's wife nonetheless. But it is her tongue that is her downfall, and, even if my father were to offer a huge dowry, I expect there would be no takers.

Honesty is still in bed, despite the smell of fried breakfast that must surely be wafting up the stairs. Honesty has never moved from her attic girlhood bedroom even though she could have taken one of the larger bedrooms on the first floor as I have, since my older sisters have long since been married off and vacated them. I am just about to offer to take something up to her when in she walks, still wearing her nightgown but looking every inch the virginal bride, with her hair freshly washed and tumbling around her shoulders like a golden waterfall, asking for black tea and a crust of bread; she dare not risk any other food as the sickness has only subsided a few days ago.

We are just finishing our breakfast when Prudence walks through the back door and into the kitchen, with her husband Fred trailing in her wake, as if they have been married for years instead of barely a week. Honesty's marriage is out of necessity, but I have no idea why Prudence married Fred. I suppose she must love him, although he is not my idea of a husband. Fred is short and dark-skinned with a mop of wiry black hair and an eye that permanently looks to the left. He is an apprentice blacksmith, although in six months' time he hopes to have his own thriving workshop out Shrewsbury way. I hear that when Prudence's helpful suggestions get too much for him, which I suspect he has discovered is quite often, he takes himself away to the forge and bangs away on an anvil with his largest hammer until the workshop is alive with sparks and his frustration is spent. They join us at the kitchen table and, with three of us younger girls present, it is almost like the old days.

Prudence must have been reading my thoughts because she says, 'Is Mercy coming?'

'No, she's only got about a fortnight to go and didn't want to risk the journey. Your elder sisters are coming this afternoon, so it's only you, Lily and Hope to help with the preparations. You can help Lily with the flowers. You had better change out of that smart dress – you don't want to get it ruined,' says my mother. Prudence opens her mouth as if to protest that her newly married status gives her some sort of immunity from the mundane wedding preparations, but she says nothing and puts on one of Honesty's old dresses.

A quarter of an hour later, my father excuses himself and says that today he and my mother will milk the cows, and, pleased to be excused from that task, I walk with Prudence to the Dutch barn to assess the condition of the wedding flowers. The barn is devoid of any hay but there are trestle tables and chairs down its centre, and cornflowers and poppies in milk churns, vases, jars and any other receptacle that will hold water dotted all around the building. Most of the flowers appear to have survived the week since Prudence and Fred's wedding surprisingly well. Percy had wanted the wedding breakfast to be at Manor Farm, but Honesty had been adamant that it was tradition for a father to pay for his daughter's wedding and she wanted to have it at home and besides, everything would still be in place since Prudence's wedding the previous week. He had protested that Manor Farm was her new home, but I expect she had smiled that sweet Honesty smile, and he had acquiesced. From the rafters hang bunches of lavender and honeysuckle; they still smell wonderful but are a bit dried out, but I am not going to climb up there and risk breaking my neck trying to replenish them. Prudence goes to the well to draw some water and I take a trug and walk down to the upper cornfields and pick more poppies and cornflowers. When I return, Prudence has already been to the garden and picked the white lilac we need, and so together we replenish all the receptacles with the water and weed out and replace those flowers that have not survived the week. We have just finished our task when Fred and my mother and father walk in carrying glasses and plates, and when these have been set on the tables Fred goes to the orchard with my father to have a smoke, and the rest of us troop back to the kitchen to help Hope with the wedding breakfast.

By noon, we are as ready as we will ever be and are sitting around the kitchen table drinking tea when Honesty walks in. She has asked for no help in dressing and so it is the first time any of us have seen her in her wedding finery. I must admit she is a sight to behold: a plain white cotton gown that hides her growing stomach, white honesty flowers in her hair, ringlets in a halo around her face, and Percy's mother's engagement ring glistening on her finger. She looks like a bride from Arthurian legend, and for a fleeting moment I envy her her bridegroom and her wedding, even if Percy is no Sir Galahad.

There are no spare seats to be had in church, as country folk love nothing more than an excuse to dress up in their good clothes and eat a free meal. The organist starts to play the Wedding March, and all eyes turn to my father and his prettiest daughter as they wend their way down the aisle. My father looks very handsome in his tailored suit still smelling faintly of mothballs. It is strange that Honesty is the only one who has inherited his fair hair; the rest of us are not redheads like my mother, but dark-haired like our Lovell grandparents. When they reach the end of the aisle my father steps to the left to join his family in the first two rows of pews and Honesty stands next to Percy, the final enactment of the ancient ceremony of giving your daughter away to the care of another man, like a prize sow. But I suppose these days it is only symbolic; there is no dowry involved and besides, Honesty has already given herself away to Percy some months ago. Not that she is the first to be with child on her wedding day and she certainly will not be the last and in some ways it is a prerequisite for a farmer to whom fecundity is everything, especially to secure your own lineage.

Honesty is now Mrs Burnell of Manor Farm, with all the expectations of largesse and patronage that elevated title brings her. I wonder if she is up to the task; I am sure I could make a better job of it if I were so inclined. Honesty looks ashen as she turns to walk hand in hand with Percy towards the church door, and I know she is praying that she can make it down the aisle before she vomits. But I expect our vicar, Reverend Pugh, who has christened, confirmed and now married Honesty, is used to that sort of thing. The newlyweds head the procession into the blinding sunshine, where Honesty manages to throw her bouquet behind her as tradition dictates. I duck out of the way in case it travels in my direction, and Honesty hurtles past me and throws herself behind the nearest gravestone. But when she emerges there is no telltale trail around her mouth or stain on her dress and she shakes her head at me and mouths, 'False alarm.' She returns to the side of her new husband, who scowls at her and then turns and smiles at the attendees and says, 'See, she hasn't deserted me already,' which causes a titter and a whispered 'Shame' from a couple of female voices at the back.

For all my mother's fussing, or perhaps because of it, the wedding breakfast goes without a hitch. My father stumbles his way through his speech, dabbing his eyes with his handkerchief, although you would think he would be used to it by now. Honesty leaves the top table twice to be sick and Percy, frowning, whispers a few words in her ear when she returns; he does not understand how she feels – how could he? – and every year for the next few years she will be in the same condition unless she does something about it. I can already see him eyeing up some of his previous conquests and come October, when Honesty will be as big as a house, I expect he will find a reason to be out late tending his herd and flock.

'That recollection is certainly more informative than talking about some foolish fireworks,' says Pomona.

'But I used to love Guy Fawkes Day. Didn't you?'

'My father forbade us having fireworks or going to a display,' says Pomona. 'He thought them dangerous. As a doctor, I expect he too often saw the aftermath of careless fun.'

'They are having a big bonfire and firework display in Leeds. Perhaps you could tag along with Rowse and O'Neill for your baptism of firework,' I say.

'Very clever. But I hardly think that would be appropriate.' Moments later she adds, 'You are joking, are you not?'

'About going with Rowse and O'Neill, yes, but there is to be a big display. Have you no female friends with whom you could attend?'

'My female friends are all back in Harrogate, and before you ask, and it is none of your business, I have no gentleman friend who might take me either,' she says, the lie betrayed by her cheeks, which are the colour of ripe cherries.

CHAPTER TEN

It is the day before Christmas Eve and the patients have been busy fashioning Christmas decorations from crêpe paper. I have been charged with threading the decorations on to string and now have miles of festive cheer pooling around my feet. The superintendent had been against this frivolity, insisting that a good Christian service, with a few well-chosen carols for good measure, followed by a decent Christmas dinner with all the trimmings, was all that was needed. But Matron suggested that the crafting of the paper decorations would be good therapy for the patients, and he has relented. If Matron's scheme is vindicated, the superintendent will claim in the new year that it was all his idea. The wards therefore will soon be festooned with paper Christmas trees, stars and snowmen. Relegated to the far corner of the room will be paper shapes of a dubious nature; even if you are mad, it seems you do not lose your sense of humour. The corporation has fulfilled its civic duty and donated money to purchase glass baubles for the whole of the asylum; Matron had to get a gardener to hang those earmarked for the wards, which are soon to be joined by our homespun efforts, way up in the rafters, just in case.

In the asylum foyer there is a twelve-foot Norwegian spruce whose aroma fills the adjacent wards. Its branches have been decorated with the remaining glass baubles, fruit, and gingerbread stars tied with red and green ribbons. Cook is proud of her gingerbread decorations; she confides to anyone who will listen that she has followed a recipe used by Queen Victoria's chef, and the biscuits have turned out good enough for Her Majesty. Visitors will be impressed that the tree imbues the asylum with a festive air, even if the patients will not get to see the huge spectacle.

At half-past two the bell rings and the visitors depart for their own celebrations, smug in the knowledge of having fulfilled their Yuletide duties. The tree is already shedding its needles. After tea, the staff who will be working over the festive period will place presents for each other under the tree; the presents will be opened after the Christmas Eve service. By Christmas morning the tree's bounty of fruit and ornaments will be harvested by an unseen hand and Matron will decree that next year she will not countenance the expense of glass baubles.

In my little sitting room, a log fire blazes and there are Christmas cards on the mantelshelf. I look inside the cards and see that they are all addressed to Matron on behalf of local businesses eager to secure her patronage; Matron should be careful that a draught does not blow the cards into the flames. I bet this chimney has not been swept for years and I would hate for there to be a chimney fire. A tower of mince pies on a plate decorated with a Christmas garland is placed on the table with the tea set. Rowse has travelled home for Christmas, but O'Neill has volunteered to work over the festive period. She will get extra time off in the summer and says that she will go to Blackpool for a week. Her mother is upset at her absence but will light an extra candle for her at midnight Mass. Gangly Langley is back, and in the intervening months she has not departed from her name.

Our session is to be shorter than usual because heavy snow is forecast and Pomona much catch an early train to Harrogate to spend Christmas with her parents, and as she carries neither bag nor briefcase I must assume that everything I say will be committed to memory. She has again been to a dressmaker and seems to have permanently discarded her manly coat and trousers; today she wears a navy fitted suit and cape and red leather gloves. She deposits her cape on the back of her chair and slides off her gloves to reveal manicured nails and a silver ring with a large diamond and two opals.

'Merry Christmas, Lily,' she says, 'have a mince pie with your cup of tea.'

'Merry Christmas, and congratulations,' I say, picking up the mince pie that has the most sugar on top. She smiles and edges her left hand towards me. I know a few things about precious stones. There was a chap down Market Street who would bite your hand off for these gems and the platinum band on which they sit. He was as straight as a die and would never diddle you. The last I heard of him, he was in Strangeways.

'When is the wedding to be?' I ask.

'Not for a few years,' she says, snatching her hand away. I wonder if her engagement will prompt an interrogation on marriage. But at least for now I am spared, as instead she says, 'I think we should talk about Christmas. Your Christmases, a proper country Christmas. A typical Day Christmas Day,' she says, laughing at her own wit.

I could give her a real country Christmas, a vision of snow and Yule logs and mistletoe and rosy-cheeked children and holly and ivy wound around a carved mantelpiece. Perhaps I will tell it later. She glances at the clock; she is hopeful that my recollection will be swift enough to be merely a footnote in her thesis. I decide to disappoint her.

Little Meadows Farm, Boxing Day 1888

Honesty and Percy are staying with us for Christmas because Manor Farm is still being repaired after a series of flash floods at the tail end of the year have left it uninhabitable. My father has sent me to the best bedroom to tell Honesty that dinner is on the table. She is lying on the bed, her right breast spilling out of her nightdress. The breast is white and streaked with veins and there is a dewdrop of milk dried on to the nipple. Elijah, her newborn, is asleep in the crook of her left arm. The day is beginning to draw in, so I haul the bedspread up the bed and cover them both with it. But Honesty is not asleep as I had presumed but is staring out of the window to the hills beyond. 'I'm sorry,' I say. 'Are you coming downstairs to eat with us?'

'Couldn't you bring me some up? I can't face going down. I'm so tired.'

The woman lying in the bed is not the beautiful bride of seven months ago. This woman is bony, with pale lips and straggly hair and aged well beyond her numerical years. If that is what marriage and children do for you then you can keep it; I am glad that I will have a farm to run on my own terms. Elijah wails and begins to root for his mother's breast, which has, despite its owner's exhaustion, involuntarily responded to the cry.

'The full works, is it?' I say. 'And Christmas pudding. I'll even try to get you the silver sixpence if you like.' That raises a smile. 'See, I knew I could tempt you.'

'That would be wonderful,' she says, hauling Elijah to her breast.

Honesty stays in bed for the rest of the day and Percy stays downstairs, getting steadily drunk on my father's best whisky. I suppose that is the way it is with babies. I take Honesty some supper at eight o'clock. The dinner I had taken her lies undisturbed, but she has made headway into the Christmas pudding. Next to the bowl lies the small sixpence I had secreted within it.

'Thanks for the sixpence,' she says, rubbing her eyes with her fists and then stretching her arms to the ceiling; without a bed jacket they look like the slender branches of a willow.

'Oh, good, you found the last one. I was beginning to wonder if someone had swallowed it,' I say.

'Shame it wasn't Percy,' she says.

Before I can ask her why she wishes Percy to choke, in the corner of the room Elijah starts to sniffle and cry out in between large gulping breaths. I walk over to his crib, pick him up and swaddle him with his blankets and sing to him the way I think mothers must do. After a few minutes his breath quietens and steadies and he falls asleep in my arms and I place him in his crib, tucking his blanket beneath him. Honesty too has fallen asleep, so I close the door gently and tell my family that Honesty is very sorry not to join them, but she is exhausted and needs her rest.

By nine o'clock, my other siblings have escaped to their homes to milk cows or pluck pheasants or some such; it is as good an excuse as any and like any good lie probably has some semblance of truth. My mother has gone off to bed with one of her heads. I sit with Percy and my father around the fireplace. They are both very merry and I must admit I have had a few glasses of porter myself. My father and Percy are discussing the current price of potatoes and how my father will have to get in extra farmhands on account of the additional winter barley he has planted. My father stands in front of the fire with his back to us. He looks diminished some-how, hunched and shrunken in a way I have not noticed before. But he continues to expound his theories while trying to hide the warming of his hands in the way he often does when his arthritis is playing up. Percy winks at me and nods his head towards my father; I find the gesture of conspiracy somehow unsettling. At about ten o'clock I take the supper plates and put them to soak in the sink in the back kitchen. 'When you go up to Mother, tell her I'll wash those in the morning, I'm off to bed now,' I say.

'Goodnight, Lily. I'll just check the cows and then I'll be up,' says my father. He hauls himself out of his armchair and staggers towards the kitchen. I have always thought that we should have had one of those signs that you see in country pubs that say 'Duck or grouse', because our ceilings are at least as low as any country alehouse. Not that my father is in a state to read anything or indeed feel the impact of the blow to his head from the kitchen door lintel; he laughs, rubs his head and walks out of the back door. Come morning, I expect we will find him curled up in the cowshed with Clarabel, his best girl.

Percy has consumed at least as much alcohol as my father but is rumoured to be able to drink a sailor under the table, especially if the sailor is paying for the liquor. As I wish him goodnight, he pulls me on to his lap. 'How about a Christmas kiss for your most handsome brother-in-law?' he says, his face hovering a few inches above mine, his arms outstretched to embrace me. He is certainly handsome, and it is a while since I have had someone's arms around me. I sit on his lap and let him kiss me. He tastes of that peculiar mixture of alcohol and cigars that is only pleasant at a certain time of the evening. I kiss him back and, encouraged by this, he puts his hand on my breast; despite my conscience screaming at me that he is Honesty's husband, I let it rest there. Then the back door opens and my father wobbles in saying he needs his knife to cut some twine for one of the barn doors that has refused to shut. I have no idea whether he has seen us, but I manage to wriggle free from Percy's grasp, jump from the chair, and stand glaring at Percy, who laughs at me.

Thank goodness for Father's return and Percy's laugh. I grab a brass candlestick from above the fireplace and run up the stairs, spilling teardrops of red candle wax on my feet. Halfway up the stairs I realise I cannot wait until the next day to know if Father has seen us together, so I lick my fingers, pinch out the candle flame and sit shivering in the darkness of the landing, waiting for my father to admonish Percy.

'How was the hay harvest this year?' I hear Percy say.

'Could have done with more rain, but managed to salvage something,' says my father.

'The winter barley's looking good, though. Had a walk over to the bottom fields yesterday.'

'Better than last year, but I'm getting a bit old for all that bending over. Just barking at the men is all I can manage nowadays. But don't tell anyone.'

'You should get yourself a farm manager to do that for you. He'll make sure the men are all doing their work, and that all your barns and sheds are secure as well. Another drink?'

'Why not? It is Christmas, after all.'

As it is my father's whisky, Percy pours two doubles, staggers over to the fireplace, and the two men plonk themselves in the fireside armchairs, warming their feet on the dwindling fire, the banging barn door forgotten. From my vantage point I can see two shapes silhouetted against the fire, my father hunched in the one chair and Percy taller than my father by at least six inches, upright in the other, but rising every few minutes to gesticulate, with his arms up to the low ceiling and then akimbo, to impress upon Father the size of his livestock or his barns, and all the time the glow of the fire highlighting his jerky movements like an automaton. If my father is going to berate Percy, he is certainly going around the Wrekin before he embarks upon it. He must not have seen us! But I cannot go back to my bedroom yet; my father is considering Percy's suggestion of getting someone else to manage the farm. This is not what I had been led to believe would happen when he relinquished the reins. I tiptoe to my bedroom, sneak out a shawl, and sit back on the landing, holding back the tears for fear I might wake the sleepers.

'You are right about the farm manager,' says my father, refilling his glass, 'but I can still do most of the work myself, and I have a few good men as well. But I have been thinking of somewhere smaller now that Hope is off in service and there's only Lily left to get married off. I've seen a decent-looking smallholding, about forty acres, over at Cound, not too far to transport the farm equipment, and just the right size for me and Dorelia to see out our old age.'

'I'm surprised. I thought you were wedded for life to this farm.'

'When I was a young man I could never have countenanced selling Uncle Herbert's farm. That's how I thought of it – his rather than mine – for a long time. I felt I owed it to him to keep it running, even in the bad times. But it will have to be sold one day and I would like it to be soon. I can give each of the girls a bit of money with what's left over.'

'I fancy Lily thinks she can run the farm for you, has been trained to do so. Maybe will even be left it in your will, like one would a son. Or she was led to believe that was the case.'

'Did Lily tell you that?'

'Honesty mentioned it.'

It is not true; I had only confided to Honesty my wish to never leave the farm. I had not credited her with enough intuition: she had seen through my subterfuge and had been busy telling Percy my desire to inherit it. I had never expected her to confide in Percy: I had thought it a secret between sisters. I wish now that I had kept my thoughts to myself as now wanting it so much has ensured that my desire will never be fulfilled.

'I never meant to give Lily the impression that I would leave her the farm, or that she would run the farm for me,' says my father. 'She's a capable girl, but she's not a son. I suppose Lily could marry and her man could run it, but a man needs his own farm, not spending his days running one for his father-in-law. Breeds resentment.'

'I know a few who would be interested in taking Lily off your hands. She's not a bad-looking girl and would certainly be a capable wife and mother. I have a couple of cousins about thirtyish who might be interested in her. They're done with sowing their wild oats and have got a bit of money behind them as well. Of course, they're not as handsome as me.'

My father laughs and says, 'I don't think that looks matter in a man, although I suppose they might do to Lily. I'm sure Honesty finds it a trial at times having a handsome husband.' Perhaps my father too has heard the rumours, but Percy does not reply; he is too sozzled to notice the barb. I want my father to stop talking now but he continues with the same disconcerting ramble. 'They just need to be financially well set up. We'll have to see about it in the new year, get the idea in motion. Get your cousins over to do some work. At least I'll get it done for free! Let's not make it obvious. We'll need to get Lily interested in that direction. But they'll have their work cut out. She's like her mother: a force of nature.'

'Needs a bit of taming, then.'

They laugh together in a way I had hoped that my father never would and my heart breaks: the one person in the world I thought I could trust has let me down.

'One more before you go out and shut that barn door?' says Percy, eager to seal the deal.

'No, better not,' says my father, getting up and venturing back out into the bitter night.

'Would you like to take a break, another cup of tea?' says Pomona. 'Get your voice back.'

My voice must have become hoarse, although I have not noticed. I must have been talking too much, giving too much of myself already. But I am glad of this hiatus, for now my story must diverge from the path of truth. I picture that path in front of me, forked like my tongue: the sordid, sinister left turn that lies seared on to the floor of my childhood bedroom; and the sanitised right turn, the Pomona truth, the less painful and less truthful iteration. She may understand the actions I took on that night, but I cannot give her the opportunity to choose.

Little Meadows Farm, Boxing Day 1888

I relight the candle and stumble into my bedroom. Thankfully there is still a good fire in the grate, although it is a blur of dancing red and orange flames. I undress in front of it and crawl into bed, burying myself beneath the covers. I feel as if I have lain awake for hours, torturing myself with my father's cruel words, and then, when sleep finally comes, I dream of my father dragging me by my hair down the aisle of our church, resplendent in its Yuletide foliage, and me not dressed for either a wedding or the season, and all the time my groom a hulking blurred shape waiting greedily at the altar. But I must have slept for a few hours or so because I can hear Percy snoring in the bedroom next door in a way that I have found, to my agitation on previous occasions, comes to him in the depths of the night.

The fire is out now, so I feel along my bedside table for matches and light the oil lamp that sits there and hang the expense. I think everyone must be asleep now, so it is time for me to go. If I am not going to be taking over the farm, I am not staying to be sold off in the new year to the highest bidder like a common whore. I go to my wardrobe and drag down the large carpet bag that lies on its roof. I bundle some clothes from out of the wardrobe and then feel my way to the chiffonier, where I take out an assortment of undergarments. From the corner of the top right-hand drawer of my chest of drawers I feel for my savings jar that lies buried in my winter scarf with my other treasures: two new unread books received as a Christmas gift. There is no room for any of my other books. I grab it all and shove it into the bag. It is still as black as coal outside; I pick up the lamp, and slink downstairs. In the hallway I put on my best winter coat and Honesty's scarf and gloves, and then, with Honesty's coat on one arm and my best hobnail boots dangling from the other, I extinguish the flame of the lamp, place it on the hall table, unlock the front door, and tiptoe out into the night.

I put on my boots as best that I can and walk from the house without a backward glance, for fear I might lose my resolve. I negotiate the drive by avoiding the gravel and finding the grassy patches that luckily are well known to me, there being very little moonlight, but they remain crunchy underfoot and each step sounds as if it echoes around the valley. The water in the troughs is frozen and the gate of the yard is laced with ice. The latch will be frozen solid; there is no point trying to open it, I will have to scale the gate, so I throw my carpet bag over, place Honesty's coat on the top rail and start to climb. But the bars of the gate are slippery underfoot and as I haul myself over I lose my footing and fall to the ground. There are shards of gravel embedded in my palms, but I have avoided a broken nose, although liquid is gushing warm and metallic down my chin and my left eye is starting to close. I staunch the blood flow with one of my scarves and hobble out of the yard and down the drive.

At the top of the drive where it meets the main road, itself no more than a dirt track, having no idea to where I should flee, I decide to trust my destination to the flip of a coin: tails will see me heading towards Much Wenlock, heads towards Church Stretton. It is light enough now to see the faces of the coin and the gravel in my palms. I start to pick at the most stubborn pieces and take a coin from my savings jar but then drop the damned thing and nearly fall over again when I bend to retrieve it. The coin is lost, but my dizziness reminds me of the pointless game we played as children where we would spin round and round until we became giddy, and the winner was the one left standing. I have an idea. A few turns of that daft game would do; I only want a direction not nausea. But I imagine that if anyone is watching I must look like a demented whirling dervish with my battered head and my left eye half closed and Honesty's best coat flailing around me.

I manage to walk the seven miles to Much Wenlock station and lie footsore and exhausted on the bench on the empty platform with both coats and two scarves wrapped around me. Owls hoot in the woods, and, somewhere in the fields, vixens screech for a mate like murder victims. But I must have slept at least an hour, because at six o'clock the station master arrives and, surprised to see a prone figure on one of his benches, prods me with his finger. I sit up and he ushers me into the waiting room and in two minutes he has lit a fire. I warm myself for ten minutes and then go to the ticket office and buy a ticket for the next train to Shrewsbury. As I pay for my ticket my heart is thumping in my chest, but the station master does not recognise me, nor does he ask any questions, not even about my bloody scarf; he only speaks to tell me there are only four trains a day to Shrewsbury but I am lucky as the next one will be at half-past six in the morning. Still, I am sure that I will be fodder for his stories down the pub for the next few weeks.

By the middle of the day I am on my third train. I have heeded no timetable or direction except that the train I board will take me away from fields and farms to the sprawling industry of the north. I must have travelled through Crewe, but after leaving Shrewsbury station I remember little of my journey other than the hope that it will take me far enough away from my past that I might never be found.

Silence. My doctor's chair is upholstered in green velvet and there are two fancy green cushions edged in red for the festive season; but it might as well be made of cast iron for the comfort it now delivers. I bet she wishes she had her notebook and her posh pen with its ready nib and dribbling ink. Now for her notes she will need to rely on her memory.

'You did ask for a Day Christmas Day,' I say.

'Why did you choose one of your worst?' she says. 'Why not one from your childhood, a joyful country Christmas – food, presents, Santa Claus. Was there none like that?'

She is obsessed with this preposterous idea of a rural idyll. A few weeks working on a farm in the depths of winter would disabuse her of this illusion, but for now a gentle chiding will suffice.

'There were plenty,' I say, 'but you would not need my words to write that fairytale; just choose any child's Christmas story book. And I thought you wished to understand me better?'

'Could you not have stayed? You had not really done anything wrong.'

'It was not the Percy thing. Even if our dalliance had become known I could have stomached my family's condemnation of my disloyal behaviour, and if we hadn't been seen by my father, Percy probably wouldn't have said anything anyway. It was my father. It was clear I was never going to run the farm, and it had never been my father's intention that I should. And even if he had not said as such, he had implied it, and how is a child supposed to know the difference? Those nights in his study, our trip to Shrewsbury together, had meant nothing. His treatment of me as a mere chattel, to be joked about, to be married off, just like all my sisters, not a favourite at all, was the last straw. I wasn't going to hang around for that to happen.'

'So, you acknowledge the importance of that Christmas. Your father's rejection of you as a farm manager must have been extremely traumatic if you felt that you had to leave?'

'If you say so,' I say. 'I'm sure you know more about these things than I do.'

CHAPTER ELEVEN

Pomona will be on the train to Harrogate by now; first class of course. Her worries about my story will be mitigated by the cheer of her fellow travellers, all eager to escape the Smoke for the festive season. Her young man – I presume him to be young but in truth I do not know his age – will meet her at the station. I expect he is a professional gentleman; her parents would countenance no less. They will exit the station and instead of a hailing a cab they will walk in the snow, which has started to fall heavily now, playfully throwing snowballs at each other until they reach her parents' house, eager to find some time for each other before spending a well-chaperoned Christmas with her relations. She will try to forget my story until after the new year, when she will drag herself from her revelries and write up the account of my Christmas long past.

She must have had an uneventful life if she believes that my disappointment with my father would make me do a moonlight flit. I would have left eventually, although not like that. But my plan is working, and that is as close to a Christmas miracle as I can hope for, until I myself am walking freely in the snow. I can only hope she does not think I must be mad for leaving my future to the flip of a coin and the vagaries of a train timetable.

As I drift to sleep that night, my mind is still on that fateful Christmas. How different life might look if the story I told to Pomona had been true.

Little Meadows Farm, Boxing Day 1888

I stumble into my bedroom, place the candlestick by my bed and undress by the firelight. I throw a few coals on the near dead fire, and, since it is Christmas, I excuse myself the bother of washing my face and hands or brushing my hair and slide into my freezing bed, wishing I had placed a warming pan there hours ago. Yet, despite the late hour and an excess of porter, I cannot sleep. Instead, I am torturing myself with the weakness of allowing Percy to kiss me and the cruel words spoken by my father.

The wind too has awoken and is rattling the bedroom window catches. I rise from my bed and walk to the window and attempt to stifle the noisy frame with a blanket. It is blowing a gale out there and snowflakes are throwing themselves against the pane. I put a few more coals on the fire and run back to my bed and snuggle down beneath the covers. Now the wind is rattling the catch on my door; up and down it goes with each gust until I realise that it is not the wind but someone fiddling with the catch on the other side of the door. Finally, the door is opened and a wedge of light from the landing is cast on to my bed. A figure stands in the doorway immobile for about half a minute and then trips down the steps into my bedroom.

'Surprise!' Percy steps into the firelight and waves a bottle of sloe gin at me that he must have taken from the pantry. 'Compliments to your mother,' he says, taking another gulp from the bottle.

I want to scream at him to get out but instead say, 'Percy, you are in the wrong bedroom.'

'Oh, I don't *think* so,' he sings.

He must be very drunk, so I speak to him like a child. 'Now, Percy, you know this isn't your room. You are next door with Honesty.'

'*Next door with Honesty. Next door with Honesty.* Ah, my lovely wife. She was a beauty, you know. No one to touch her, or so she tells me. Not now, though. Bony bitch. She was a bonny bitch, honest she was,' he says. 'Now how about finishing what we started downstairs?' He starts to fumble with his trousers and pull at his shirt, but he cannot thread the buttons through their holes. He swears and rips the shirt from his body, scattering buttons across the floor like confetti, and then flings his shirt, vest and trousers at my hat stand. They miss the stand, of course, and fall to the floor. When he turns to me, he is naked except for his garters and socks and stands in front of my bed, illuminated by the firelight like a grotesque music hall turn. It is a pity that he has not drunk more of my father's whisky. He wrenches the bed covers from my grasp and tries to get in beside me; I am panicking now, kicking out at him wildly. He falls to the floor with a thud.

'Well, aren't you quite the tease,' he says, laughing and rubbing the inside of his thigh with his left hand before moving it upwards to his groin. 'That's going to be a decent bruise. I'll tell Honesty one of the heifers kicked me. That wouldn't exactly be a lie, would it?'

I retreat to the far corner of the bed, pulling the covers around me, and he kneels on the space I have vacated. He tears his hand away from his groin and presses his index finger to his lips. 'Now you wouldn't want to start shouting and wake poor baby Elijah, would you, and have Honesty come running in here? I'm not sure what she would call you. And I'm sure your father would have a few choice words too. I'll just apologise and blame it on you and your father's whisky,' he says, 'makes you frisky, you know.'

His speech is becoming less slurred and for a few seconds I wonder if he will sober up and realise what he is doing and slink back to Honesty's room. But instead, he leans over and pulls the covers from my grasp and traps my wrists under his left hand; I can feel my veins pulsing against it. With his right hand he is forcing up my nightgown. I work my right wrist free and lunge at his face but only succeed in painting his cheek with streaks of coal dust so that he resembles the heathen savages I read about at Sunday School. He raises his right hand high above my head and slaps me across the face with a force that knocks me into the wooden headboard. I can feel my left eye starting to close.

'I could always go next door and wake up that bitch myself. I'm sure she would be more accommodating than you. Conjugal rights and all that.'

I would like to say that I was not thinking of myself but of Elijah lying peacefully in his crib and of Honesty lying exhausted in her bed, only to be woken and slung around like a rag doll and him pushing himself inside her. But I am beyond thought, and, if any thought exists, I cannot speak it. There is a ceiling rose in the design of a wreath of roses above my bed. Two of its leaves are missing. Years ago, when we were scrapping, I had flung one of my hobnail boots at Mercy; she was always light on her feet and had ducked and the boot had taken chunks out of the plaster. We did not tell my mother or father, and, as the candle-holder was never filled, they never saw the damage. The damage was at three and nine o'clock and it must have been a hefty shot to have denuded both sides of the wreath. Percy's face is hovering above mine, and he is trying to force himself inside me. I determine to catch a train and go to Baker's Builders' Merchants in Shrewsbury to get some plaster. Surely the repair would be easy; I was always handy with a trowel. It would be as good as new. I would buy some candles as well. In his haste for release he seems to be having trouble locating any orifice and has had to take his hands from my wrists to turn me over for easier access. I reach out and try to grab at something, anything, and my outstretched fingers find the candlestick on my bedside table. I wriggle across an inch – he has his full weight on me now – and smash it into the back of his skull. He falls on top of me and I shove him on to the floor, and then hit him again. He whimpers and then is silent, sprawled out on my rag rug like a drunkard. I stumble to the fireplace and light the candle with the dying flames. The base of the candlestick is sticky with his blood and bits of bone. I poke his chest with my foot and bend down to listen for any breath; there is none. They say you should put a mirror to someone's mouth to check for breath, but the only mirror is attached to the dressing table, so I grab his wrist and feel for a pulse; there is not a flicker of a beat. My naked brother-in-law is dead on the floor of my bedroom with his head and face bashed in.

I open my mouth to scream for Honesty or my father and then

realise how this will look. They will say I encouraged Percy into my room, into my bed, and that, when he was all set to do the deed, I changed my mind and attacked him. I could say a robber – perhaps a vagrant, you see quite a few on the roads around here – broke in through the window with the loose catch and Percy rushed in hearing the commotion and was attacked. But surely he would have put on some breeches or a nightshirt? I look at the clock and realise I have been sitting in my chemise staring at him for half an hour and that I am covered with gooseflesh. But I cannot stay here until morning. I shove the bloody candle-stick and everything out of my chest of drawers into a bag, shut my bedroom door, and run down the stairs and grab a handful of scarves, coats and boots from the hall stand and run barefoot down the drive, ignoring the frozen gravel cutting into my feet at every step.

I should at least have until breakfast time, as Honesty will think Percy has slept off the excesses of the night before downstairs. They will be after me soon enough then, unless they think I have been kidnapped and Percy has been killed trying to defend me. But would anyone believe Percy would do such a thing? And why would my clothes and money be gone, unless the kidnapper took those as well? I cannot take that chance; they will never believe it was self-defence. I need to get as far away from Little Meadows as possible before they are on to me.

CHAPTER TWELVE

It's Christmas Day in the Madhouse
And the tables are all a-heaving,
Replete with food, but when we withdraw,
None of us is leaving.
Our benefactors gave us beef,
Not knowing that their do-gooding
Would usher in three long days of cold meat,
With just as cold rice pudding.
No work to do in the laundry,
No washing, no ironing, no steaming
There will be no dissent today
Just opiates and no screaming.
A toast to Christmas and New Year,
Let's all be hale and hearty,
Let's misbehave because we know
They've cancelled our New Year Party.

'Thank you, Miss Lily Day,' says Matron, climbing the steps at the side of the stage and shooing me back to the dance floor. She walks to the centre of the stage and says, 'Not as billed, but an inspired interpretation of that well-known ballad. In reply to Miss Day's statement and in anticipation that it will not cause any bad behaviour, I can confirm there will be no New Year's Eve party this year. Now I know you have all spent months making your costumes and are disappointed, but, as you well know, we do not have the staff to oversee the celebrations.'

Cries of 'Oh, yes, you do!' erupt from the audience and then the boos and hisses begin. Matron tries to quieten the room with her steely gaze and an index finger to her lips like a schoolteacher, but, when this fails, she shouts out, 'This is not a pantomime,' only to receive the reply that she should surely have expected. She sends three attendants into the audience to weed out the noisiest offenders, and a threat of incarceration in the seclusion cells restores a degree of order. She scans her order of performance, and, as I am the last on the bill, she says, 'Now, does anyone else have anything that they would like to perform before we retire? No? Then please show your appreciation to all our performers and the asylum band.'

We clap and whistle and stomp our feet and cry out for more as the time is barely ten o'clock, but this is already an extension of our usual bedtime by two hours, and we must always adhere to the schedule. Matron, attempting to rise above the hullabaloo, shouts for us to line up, and we are shepherded into rows by the attendants. Resigned to our bedtime like belligerent children, we fight our way out of the ballroom, our Christmas concert over for another year.

The concert, with its mix of music hall songs and popular

classical arias, has been the highlight of a day of festivities, a day without work, a day designed by the superintendent to give an aura of normality to an abnormal situation, to abnormal people. There have been two church services: Holy Communion in the morning followed by a carol service in the evening. In between, we have eaten a Christmas meal in the refectory, whose rafters have been hung with holly and ivy and in the corner a small tree decorated with the same. The Christmas Day meal we have enjoyed, with its choice of goose or beef and, for afters, plum pudding and custard, is a repast far better than many have been used to on the outside.

Some of the patients have been collected by their relatives and taken away for a few days for a trial run of their sanity. A sister of Queenie's has emerged, newly widowed, with a large hotel on the seafront in Blackpool. They look like twins, both as tiny as wrens and matched in their tweed, and with Queenie out of her nightdress for the first time in years and with her hair all done up, looking ten years younger than the previous day. 'This is my little sister May,' says Queenie, giving her a quick hug as if she had but seen her last week, while May looks at the floor, contemplating her thirty-five-year absence. Queenie is now residing at the seaside and was even talking of paddling in the frozen sea; we are all jealous of her escape and secretly hope it will rain cats and dogs.

Elise has not been collected, but her family left a huge parcel on Christmas Eve wrapped in red silk ribbons and bows and inside, when she was finally persuaded to open it, was a dress that she will not wear and handmade chocolates she will not eat, and which by noon on Christmas morning had been demolished by the rest of the patients.

In the ward, the patients' Christmas cards are strung high up on the picture rail. I have received no cards, but I have had a gift from Pomona in a box passed to me at our last session. 'A gift for you; keep it secret,' she said. It was small, book-shaped, and wrapped in Liberty-print wrapping paper. I shoved it into my apron pocket and when I reached the ward I hid it between the bed and the mattress, just like in the old days. I unwrapped Pomona's present this morning in the privy, careful not to tear the paper, but it was not a book as I had suspected but a small square box, lined with grey silk, and, inside, a cream silk square decorated with red lilies. She had placed a note inside that said lilies signify rebirth, that she wished me a Happy Christmas and New Year, and that I must hide the square to avoid its confiscation or theft. As an afterthought, she had crammed more words underneath that said she hoped that I 'could be trusted not strangle myself with it', and, a little further down, 'nor anyone else'. How I would strangle myself with such a small square I do not know, unless she thought I might choke myself to death by shoving it down my throat; but I tied it to the string of my drawers anyway.

When I go to sleep I dream of walking through Christmases long past – chaperoned not by a Dickensian spirit but by Pomona, wreathed in scarves. In the background lies a scaffold and a rope of pure silk, and all the time Pomona is haranguing me with her shrill tones and her infernal notebook, and, when I wake, I feel I have not slept at all.

I still have not shaken the sense of her presence two weeks later when she arrives back in our little room.

'A belated Happy New Year, Lily. Did you make any

resolutions?' says Pomona, wrapped in a mink coat, a Christmas gift from her fiancé.

'My resolution lasts all year long,' I say.

'And what is your resolution?'

'To get out of this place.'

'That is a very good resolution, and more achievable than those that most people make.'

Today we are breaking rules as we all huddle together around the inadequate fire, hoping Matron will not check in on us.

'This is nice, Lily, we ladies all together instead of us all sitting four feet away from each other, although I would have thought Matron would have made sure a fire had been lit to air the room before today,' says Pomona.

'It's warmer than the ward,' I say, grateful for once for our time together.

When, with much reluctance, the girls are dismissed, Pomona refills our cups, and I take a gulp of the scalding tea.

'Can you me tell what happened after you had fled the farm?' she says. She takes her pen and notepad and writes *L. Day's Flight*, as if I have suddenly sprouted wings, and double-underlines it with quick strokes, in anticipation of its importance to my story. I tell her what she needs to know.

A first-class carriage somewhere on the Northern Railway Network, 27 December 1888

I have treated myself to a first-class train ticket, as I need the comfort and privacy that other classes will not give me. I have been travelling for six hours and now I am on a train to Leeds. I have had to untangle myself from my layers to sip the tea the waiter has just served, and for the first time I look around the carriage. Trade in first-class tickets to Leeds is sparse today and there are only four of us: two old dames in their finery out to visit their offspring for a late Christmas celebration, and a middle-aged vicar asleep in the corner who is jostled awake at every station by the train's cessation of movement. Thankfully none of them tries to engage in conversation with me.

After two hours we pull into Leeds station, and I have to shake the vicar's shoulder as he has remained asleep and, if Leeds is his destination, I do not want him to miss his stop.

'God bless you, my child,' he says, trying not to stare at my bruises.

I cover the left side of my face with my scarf and say, 'Thank you.' I am going to need help from anywhere I can get it if I am to survive. But Leeds seems a good enough place as any to alight, and far enough away from my home that my family, if they even wish to, will not find me.

It is a shock: all these people and noises and smells. Street vendors, ladies in their finest clothes, factory workers in their caps and scarves, beggars in rags, children with no shoes. Shops, factories, trams, pubs spilling out their drunken clientele; it is a far cry from Shrewsbury, even on a market day. My first-class ticket enables me to visit the waiting room. I am the sole occupant and after I have used the privy I survey myself in the washroom mirror. I need not have worried; my face is a little blue in places but the suspected black eye has not yet emerged, so I have no idea why the reverend was staring at me; perhaps he could see some-thing I could not. My stomach growls to remind me I have not eaten since the previous day, so I buy the local newspaper from the platform vendor and ask him for directions to the nearest tea shop.

Two Eccles cakes and a pot of tea later, I am ready to find a place to stay. I do not want one of those doss houses that I have heard about, but when I look at the advertisements for lodgings in the newspaper I realise I had had no idea how expensive they could be, and me with no work either!

Two hours later, I have purchased the plainest of black dresses, even if it does cost me an arm and leg: if I am to get a job in a factory and be accepted into a smart boarding house, one look at my ragtag farm clothing will have the door of both establishments slammed in my face faster than you can say Jack Robinson.

Mrs Jackson's boarding house for respectable young ladies occupies a corner plot on the confluence of a street of newly con-structed villas and a street of older town houses. The house is of red brick with a slate roof and, inside, it boasts a long tiled hall-way, three reception rooms, a kitchen, a scullery, four bedrooms, a bathroom, two attic rooms and a large cellar. The front steps lead directly to the street, but at the back, accessed by French windows, is a lawn shaded by mature rowans and elms. It is going to cost me fifteen bob a week for a clean bed and a good breakfast, another sixpence a day if dinner is taken. Thank goodness I have changed into my new dress, as the lady says she has a room for me on the first floor and I can move in right away.

I have been cossetted on the farm, not known the cost of

surviving without support, and for the first time I wonder if I have been foolhardy in leaving as I did. Mrs Jackson's establishment is certainly out of the range of most working-class women, and I will be stopping for only a couple of weeks, but that gives me time to find a job and, unfortunately, time also to resign myself to the fact that when I leave, I may have to reside in a doss house for the foreseeable future. But for now my bedroom is warm and clean, and as I lock the door I am in my own domain, completely reliant on myself, and I begin to look to the future, my autonomous future, with some hope.

'Yes, it is wonderful to have autonomy,' says Pomona. 'It must be awful that in here you do not have any.'

'I expect that's why some patients try to take their own lives. It might be an act of autonomy rather than an act of madness.'

'Well, we will not have you taking yours,' she almost shouts, suddenly scared by my tone.

'Not me, not on your life,' I say, which confuses us both, and she takes her leave, saying we will meet again next month.

I thought the inclusion of a vicar in my story would lend it some authenticity, even though, as soon the words left my mouth, my vicar sounded like a stock character in a murder mystery. But Pomona seems to have accepted what I have told her – interweaving lies around some truth always constructs the best falsehood. I cannot tell her the real story of my arrival in Leeds, of course. Now I've chosen this path, I must follow it all the way to its destination, wherever that may be.

A third-class railway carriage somewhere on the Northern Railway Network, 27 December 1888

Dressed in my coats and scarves, I am hiding myself away from my fellow passengers and the police, who I cannot be sure are not already looking for me. Every new passenger entering the carriage has my heart pounding so fiercely that I think that the noise alone will give me away. My head is aching and oozing, and my arms and legs feel as though I have crawled up and down the Wrekin ten times; I presume that I look a dreadful sight. Not as much of a sight as Percy must look, though. Poor Percy; I have broken the sixth commandment and must surely be punished, even if it was self-defence and he brought it on himself.

Waiting for my train at Shrewsbury station, I had had time to think, and had considered going back home, to try to explain it all; but cowardice or wisdom – who can tell? – got the better of me, and so now I am on a train from Manchester and have been travelling wherever the rail track has taken me for about six hours. A young woman has boarded the train; I can smell her cheap perfume even through all my layers, and through a gap in my scarves I can see she is looking down her nose in my direction. I am half tempted to sling away my disguise and ask if she would 'care to cross my palm with silver, dearie'. But she decides she has already spent too much time on me and turns away, telling anyone who will listen that she is off to Leeds as there are plenty of positions to be had in Leeds and that she is now in a better position to get a position. I know the position I wish her to be in, but she has at least given me the semblance of an idea that Leeds would be my final stop, and that my future lay in my disappearance into the throngs who toil in the apparently myriad industries that flourish there.

When I had boarded the train in Much Wenlock the platform had been empty, but, as each hour has passed, the station platforms have become progressively busier. At Manchester the station is a cauldron of life: the solicitors and bank managers alighting from first class; the clerks and shop girls from second; and the poorest from third, all disgorging from the platform and spilling out into the streets where cabs and omnibuses are waiting to whisk those with means off to work; those too poor to afford even a few pennies for an omnibus, having spent the little they had on a train ticket, walk to their employment. But luckily, as the train is approaching Leeds station, half of the passengers have disembarked and I am left in the carriage with two old dames and a gaggle of shop girls not yet able to afford a higher-class ticket, and the noisy one, hunched in the corner. I am sure that she will find the position she covets and will soon be elevated to second class with her cheap suit and even cheaper smile.

At all the other stations I had hobbled off the train shrouded in my coats, bought the cheapest ticket to the next largest town or city and, standing on the outer edges of each platform, there being no waiting room for third-class passengers, had avoided contact with everyone save the ticket clerk and inspector. But as I must now venture out of the station, I wait until the other passengers have alighted and then step gingerly from the train on to the platform. No porters rush to take my bags, and not even the street urchins who would usually fight among themselves and risk a backhander from the porter to carry your luggage for two pennies venture towards me; I must look a worse sight than I had imagined. I hobble to the ladies' waiting room, hoping I will not be thrown out, but, the next train not being due for half an hour, the room is devoid of any passengers and the porters are using the lull to have a swift cup of tea.

On the farm we children would always have our share of cuts, scratches and bruises. I would like to say it was from the implements, or the animals, but mostly it was from fighting with each other. There were too many of us really; one day we would have an alliance with one sister, the next she would be a sworn enemy. The washroom mirror reveals 'Two Lovely Black Eyes' as the song goes, far worse than any childhood skirmish, as my lids and sockets have erupted into a rainbow of blues and purples, one colour for each eye, like hydrangeas blooming side by side in different soils. My upper lip, which I had not thought to be badly bruised, is swollen and bloodied; no wonder the passengers have given me a wide berth. I take out my handkerchief, wet it with water from the basin and ease off the congealed blood. I will need something to cover up all the bruising, as I am not going to be presentable for a least a week and the bruises will delay my plans for getting employment for at least a few more days after that.

Leeds has wonderful shopping arcades which, along with its music halls and parks, have transformed it into a vibrant centre of entertainment; or at least that is what the council, questing for city status, would wish you to believe. More arcades are in the pipeline, but it is a water pipeline that the neighbouring properties most desire, as cheek by jowl with these monuments to consumerism are some of the meanest streets in Leeds.

Thornton's Arcade is built of cast iron and glass in the Gothic style and is said to be an excellent example of the trend if you like that sort of thing. Inside, the shops look pricey, but it's below freezing outside, and the arcade looks invitingly warm and devoid of shoppers, so I step inside. The shops' windows are weary with the remnants of festive fayre for the well-heeled: a toy emporium with dolls, toy soldiers and clockwork trains; a haberdasher's with 'gifts for the discerning lady and gentlemen'; an outfitter's with its windows framed by cravats and scarves draped into bows; and a sweet shop, forlorn, its window denuded of its festive delights. I head for a shop called The High-Class Ladies' Outfitters, hoping the lack of an imaginative name will be reflected in its stock. As I step inside, the shopkeeper, duly summoned by the bell for there seem to be no assistants, comes from behind the counter and re-gards me with the look of someone who has found a penny and lost a shilling.

'I need a simple black dress and a veil, off the peg, something suitable for mourning; do you have anything?' I say.

Her pursed lip soften into a flat shopkeeper's smile, somewhere she must judge to be between welcoming and sympathetic. 'I'm sorry for your loss,' she says.

I decide to offer an explanation in case she starts to pry. 'There was an accident.'

'Oh, my dear.'

'I survived, just, but my poor husband . . .'

'I'll see what I have in stock.' Looking me up and down, she says, 'Under all those clothes I expect madam is very slim. I am sure I can guess your size. Years of working here have made me particularly good at that. Black is still a popular choice, but the fashion is for grey and beige – but of course you need black for mourning. I do have a small selection of black dresses, and I can always order one for you.'

'I really do need it today,' I say.

'Well, then, perhaps this,' she says, offering me a dress so dowdy that even our Queen, a professional mourner not renowned for her frivolous attire, would have rejected it. 'No? What about this? A little dearer, but worth it. Plain but stylish, with a high neckline and long puffed sleeves which lift it from the everyday, don't you think? Makes it look distinguished. And it will cover madam's arms and neck. Most ladies buy the jacket that completes the ensemble, but I'd have to order that in for you.'

I decline her invitation to help me into the dress, fearing what will be revealed when my clothes are removed. I had imagined the damage a good day's festering might have wrought, but it is far worse than I had expected. As I undo my blouse buttons my shoulders are revealed to be the same hue as my unfortunate eye sockets. But the shopkeeper is correct: the dress envelops me like a black shroud. It is a little large in the waist, but my shoulders are those of a yokel, having grown sinewy from farm work; I cannot be squeezed into a smaller size, and I do not have the time or money for bespoke attire.

I gather up my clothes, so shabby next to this new dress, walk to the till and say, 'I'll take the dress. I will keep it on. I'll not require the jacket.'

'As you wish. I must say it suits madam very well. Does madam require a bag for her clothes?'

'I do, yes – and the veil?'

She shows me the only two black veils that she has in stock. I choose the cheapest: I will only need it for a week or so. I put it on and my transformation to grieving widow is complete.

I take a cab to a boarding house where, according to the dress shop's proprietress, a decent widow may rest unmolested. It is going to further diminish my meagre funds. The landlady, Mrs Jackson, passes me the register, and, grateful that I am wearing Honesty's best Sunday gloves, I invent Mrs Wenlock, a poor young widow who – and here I draw on the description of my mother's engagement ring – has had to sell her twenty-four-carat gold ring set with diamonds that had been a gift from her husband's grandmother and would have gone to our son had we been fortunate to have one, to pay for the funeral. All this in my new widow's weeds; it is quite the performance.

I will be staying in my bedroom for a week, a fire burning in the grate that has cost an extra shilling for coal and blacking but has allowed me the luxury of reading *Bleak House*, a Christmas gift, without interruption. During that week I propose, for the sake of propriety, to only leave the house on the day of the 'funeral'. Within an hour of my arrival Mrs Jackson accosts me in the hallway and asks if I would like her to accompany me at this sad time. I refuse her offer and say that I will be much better off alone with my grief.

A few days later, I find Mrs Jackson outside my bedroom door when I put out my evening tray – in sympathy for my predicament, and for a few extra pennies, she has been bringing all my meals to my room. Today was the first time I have left the lodging house, and I think she has been lying in wait for me, but I do not comment. She asks me if I would care to join her for a small sherry in her sitting room, and she has been so accommodating that I feel it would be churlish to refuse.

Her sitting room smells of pot-pourri and recently lit gas lights, and is stuffed with furniture: a chaise-longue; two sideboards; a Welsh dresser that is pressed up against the window and must block out any natural light; and in the corner a piano that I have not heard her play. We sit in two leather button-back chairs squeezed into the centre of the room, separated by a small table on which she has placed the sherry and two cut-glass clippers. She pours us both a good measure and after a small sip says, 'How was the funeral?'

'Just me, the vicar and my in-laws. It was a nice service.'

'It's such a shame you had to sell your ring to pay for it. Did your in-laws not help with the costs?'

'No. They were not able.'

Mrs Jackson frowns sympathetically. 'Another?' she says, before I am halfway down the first glassful. She tops up my glass with the sickly stuff without refilling her own. 'How long had you been married, if you don't mind me asking.'

'Six months, but we had known each other for two years.'

'And then the accident. Was it in the mills? One hears of so many accidents there these days.'

'No, he was stung by a bee. He couldn't breathe afterwards. Died gasping for his last breath.'

Mrs Jackson raises her eyebrows. 'That was very unlucky. And unusual. I would not have thought there were many bees around at this time of year.'

It was a stupid idea to say he had been stung by a bee. I had become too sure of myself. I should have kept the lie much simpler, said he died in a mining accident. Perhaps I am not so good at this subterfuge as I thought.

'Tell me, where did you meet your husband?' she says.

'We met in church. Harvest festival, it was,' I say.

'Like me and my Alfred. Sunday School sweethearts since we were thirteen.'

I look around the room for any photographs of Alfred or any evidence of a male presence.

'Oh, you won't find any photographs of him. He ran off with the maid back in the spring of '85. An old man's fancy, I suppose. Not seen hide nor hair of him since. Good riddance to bad rubbish, but don't tell anyone I said that.'

'Of course. I didn't like to presume. I thought perhaps he worked away or had passed away.'

'Like your poor man.'

'Yes indeed.'

I fidget with my veil and smooth down the sleeves of my dress, which have puckered at the elbow. Picking up the glass, I gulp down the remains of the sherry, put the glass on the tray, get up, walk to the door and place my hand on the doorknob. Turning, I thank her for the sherry and tell her I will require the room for another week.

A few days later, as I had hoped, my body has started to feel less like a malignant appendage and my black eyes have faded to yellow. I leave the boarding house, take an omnibus to somewhere the driver says is no part of town for a lady to loiter, and seek out a second-hand clothes shop. There seems to be quite a trade in worn garments: a whole row of shops with dirt-encrusted windows and the floor tiles at their entrance, inlaid with the name of some long-forgotten business, unswept, and inch-thick in grime. I choose the establishment with the cleanest windows, but the owner and the clothes still smell of sweat and dirt. I take the veil out of my bag and hand it to him. He holds it up to the meagre light that has managed to squeeze through those filthy windows, sniffs it, brushes the silk against his cheeks and runs his dirty nails along its lace borders so that I fear he might pucker it and render it worthless. He says that most of his clientele work at night, and that there would be a right catfight over my veil, and jokes that they will use it to cover their modesty, if nothing else. He laughs and nudges me with his elbow. I smile in an attempt to tolerate him as one tolerates cow muck: it stinks, but you know it does wonders for the soil. He offers me two bob, which I refuse, and after a bit of haggling we negotiate three and sixpence; the amount is still only half of its cost. But the veil is now of no use to me and so I pocket his begrudging payment and, having discarded my widowhood with my veil, I emerge into the bleaching sunlight, still bruised, but thin and yellow enough to become the sallow Miss Williams. If the police are still looking for me it's going to be hard to find a Miss Williams among the millions; and my family will never find me with this name. I could use some make-up to cover the remaining bruises on my face, or at least some bright lip paint to detract from them; but make-up is for actresses and whores, and I am neither.

CHAPTER THIRTEEN

After a month, two-faced January has arrived in early February. Cold and spiteful, it is spreading the usual round of influenza and pneumonia; in the isolation ward, those already weakened by phthisis are dropping like flies. Their bodies loiter in the morgue, waiting for dissection, or for the soil of the infirmary graveyard to thaw so that they may be interred. To mark their passing, Superintendent Sharp will say a few words of remembrance and then wooden crosses bearing their names will be hammered into the unyielding ground. After a year, grass will cover the mounds, and the gardeners will clip respectfully around each hump; in five years the crosses will rot; in ten years the mounds will be flattened with savage spades and their passing will be unmarked save for an entry in the asylum register. A few lucky corpses will be claimed by their kin and borne off for a Christian burial. Matron flits between the wards, her cape flapping around her waist. Today she is a vulture, scouring the wards, sniffing out the sick and diseased. I am never ill; I put it down to a mixture of country food and stubbornness.

I must have slept badly as I am jolted awake by the first bell, when usually I am awake well before six o'clock, whatever the season. Rowse is helping to get the patients washed and out of their beds. Elise never desires to rise from her bed save for the obligatory visit to the water closet and I swear she would use a gazunder if she were not so much of a lady; the weekly changing of sheets is a torment to her as she hates the smell and feel of the starch and will only settle when her sheets and nightgown have been impregnated with the sickly-sweet odour of her body. But today she is missing; not scrunched in a ball at the bottom of my bed nor swaddled down in her own against the cold – she feels the cold very much, whereas I am immune to its charms.

'Miss Rowse,' I say, 'where is Elise?'

She looks momentarily confused but then says, 'I believe she was taken to the infirmary early this morning.'

'Oh. I didn't know she was ill; she seemed more like her old self yesterday. She didn't come to me.' I wondered if she had been too weak to be able to rouse me from my sleep or even climb onto my bed. 'What does she have? Is it the phthisis? Elise is frail at the best of times; this will surely see her off.'

'My shift started at a quarter to six this morning and Elise was not here when I came into the ward. Perhaps you could ask Matron.'

Matron is not on the ward this morning so I must wait until the afternoon, when my shift in the sewing room has finished, to accost her. After I am released from my labours, I do not go to the day room but sit with the infirm patients waiting for Matron to do her rounds. At half-past five Matron is working her way down the ward, squeezing into the inadequate space between each bed, asking the obligatory questions and receiving the obligatory answers.

'How are we today, Lily?' she says.

'We are well. Not so Elise. Where is she? Miss Rowse says she was taken ill.'

Matron walks over to Rowse and whispers something to her. I hope the indiscretion will not stop her from escorting me to my sessions with Pomona. Matron walks back to my bed and says, 'It is none of your concern but if you must know where she is, and it seems you already do, Dr Roberts recommended that we take her away for treatment. We did so in the early hours as to not excite anyone. Do not worry, it was nothing contagious.' On Matron's wards, no contagion is allowed to surface without being swiftly expunged, and, should such a contagion dare to arise, it must surely be the fault of us lunatics.

'I am not worried about contagion. I would like to see her. She must be very scared, away from everything she knows.'

'That is not possible. She will soon be back on the ward and much recovered. As the doctor says, a fat and well patient is a curable patient.'

Rowse gives an intake of breath as we both realise what they have done. My first impulse is to run to the infirmary and drag Elise back to the ward. I would have done it, too, a few months ago, and I wonder how this girl has inveigled her way into my affections without me noticing and that she is indeed my pet, as Queenie disparagingly called her. I decide to wait until after tea, a meal of bread and butter and cake that we eat at six o'clock; it is called tea because it is of an insufficient quantity to be called dinner. There is then a gap of three hours before lights out and so there is a small amount of time to conduct my plan to rescue Elise. Not that I have a distinct plan, but, as Matron has told us, this month the asylum is short-staffed, and so, in the absence of locking us all up, we can get away with murder.

I sneak to the washroom; two attendants are taking a short break, hiding from Matron, whispering together in the shadows along the unlit corridor adjacent to the open door of the washroom. They are still talking when I have finished, and I shuffle around the door and edge my way along the corridor. I am unsure where the infirmary is located, and I meander down three corridors before I see a sign for it. In the distance I can hear hammering and sawing and the sound of men whistling and singing coarse music hall songs that will bring Matron over if they are not careful. The workmen are employed in the continued expansion of the asylum; the governors have decreed that more wings must be built for the increasing number of lunatics, an epidemic of us, and so eventually the asylum will have more wings than a poulterer's cart at Christmas.

After the first rush of fever has subsided, I realise I have still not formulated a plan. I have a mad, melodramatic idea to grab a uniform from the laundry and pretend to be an attendant, rescue Elise, and bring her back to the ward. The acquiring of the uniform would be simple as I am well used to the layout of the laundry, and if questioned would say I have been sent by Matron to resume my work there; but without an attendant's hat, and with my madwoman's eyes and hair, I would be fooling no one.

But the decision is taken from me, for down the corridor, naked except for a thin gown that is flapping wildly behind her, is Elise, pursued by two nurses. She lets out a growl like a bear and runs to me, wrapping her arms around my neck and trying to wind her legs around my waist; but she is too weak and dangles in front of me, the growl subsiding to a banshee's wail. I can feel her wrists digging into my neck and so I grab her waist and hoist her on to my shoulder like a baby. She is so tiny, minuscule, and without her usual flannelette nightgown I can feel her ribs rubbing against my chest. But that is not the worst: when she turns to face me, her arms and face reveal a patchwork of bruises; one of her front teeth is missing; her lip is split in three places; her nose is bloody and swollen like a boxer's; and, through the tangle of her hair, patches of her scalp are revealed.

Beneath the sobs, her breathing is becoming laboured. I can feel my resolution to behave starting to crumble and bile is rising into my throat as I shout out, 'You bastards, how could you do this to her?'

The two nurses take a step back, unsure how to handle this angry lunatic who is towering over them with one of their charges clamped to her shoulder. And so, in the time-honoured way, they blame someone else. 'It was Dr Roberts. He authorised it. He made us do it,' says the more intrepid of the two.

'But I expect you helped. Was it you who held her down while she was screaming, or perhaps you forced in the feeding tube?' And, turning to the other, 'Perhaps it was you who mixed the milk and eggs and fed them into the funnel.'

Elise is in such a state that I know she cannot go back to the ward until she is healed; but I need to make sure they do not try to force-feed her again. 'Here,' I say, loosening Elise's hands from around my neck, 'take her back to the infirmary.' Elise starts to scream again and grabs at my hair, but the nurses prise it from her slight grasp and drag her, whimpering and spent, down the corridor to the infirmary; no doubt she will be sedated on arrival.

I turn my back on them and stomp towards where I think I remember Matron's office is located, as she must have scurried back there by now. I expect to be accosted at every turn, but what with the understaffing, and the expectation that anyone going in the direction of the old part of the asylum has been sent to Matron and will undoubtedly have an attendant in their wake, I remain unchallenged. Matron's office is not signposted, and it has been almost a year since I was last in her lair, but when I round the corner I see the corridor of portraits stretching out before me. I halt my stride and tiptoe to her door. To the right of the door is a painting-shaped area of wallpaper more vibrant in colour than the wallpaper that surrounds it; some old codger must have been demoted to the attic to make room for a portrait of Superintendent Sharp, or perhaps even one of Matron; but Matron will never retire, and I expect she will be carried out of here in a box. I wonder if they will choose a photograph for the portrait instead of an oil painting. There is a photograph of me taken when I first arrived. I have not seen it, but it will be in my file and, considering what took place before I was sent here, I expect I look like most people's idea of the madwoman in the attic. But a professional photographer will take the photograph for the gallery, and the worthy will be recorded, poised and in all their pomp for posterity.

I hammer at the door and walk in, although my first inclination was to burst in and ambush her. 'Elise,' I say. 'Why did you let him do it to her? You could have protested. Force-feeding will kill her. You know it didn't work in her previous asylum.'

'Ah, Elise Duchamp, in your ward,' she says, in a low, practised voice, as if a lunatic bursting through her office door is an everyday occurrence.

'Have you seen the state of her? Lord knows where they went with their bloody tubes.' My tongue is freer than it has been for months, and Matron is feeling the full force of my anger.

'Yes, she did resist the tube down her throat even after they had used the mouth clamp, so I am told. Feeding her through her nose was the only alternative.'

'The alternative would have been not to have done it in the first place! I was starting to feed her titbits. She was *responding*.'

'Well, you are not a doctor, and a doctor thought it necessary, in fact essential.'

'So essential that she was spirited away while no one was awake and now you have nearly killed her.'

I have my two hands on her desk now and am leaning over it, towering above her, my face inches from hers. Matron is turning as pale as poor Elise. She reaches under the desk and pulls at something, and ten seconds later two attendants burst through the door and attempt to manhandle me into a straitjacket. But these girls are novices, fresh off the ship, and trip over each other as they give chase. I run around the room pushing over furniture to barricade myself against their advance and then hold my arms aloft and wave them around like Loïe Fuller. Matron joins the fray and instructs them to each grab one arm and yank it down and at first there is confusion as to who should grab which arm until Matron shouts out, 'Kelly the left, Maguire the right,' and they corner me behind the aspidistra and restrain the correct limbs. Matron holds out the sleeves of the cursed garment and shoves my arms into it, and, while the attendants hold my arms fast to my chest, Matron secures the buckles at the back and the sides, until I am trussed up like the proverbial goose. But they have received a few mementos for their trouble; the girls are going to be feeling their introduction to asylum life in the morning, and Matron will have some fetching lumps and bruises on her shins and knees that she will mask with the blackest of stockings.

'Take her to the seclusion cell,' says Matron. 'If she calms down after a few hours in there, see if you can get a bed restraint on to her wrist instead of that jacket. And remember to put it all in the restraints book.'

'The padded cell?' says Maguire.

'No of course not. Would I not have said so?' Matron snaps at the girl, who, having withstood with fortitude the onslaught of my clenched fists for five minutes, for which she must be commended, is now on the brink of tears at Matron's stinging reply. 'Would I have requested just shackles if I thought there were any prospect of self-harm? Day is not a danger to herself.' She does not add *just to everyone else*.

Matron's office lies outside of the asylum's maze of wards and corridors, and I must be dragged down three corridors and through two wards to reach the seclusion cells. I refuse to walk, so three attendants, for we have garnered another by now, must drag me backwards, still struggling and kicking, through a sea of faces. Those patients who are medicated cheer my performance while others, their senses not curdled by medicine, look on and shake their heads. I dig my heels in the floor and leave a slug trail of scuff marks, for which my ankles will later surely suffer, but for now I am anaesthetised by the euphoria of my small triumph and am back at school, returning to the classroom after another caning in the headmistress's office.

After two days of cursing and throwing herself against the cell wall, Hopkins, the patient in the next seclusion cell, has been carted off to the padded cells. She is a teenager and a novice at this imprisonment lark; only placidity will get you released, and I am hopeful that after my conversation with Superintendent Sharp, who visited me this morning, my liberation, albeit only as far as the ward, will come in the next few days.

The padded cells are at the rear of the wards, but the original six seclusion cells are buried beneath the asylum like a row of oubliettes; unlike the oubliette, each cell has a door with an inspection window, and every half-hour, in the guise of caretaking, the plate will slide open and an attendant will gawp at the maniac as in the good old Bedlam days. In the cells, everything that can be picked up and thrown is nailed down: the bed, the table and chair, and even the chamber pot. I am sure they would nail me to the floor if they could, but instead I have been relieved of my straitjacket and am tethered by a leather strap to the bed.

At one o'clock, for even in the depths of the asylum those

blessed bells can be heard, the window plate is pulled back and Matron peers in.

'Good afternoon, Lily. May I come in?' she says, as if I have a choice in whether or not she enters the cell.

'Welcome to my humble home,' I say. 'Sorry about the state of it but I have been in much demand today.'

Pomona has not visited, although she must have been told of my misdemeanour. I expect she thinks that all her hard work has been for nothing.

Matron unlocks the door, steps into the cell, and deposits my food tray on the table. Today it is mutton stew; the smell wafts under my nose and my stomach growls in anticipation but I have never been keen to eat under another's gaze. Today must be Matron's turn to ensure I do not choke myself. In here it is the everyday things that you miss, the things that mark you out as different, like the privacy of eating alone; like a real knife and fork that a sane person would use without thought, not the round-ended ones that we are forced to use to stop us from stabbing each other.

'Please eat it while it is warm,' she says. 'I hope you are calmer. I know Superintendent Sharp talked with you this morning about the incident and what your consequent treatment will entail. Do not look at your time in here as a period of seclusion: it is not solitary confinement, nor is it a punishment for your actions, but, rather, a respite – time away from the stresses and strains of the ward, a time for quiet reflection.'

'Perhaps you should vet the other residents, then.'

'Yes, it was a mistake not to send Hopkins to the padded cells straight away, but now you are the only patient in seclusion perhaps you can get back to the true meaning of asylum: that of a place of sanctuary and refuge.'

'You make it sound like a week away in Baden-Baden.'

'Now that is something I would enjoy.'

'But that would be your choice, not a decision foisted on you.'

'But this is a decision foisted on you for your own good. While you are here you will have a chance to think about your outburst. I would encourage you to rest or to read. Some asylums encourage sewing, although I am a little dubious about the safety of that enterprise.'

'I would rather recuperate by walking in the gardens – in a straitjacket if necessary,' I say, acknowledging her version of my culpability for the incident. Now is not the time to protest that I was surely provoked, and that I was not the one to initiate the fracas in her office.

'We cannot always have what we want,' she says, and from her apron she extracts a book and places it on the table. 'It's my current favourite book. Take it in the spirit it is meant. I realise that your outburst was born of your affection for Elise, and I was at least partly to blame for your reaction. On reflection, I should, as you said, have tried to stop them. Your reaction was not abnormal.' She pushes the book along the table towards me. 'Would you like to read it?' she says.

'I would very much like that,' I say, astounded by her admission of complicity.

'If you cannot travel to Baden-Baden, at least you can travel through time to another world,' she says, with a smile so unexpected that it is more unnerving than her scowls. It suits her; she should try it more often.

She looks at my half-eaten plate of food. 'Finished?'

I nod, and she scoops up the tray. I lay the book on the centre of the table; it is pristine. I turn to the first page and Matron steps back into the corridor and says, 'Keep it,' as she locks the door and slides across the window plate.

High up on the back wall there is a square aperture, no more than six inches by six, protected by a wire casing that lets in a small amount of air and light and birdsong, and if I try hard enough to listen to it I can block out the screams, even my own. There will only be natural light till about four o'clock and after that the cells will be plunged into a dimmed light to soothe our souls. But the semi-darkness is at least an improvement on the total darkness that was used to calm me on my last visit here. How a dark, dank, claustrophobic cell could ever have been used as a treatment to calm even a sane person, let alone a lunatic, I do not know, and nor, now, does Superintendent Sharp, who has forbidden its use.

By three o'clock the following afternoon I have read the first twelve chapters of *The Time Machine*, and am eager to start the thirteenth before the light begins to fail when there is the turning of a key in the lock and the door is flung open.

'Matron says you are to go back to the ward,' says the attendant, one of the steamship girls who had pursued me around Matron's office.

'But I have a chapter to finish,' I say, holding out the book.

'Pick up your stuff.'

I turn my hands palm upwards, hold out my wrists, and shrug my shoulders. The manacles have irritated the scars that lie there, and they are beginning to itch. The attendant extracts a key from a keyring that hangs from her waist and unlocks the shackles. I run around the cell and neigh like a horse let free to roam a pasture.

'Move it, Dobbin,' she says, and I gather my possessions, and follow her in silence back to the ward.

Leeds, 12 February 1898

Pomona Fairchild's notes on Miss Lily Day (Hysteric, Sunnyside Lunatic Asylum)

Subject in solitary after attacking Matron and is probably subdued with opiates.

Superintendent Sharp forbids me to see subject for two weeks.

After outburst due to discovering sickly child has been force-fed, I am becoming convinced that subject does in fact have hysteria.

CHAPTER FOURTEEN

The promise of spring has bypassed Leeds. Winter white has been supplanted not by burgeoning green, but by a sea of sepia; trees, lawns and mounds of raked leaves all cleave to brown mediocrity. In the woods, even the brazen snowdrops, usually the first to show their heads, have remained hidden under the roots of beeches and elms. Only the yews in the graveyard show any sign of life. But all is verdant within my little sitting room. There is a decent fire in the grate, and I want to stay here forever and stare out of the window. Encouraged by the previous bending of regulations and my apparent slip back to sanity, my girls are trying to edge their chairs closer to the fire. Not that I blame them: it is colder than the North Pole on the ward. Rowse has a cut on her lip and a bruised and bloody nose; I expect it is courtesy of Cissy in the geriatrics' ward, who is always free with her limbs. O'Neill is missing, replaced by a silent Langley; I thought it must be near her time, but Rowse tells me she is due back in the asylum in a few weeks.

'Has she been ill?' I say.

'You could say that. It's not contagious, at least I hope not,' she says, laughing.

I like this girl who does not tell on her pregnant friend, and while we wait I do not sigh as she feels the need to converse. I do not mind being a surrogate O'Neill. She has an assignation with her new beau and is excited to tell me about it.

Pomona is late. I wonder if she charges by the hour or if I am a fixed-rate project? That is, if I *can* be fixed. Matron says that Pomona has decided that we will have more regular sessions from March as we have missed too many sessions due to Pomona's absence in autumn and my incarceration earlier this month.

'Lily, I have some awful news,' Pomona says, entering the room from the door to the asylum and plonking herself in the chair, taking a mouthful of her tea and encouraging me to drink mine before she delivers the bad tidings. 'There is no easy way to say this, but I have just come from Matron's office, and she tells me that poor Elise passed away a few days ago from septic pneumonia. I know you were close to her.'

'Why wasn't I told earlier?' I say, taking long, low breaths to try to stop myself from shouting.

'I think Matron wanted me to deliver the news. She hopes I will be able to console you and persuade you not to let it hinder your progress.'

'More likely Matron feels guilty. It must have been an infection caused by the force-feeding. I hear it often happens,' I say, fighting back a stupid tear.

Pomona, of course, notices. 'It is perfectly reasonable to shed a tear, Lily. It is to be expected,' she says.

But I did not cry for Maggie and I will not cry for Elise, even if she has become dearer to me than that old bat could ever have been.

Pomona hands me a cutting from the *Yorkshire Evening Post*. 'For you to keep,' she says, holding on to my hand in a gesture of comfort she must have learned. This time I am the one to withdraw from the connection.

> **DEATHS** On the 22nd February, Elise Duchamp, eldest daughter of Mr. and Mrs. Edward Duchamp of Headingly. She trusted in her Saviour, and she now rests in Him, who has released her from all earthly pain and suffering, having fallen asleep in Christ.

'I didn't know that Elise had younger siblings, but then anyone would have thought her an only child, since only her parents ever visited. Perhaps they have all been released from earthly pain,' I say.

'I did not know you were religious,' says Pomona.

'There is a lot you don't know about me,' I say.

'Then I hope your faith will bring you some comfort. Do you feel up to continuing? Perhaps it will take your mind off this awful Elise incident.'

Poor Elise, her short life relegated to an 'incident'. Relegated to 'poor Elise'. Since she was deposited in here, she never really had a chance. Talking about my past is unlikely to lessen the sadness that I unexpectedly feel. I should have tried harder with her. I should have been the mother she craved.

'The last time we talked, you had spent a week or two resting in Leeds. I would like to hear about what happened to you next,' says Pomona, dragging me from my reveries enough to be able to continue my story.

Leeds, 10 January 1889

There is a card placed in one of the windows of Hofstein's Clothing Factory. They require a buttonholer, no experience necessary, ten shillings a week, must be a quick learner. They know that there is no need to advertise in a newspaper, as potential employees, streaming from rural backwaters to the industrial towns and cities, are ten a penny. It is a pittance really, but so is all menial work, and I have no idea what a buttonholer does, but I need a job quickly and cannot afford to be fussy. The factory supervisor, Mrs McKie, an ancient Scottish woman, walks me through the workrooms, noisy as hell, bursting with cutters, seamstresses and finishers and, at the bottom of the pile, the buttonholers. She asks me to study the work of the buttonholers for a few minutes while she attends to a crisis in the cutting department. I am none the wiser when she returns, but we continue our tour of the factory and move on to the storeroom, the repository for the factory's sweated efforts, rows upon rows of ready to wear suits, to be sold to men and boys so that they can pretend to be gentlemen. If there was an interview it consisted of asking how closely I had watched the buttonholers, and could I act upon basic instructions; I must have passed because I am to start in two days' time.

There has been a hard frost, and the next morning, as I open

Mrs Jackson's front door for the last time, passers-by hurrying to work are sliding along the pavements and I am grateful for my humble hobnail boots. I have three pounds and five shillings in my purse, over two months' wages to some people, so I could stay another month before my funds run out, but my buttonholer's wages are not going to buy very much in the way of luxury, and I need to find a new lodging house, where I know I will have to share a room with other women. Standing on the doorstep, I have a lump in my stomach the size of an apple; I want to spend the rest of my savings and run back inside to the bosom of Mrs Jackson. But it is one of those frozen midwinter mornings when the sun is gathering its strength and is beginning to forge its way through the meagre clouds, and, despite the frost underfoot, the day ahead feels almost spring-like and full of promise. And so, despite my misgivings, I step out into the sunshine.

There are lodging houses on every street corner in the poorer and even the richer quarters of Leeds, since, like every other industrial town and city, it is awash with young women all hungry for work. The country is heading towards the final decade of the nineteenth century and young women want to be more than their mothers could have dreamed of. But, although they are united by gender, in their living arrangements they are separated by gentility: the professional women – clerks, typists and bookbinders – who can afford a more refined establishment, and the others: laundresses, tailoresses and factory girls, who take what they can get.

There are at least a dozen cheap lodging houses within walking distance of Hofstein's, so it seems sensible to choose one of these since, having paid my rent, I do not wish to pay for an omnibus to work as well. There is card advertising a bed for rent in the window of Mrs Needham's lodging house. The law requires lodging houses to cater for only one sex; lower-class ones which allow both sexes are often nothing more than brothels. It seems prudent to wait to see if there are any unsavoury characters entering or leaving her premises. After ten minutes of walking up and down the street, there does not seem to be anyone loitering, except for me. It is bitter out here, the frost has not yet thawed despite the emerging sun, and so I knock at the residence of Mrs Needham and a woman of about thirty years of age with dark hair and darker eyes opens the front door. I am wearing the clothes I had on when I fled the farm and have stashed my best dress in my bag, as I do not want the proprietress to take one look at my posh black frock and try to fleece me over the rent. I pass the doorstep scrutiny, and she invites me in and says she is offering a bed in a room for three bob a week. The place is no doss house, but neither is it anything like the standard of Mrs Jackson's boarding house. Mrs Needham says that she knows that this is pricier than some establishments, but if I am comparing her house to those places that let you pay by the day then I must consider that they are no more than hovels. She will provide a bed with a straw mattress and bed linen that will be changed every week, and the use of a bathroom, kitchen and sitting room, but I had better be quick as she has had quite a few enquiries. I suppose she would say that. I follow her up two flights of stairs to the attic, a room that was more than likely used for servants in the past. There is a small fireplace, three beds and three tiny chests of drawers; there is no room for a wardrobe, and barely a whisper between the furniture. But it looks clean, so I tell her I will take it.

*

'What was it like, having to share a room like that? You had not done that, I assume, since your childhood. I would deplore the lack of privacy,' says Pomona.

'Yes, having to climb up to the attic was like being back at Little Meadows, when Honesty and I had the top rooms, although even then we had our own room and a lot more space. But it wasn't so bad. I suppose it reminded me of what I had lost, or I should say the camaraderie I had thrown away when I chose to sever myself from my family. At Mrs Needham's there was always a fire in the bedroom grate and someone in the house with whom you could have a conversation or from whom you could scavenge a bit of bread when your funds were running low. And, true to her word, Mrs Needham had the bed linen changed every week and we never had bed bugs, a rarity so I learned from some of the girls at Hofstein's, and even if I did sometimes find one of the girls flopped exhausted into my bed, we never had to top and tail. Some of the other girls had very suspicious working hours, but I didn't ask them about it, and they in turn did not interrogate me.'

Pomona sits forward in her seat. 'Would you say that having to share a bedroom with these women forced you to form some sort of relationship with them?'

This must be what Pomona wants to hear. Not the fact that I hated not having any space of my own to move, to read, or even just to think without interruption, and that the women would try to drag me down to some low public house most nights of the week. And not the fact that I had to keep my money down the leg of my stockings for fear of it being pilfered by my thieving room-mates. I pause, as if considering.

'It did remind me of being with my sisters, especially as one of the girls was the spit of Honesty.'

Pomona presses her hands together. 'Excellent. I believe we are making good progress. I am really beginning to see your character. Shall I arrange with Matron for us to have a session in a fortnight?'

'I will have to consult my appointments book,' I say.

'Yes, please do that,' she says, smiling, and then leaves me unsupervised for ten whole precious minutes until Rowse and Langley arrive.

CHAPTER FIFTEEN

It is good to feel soil between my fingers again. It has been nearly a year since I first voiced to Pomona my desire to work in the garden, but finally it has happened. She must have convinced Matron or the superintendent or whichever of our betters decides these things, and they have agreed to her request, and I now have a garden of my own. Both my garden and I are, as they must be, hidden from the public gaze, but as I am in full view of the asylum I am thankfully unsupervised. Every Tuesday and Thursday afternoon you will find me here, whatever the weather. On these days my skin and nails are caked with soil, and I love it! I only have a small plot, about ten feet by twenty, down by the woods where the soil is very boggy; just the sort of place to bury a body if a person were so inclined. I have been given the plot because no one else would wish to garden here, but I do not care if I have to dig down six feet to reach some decent soil. It is mine, and I will see it flourish!

Early spring sunshine has finally broken through the cloud and warms my back as I turn away from the asylum and start to dig.

Through the winter months, the ground now slowly yielding to my spade has not been boggy but frozen like permafrost; but at the beginning of the month the frost started to thaw and break the soil into manageable clumps. But the area is still riddled with horsetail, nettles and docks, their natural antidote, all fighting to survive beneath the huge brambles and willows that thrive at the edge of the woods. It is difficult to carve my way through it all with the tools I have been given: a spade, a trowel and a trug, hardly the ideal equipment to make this soil viable. Every few minutes my spade's blade finds a still-frozen clod of earth and jars my foot against its shoulder, and I am cursing out loud that I do not have a fork to loosen the soil, which would be much more useful but which has for the moment been forbidden by Matron. I think she worries that I might skewer myself or someone else with it.

I must work in my dress and apron, which is both impractical for movement and a bugger to keep clean. In a few weeks I will ask Matron if I may be allowed to wear trousers and have a garden fork; for the moment I am just grateful to be given the opportunity to be here. I must be doing something right. I am allowed out here from two o'clock until either the light fails, or the bell calls me to tea. Come the summer therefore, I will have four glorious hours to myself, even if it is for only two days a week.

Today I am trying to dig in two barrowloads of muck, which I am hoping will help with the drainage, and if I am quick enough I will be able to sow some carrots, radishes and peas in raised beds by the end of the month. Hopefully I can get Matron to sanction the purchase of the necessary wood, and I can beg some decent topsoil from the gardeners, who I suspect look upon my little garden to be as much a frivolity as the eighteenth-century folly that lies, ivy-covered and in ruins, at the far end of the grounds.

Pomona arrives wrapped in another new coat against a biting March wind. She dismisses Rowse and Langley, sits and pours our tea but declines any biscuits and says that in the future I may have them all. I take a shortbread, place it in my saucer and put the remainder of the biscuits in my apron pocket.

From her bag Pomona extracts her notebook. 'Tell me something about your time at Hofstein's,' she says.

'Oh, I wasn't there for very long,' I reply airily, cautious of giving specifics that I might not be able to keep track of.

'Why ever not? You seemed to be making quite a home for yourself in Leeds.'

'I did, and I progressed quickly, too – from a buttonholer to a cutter in mere weeks, and then after another few weeks I was let loose on sewing suits. And I began to design and make dresses for myself: the chief overseer had a bit of a thing for me and let me use the factory machines in the wee hours. I found I had quite a talent for it. But then a new girl started in dispatch, a girl from my village, one of Honesty's friends. I took care to avoid her and she did not seem to recognise me with my chopped hair, but I felt sure she would eventually, and then she would tell my family where to find me. And I wasn't ready for that. I had only just started to find my own feet.'

'Yes, I can see that,' says Pomona. 'The need to progress on your own terms. Were you there for much longer?'

'Two more months, then I moved to Manchester. By that time I had realised that the girl was never going to recognise me, but neither had I progressed any further at Hofstein's, so it was time to move on anyway, and the lure of a city with greater opportunities was too much to resist.'

'Was it not a wrench to leave all that behind?'

'No. It was not the first time I had left a life behind, as well you know.'

'I do. And when *did* you last see your sisters?'

'I haven't seen any of them since the morning I hightailed it from the farm.'

Pomona's eyebrows rise. 'Have you not contacted them? Do you not think your parents and sisters will have been worried about you? It's been nearly ten years.'

'I didn't think they would want to know me since the events of that Christmas, and they have not tried to find me, so I can only presume that I am correct.'

'I think it may have been difficult for them to find you – much easier for you to contact them. Were you not tempted to hold out an olive branch? I would hate to be away from my family or have them think badly of me.'

I imagine that they could not think any worse of someone than when she has murdered a family member; it is a sin that cannot be forgiven. But I do not think Pomona would be able to handle that revelation. She has no notion of self-preservation; the only preserves she knows are the ones her mother's housekeeper buys from her expensive grocer's. So instead, I say, in my best Pomona voice, 'One gets used to it.'

'I expect one does,' she says joining in with the joke, 'although I always wish for my parents to be proud of me. Especially after Edward.'

'Your brother? What happened?'

She closes her pristine notebook as if it might somehow record the confidence she is about to bestow; but it is of no relevance if she tells me. 'My clever, handsome elder brother. Sent down from Oxford a few years ago. It was such a shock to my parents; it tarnished the golden boy's lustre for a while.'

'Is that why you wanted to succeed as a psychiatrist – so you could prove yourself just as competent and they would be proud of you?'

'You would think they would be, wouldn't you? Anyway, enough of me. The girls will be here soon and, after all, it is you whom we must seek to cure.'

She disappears through the door, five minutes before her time, despite her late arrival. But no matter – that part of my story has come to an end, and I have told her what she needs to know. As I leave the room with my babysitters, I congratulate myself for keeping my secrets even closer to my chest.

Hofstein's Clothing Factory, Leeds, June 1889

There are two men hanging around outside the factory gates. They have been there for two days, walking up and down the street, observing the workers arriving and leaving and the deliveries in and out and writing things down on a clipboard. It has been raining continuously, but there they are regardless, watching and writing.

I am already nervous about being recognised since the arrival of that girl from my village, and now this. I walk past them with a large scarf wrapped around my head, disappearing into the throng of similarly attired women and girls.

It is a Tuesday afternoon, and I am on a shift in the finishing room when I spy one of them out of the corner of my eye shaking hands with Mr Hofstein and being ushered upstairs to the private rooms. Mrs McKie comes over and instructs me to go upstairs and make tea for the visitors with the best china out of a cabinet on the landing. I protest that I have never been to the hallowed area and that Nellie should go as she used to work in a tea shop, but she says that Mr Hofstein specifically asked for me and gives me the key to the cabinet from a keyring that she wears around her waist. I did not think he knew who I was, but with my height I must stand out – unless he has been instructed by the visitors to send for me specifically.

I cannot refuse. I walk slowly up the stairs and take the china from the cabinet on the landing. It is dusty, so I give it a swill in the upstairs kitchen, make the tea, put a few biscuits on a plate for good measure, and walk down the corridor to the boardroom. It is all wood panelling and polished oak, a world away from the noise and dust of the factory. I knock on the boardroom door and am told to enter.

As I open the door their conversation stops, and I deposit the tray on the huge oak desk and try to stop my hands from shaking. I am keeping my head down, but I would gamble they can hear my heart sounding as though it is ready to jump out of my chest. I offer to pour the tea, but they decline, so I leave, closing the door behind me, and, as there is no one on the upper floors, put my ear to the keyhole. I cannot hear all of the conversation, but they are saying something about looking over the factory and talking to the staff and can Mr Hofstein have an alphabetical list of his employees drawn up?

The thing I hoped would never happen has happened. I walk back to the shop floor and want to rush through the front door and run away, but that would seal my guilt. At least I was astute enough to choose the name Williams; with hundreds of workers in Mr Hofstein's employ, my interview will not be for a few days. And Lily is a common enough name: there are a bunch of us working here. At afternoon break Mrs McKie tells us that we are to be interviewed by factory inspectors, but I know they are police officers: I can smell it on them.

It is time to leave. The next morning, I pack up my few possessions in my carpet bag and sneak out of Mrs Needham's back door before any of the other girls are out of bed. I don't expect them to care very much, but neither can I bring myself to feign a heartfelt goodbye. With any luck there will be another girl in my bed before it has even grown cold, and it will be as if I was never there at all.

CHAPTER SIXTEEN

In like a lion, out like a lamb, that is what they say about March, but not this year, as the late March winds are throwing themselves against the glass of the French windows roaring to be let in. But I can ignore the weather as I sit by a good fire in my little sitting room, alone, awaiting Pomona's arrival, my attendants having had to race away to some crisis in the washroom. The end of March is also the anniversary of my first session with Pomona. A year older and even though I may not be a year wiser, hopefully Pomona is, even though there is much more of my story to tell. The jenny wren has not visited us since that first session; I am not sure if that is a good or bad omen.

Five minutes later, Pomona stands outside the French window fumbling in her coat pockets for the key while I sit in my chair, useless, as the wind and rain continue to assault her. Finally, she locates the missing key, unlocks the French windows and steps into the room, trailing water and leaves on to my carpet.

'Let's draw the curtains to block out this awful weather,' she says.

'It's a lazy wind out there,' I say.

'Lazy?'

'Goes through you instead of round you. But I like to hear the wind and the rain against the windows, knowing we're warm and dry inside.'

Pomona is a fair-weather person. She tells me that she hates the cold weather as it chills her bones but does not acknowledge that it gives her a chance to parade her new clothes; and spring behaving like winter is even worse for her: since the ditching of the mackintosh, she no longer knows what outer attire to choose. She is pale today and her hair is greasy; as she pours our coffee she attempts to hide her ragged nails, which have returned. I am tempted to ask her what is wrong, but ours is not that type of relationship. She picks up her pen. I see it as a signal to continue.

Manchester, June 1889

The train journey from Leeds to Manchester takes only an hour, so I have treated myself to a first-class ticket. For a wonderful hour I have stretched my legs and moulded my body into the upholstered leather seats. I am wearing one of my own creations in cream satin and on my feet are my new brown leather brogues, courtesy of one of Mrs Needham's residents, who will be cursing me to high heaven by now for having borrowed her best pair of shoes. Well, I couldn't travel first class in my best dress and my hobnail boots, could I? The waiter trundles between the seats with his trolley and asks if madam would like to take tea. Madam would, of course, and madam is grateful for being referred to as such without any hint of irony.

A few miles out of Leeds, the stream of factories gives way to pockets of open countryside and then the mills, solid and grey, scarring the landscape. We stop to take on water at Huddersfield; a line of horses with their cabs behind them stand with their heads bent, uninterested in our arrival, weary from their labours, waiting for the train to disgorge its passengers. Then onwards past Huddersfield to open fields where wheat dips like ripples on a pond in our wake and sheep on hills regard our progress with glassy eyes. I have a fleeting thought of catching a train to Crewe and tootling back to Shropshire, or perhaps onwards to Wales with its vast swathes of nothingness, where a person might farm sheep in splendid isolation. But both are impossible; I would need forgiveness from my family for one and money for the other, neither of which are currently forthcoming.

We rattle into Manchester at a quarter to eleven. As I step off the platform two porters jostle with each other for my patronage, a far cry from my arrival in Leeds, when my dishevelled appearance had precluded any chance of a receiving a tip. The victor, a swarthy man built like a wrestler, steps forward and offers to carry my baggage. He asks where I am bound and then hails a cab, loads my baggage, and tells the cab driver to take me by the shortest route – none of that driving round and round nonsense. I am still in the throes of my largesse, and I give him a whole sixpence, which I hope will make his day.

The driver drops me at a tea shop in the centre of the city of the kind that I would normally avoid, but today I enter the pricey establishment and order tea, and eggs on toast. I have purchased a copy of the local paper at the station, and after I have eaten and drained my first cup of tea I turn my attention to the employment section; surely in a city of half a million souls there must be a decent job for another one. I have my sewing skills, and my farming skills, but the latter will be of no use in a city centre, and I want to try something other than tailoring. My eyes are drawn to a large W at the end of the list where a music hall wants a whole load of turns. I cannot be a lady contortionist or a male low comedian, but I could play to type as a tumbling clown. The thought cheers me up a bit and I laugh out loud, attracting stares from the other customers. Then, at the very end of the list, wanted, for fifteen bob a week, female server, must be sober, diligent and honest. It seems just the job for me, so I have another cup of tea, buy an Eccles cake for later and within fifteen minutes I am knocking at the stage door of the Euphrosyne Music Hall.

Receiving no reply, I hammer on the door and a slurred male voice tells me to go away, they are not open. I hold up the newspaper and shout that I have come about the position of server. He opens the door a few inches, looks me over in the way my father used to look at the rams he wanted to rent to service our ewes, and ushers me inside.

'Any experience?' he says, without preamble.

'No, but I'm a quick learner. When I worked in a tailoring establishment I went from a buttonholer to a cutter to a seamstress in a matter of months. And I'm used to hard work.'

'Read and write and add up?'

'I was always top of the class in school.'

'Wonderful. The job's not every day of the week, just when we are open. That's Thursdays, Fridays, weekends, bank holidays and

Saint Mondays. About twenty-five to thirty hours a week, more if we are very busy, but you get paid extra for that. Fifteen shillings a week and you get to keep your tips and all the free food you can eat. But no taking any food away with you.'

'I'm used to unusual hours. I used to work on a farm. No day off there; cows don't know it's Christmas. Geese maybe do.'

He chooses to ignore my attempt at humour. 'Start tomorrow, if you want it,' he says, and opens the door, gesturing towards the street with his outstretched arm.

'What time I should I start?'

'Six o'clock in the evening, and don't be late. I'm Stan Evans. Your boss.'

'Pleased to meet you, Mr Evans. My name is Lily,' I say, but he has already slammed the door.

I find a grubby hotel for the night, which costs me four shillings for dinner and a private room. After dinner I scour the newspaper for a boarding house or a cheap house to rent; I cannot again countenance the lack of privacy of a cheap lodging house. A house turns out to be way beyond my means, and even a boarding house is beyond what my wages alone would cover, but I propose to supplement the rent with my savings, until I can find other means of obtaining extra money. The next day I view a few within walking distance of the Euphrosyne, but it is Mrs Bradley's boarding house at No.2 Mount Road, for sixteen bob a week that will become my new home. Clean and tidy and with a shaded back garden and lodgers who, according to the proprietress, keep themselves to themselves, it seems ideal. Mrs Bradley tells me she is an absentee landlady but that does not mean we can have all and sundry in our rooms, because Florrie, the ancient maid, lives on the premises. Florrie staggers in and smells as if she is used to partaking of a tipple or three – just the sort you can bribe to keep the back door unlocked for you if you need to come back late. I tell Mrs Bradley that I will take it; the cost will have to sort itself out.

'That was very brave of you, to start another job for which you had no experience and to rent a room beyond your means,' says Pomona.

'It was a necessity and a challenge. Foolhardy, some might call it, but have you never felt the excitement of treading into the unknown?' I say.

'When I went to university.'

'But you still had the trappings of home: servants and all that. And you had the safety blanket of going back home if you failed.'

'And admit defeat? But you are correct, I did have that blanket, although blankets can smother as well as comfort.'

Here at last is the probable cause of her discontent. 'Yes,' I say, 'I suppose they can.'

CHAPTER SEVENTEEN

Spring has finally arrived; in the flower beds, tulips and daffodils have erupted from their frozen sleep, and, in the woods, anemones and primroses have replaced the blanket of snow with their own pale carpet. But the arrival of spring has wrought the departure of Langley; Rowse tells me she has taken a new position at the local hospital.

'Who will replace her?' I say, looking down the corridor behind her for another attendant.

'No one,' she says, smiling. 'Matron has told me that only one of us will be needed to escort you to these sessions and back to the ward or your work. You must have done something to please her.'

While we wait, as usual Rowse talks about her beau and their outings, and I do not mind. It is good to hear how wonderful and terrifying life can be outside of the confines of the asylum.

'I went to the music hall again, the City Varieties, last night,' she says. 'Do you know it? Matron mentioned that you used to work at a hall.'

'I have never been to a music hall,' says Pomona, walking

through the French windows and catching the tail end of our conversation. She waves Rowse away through the other door and says, 'The theatre I have been to many times. Only last week my parents travelled to see me, and we saw a marvellous production of *King Lear* at Leeds Grand Theatre. Father says he thinks the music hall is too raucous and rough, not the right environment for a lady at all.'

'Has he been to one?'

'I have not given that any thought, although he must have formed that opinion from somewhere. Not that he has ever admitted to going,' she says with a grin.

'I expect he thinks it too low-class, too coarse, though we used to get our fair share of middle-class gentlemen in there, of all professions. And some upper-class too. *Slumming it*, they liked to call it, though the Euphrosyne was no slum. And we were starting to get more unescorted ladies, especially those coming in gaggles from the factories. I think you might enjoy it if you let yourself. When I get out of here, I shall take you for a night out to the music hall.'

'Definitely,' she says, 'but don't tell Father. What shall we see?'

It will not happen; there is as great a social chasm between us as between Pomona and the attendants. But in another life we shall go to the Euphrosyne and drink beer and eat bread and cheese and boo and hiss at the dreadful acts and whistle and applaud the half-decent ones. On another night we will dress up to the nines and she will take me to the poshest theatre and between acts she will whisper to me behind her fan, explaining the intricacies of *Hamlet*, not knowing I have read it twice.

'You usually get a bit of everything: acrobats, singers, magicians, dancers, novelty acts. Though I think I should take you to see Vesta Tilley; she's very popular, funny but not crude and unlikely to provide you with the shock that your father warned you about. Highest-paid female performer in England, they say. And all this dressed as a man. Just like you used to be in your mackintosh.'

She chooses to ignore the remark and instead says, 'It sounds so exciting to be working there. Paint me a picture of your time at the music hall.'

'Warts and all?'

'Yes, warts and all.'

I think for a moment. 'Before I started working at the Euphrosyne,' I say, 'I had an image of a server as being akin to a serving wench. She would be young and uneducated, but coquettish and uncouth, with a mouth like a cesspit. I imagined her being all trussed up in a black corset but with the bow on the drawstring of the garment slightly unravelled and with her bosom overspilling her beer-stained white cotton blouse as she bends to place the refreshments on the table, as regularly as she spills a few drops from the jugs of ale.'

I look at Pomona, who is smiling. 'And was it not like that?' she says.

'No: the Euphrosyne required all its waiting staff, or servers as they insisted on calling us, to be smartly dressed in order to raise the tone of the place and appease those busybodies who thought serving in such an establishment was no job for a woman. Those who flouted the rules were the ones who needed to earn a few extra bob after, or sometimes during, their shift. But most were like me, buttoned up to our necks and clothed in layers down to our ankle boots to avoid the unwanted advances of the punters; not that it always helped, but at least it did not give them any encouragement, and we did not get mistaken for the professional whores who walked up and down between the tables.'

'How many of you were working there?' Pomona asks.

'I was one of six girls working there as servers and there were two who just worked Friday and Saturday nights when the music hall was at its busiest; I did not ask what they did the rest of the week. There were male servers as well, those who had not quite passed muster as waiters in the posher establishments and yet still considered themselves a cut above us and I suspect got paid a higher wage; but it was the girls the men came to see. On nights when we had many turns or when one performer was requested to do lots of encores, I would often not get to my lodgings until the small hours, but even so, the working hours were shorter and better paid than the factory, especially if you counted the tips.'

'And what did it look like? Was it in any way similar to the theatres I have visited?'

'The building was once a cloth warehouse, but it had lain vacant for over twenty years and fallen into disrepair, until it was purchased in '87 by Mr Ezra Lloyd. Apart from being covered in pigeon shit, the roof and front façade had remained intact, but Mr Lloyd must have spent a fortune on the refurbishments of the interior; he installed boxes and seated balconies accessed by an impressive winding staircase, a stage with a proscenium arch, curtains, wings, lights, the lot. Below the stage was the orchestra pit and the rest of the ground floor was given over to the auditorium, fitted with as many seats and tables as could be shoehorned in. To the left of the auditorium was the bar, and behind that the kitchen and to the right a smoking saloon for the men.'

'Most interesting – I have a clear picture now, thank you. And did you ever meet the owner?'

'He only came to the Euphrosyne a few times a month, usually on a Saturday, to check on the takings. We called him Old Ezra although no one, not even Stan, knew his real age and he could well have been only in his thirties or forties; he had a head like a boiled egg and hid the baldness under a series of large felt hats decorated with feathers, flowers and the like, and, as he was five foot nothing and about eight stone wet through, he looked like an old man whose entire body had wizened and shrunk since the youthful purchase of those extravagant hats.'

I glance at Pomona to check that this is entertaining her sufficiently. She is leaning forward in her chair, which I take as encouragement.

'When Old Ezra visited, he was known to wait in the stage wings watching the turns, and if any of them showed promise he would discreetly ship them off to London to perform in the other establishments that he owned. We lost a lot of great turns that way, although there were always more performers queueing up to have their taste of stardom; and, for the female performers, the gaggle of chanteuses, dancers and contortionists, the ultimate prize that a little fame might bring: a small chance of bagging themselves an aristocratic husband.'

'But that was never your intention?' says Pomona.

'Of course not – nothing was further from my mind. I just wanted to work, and be rewarded with more than a pittance for my efforts.'

'And yet, it did not cover your rent at the boarding house . . .'

'Indeed it did not.' I decide that I will tell her the truth about the way in which I solved this problem.

Euphrosyne Music Hall, Manchester, June 1889

It is my first day at work at the Euphrosyne. It is only four o'clock in the afternoon, but I am leaving early as I am going to try my hand at supplementing my income with a little pickpocketing. I have bought a second-hand coat that was probably fashionable twenty years ago; it is in excellent condition, long with deep pockets, just right for the job. I have never done this before, and never would have needed to if my circumstances had been different, but I need to earn the extra to pay for my lodgings, and I expect I will not be able to rely on tips alone. I had heard the girls at Mrs Needham's talk about how you must create a distraction, pretend to walk into someone, and then, while they are busy apologising, nab their wallet or a few pennies they might have in their pocket.

There is an old gentleman walking towards me. He has a walking stick and is a bit doddery on his feet but looks as though he could be worth a bob or two. He smiles at me, something I had not expected, but it gives me the excuse to smile back and chance to walk into him, feel around in his pocket, apologise and walk away. Two sovereigns on my first foray into crime! I did not think it would be that easy. Really, people should be more careful with their money.

I am halfway down the street when I feel a hand on my shoulder, and I am swivelled round to be confronted by a police officer. 'This gentleman here says you have just stolen two sovereigns from him,' he says.

'I can assure you, officer, I have done no such thing,' I say.

'Then you won't mind turning your pockets out, will you?'

I think about refusing – he would not treat a well-to-do lady this way, asking her to practically disrobe in the street – but he is talking about taking me down to the police station, and I cannot be late to work on my first day. I turn my pockets out slowly, first my coat pockets and then my skirt pockets. There is nothing there, of course.

'Sorry to bother you, miss,' he says. I wonder if he thinks I will make a complaint to his superiors.

'We all make mistakes, officer,' I say, and walk away with a slight limp, the sovereigns digging into the instep of my boots.

The Euphrosyne does not open its doors until seven o'clock, but when I arrive at six, there is already a queue forming outside and around the corner of the street, with punters jostling for position to get the best seats. I push my way through the throng, explaining that I work there, but still get shouted at and manhandled for attempting to jump the queue. The entrance door is locked so I must knock five times before Stan opens it an inch, as is his wont, and shouts that they are not open yet. He has forgotten me, but opens the door another foot to squeeze me in when I explain he had hired me the previous day.

'Yes. Tilly, isn't it?' he says.

'Lily,' I say.

'Go to the kitchen and get some instructions, Tilly, and next time, come in through the stage door. Johnnie will let you in if you smile at him nicely.'

'I didn't think there would be such a queue.'

'Yes, very popular we are, and for tonight only, sixpence in the auditorium and two shillings in the boxes. I expect we will have to turn some away. Governor's idea to drum up some extra punters, go back to the fifties' prices for one night only.'

The Euphrosyne is a different world. The darkness and then the spotlights and the smell of the quicklime and the heat and the noise and the cheers and the catcalls and somewhere in the middle of all of it Stan is pulling me aside and telling me I am doing a grand job. Backwards and forwards from the bar to the tables I go for the best part of four hours and then afterwards, when the punters have all gone happily to their beds, the clearing up for the next night begins: wiping the tables, sweeping the floor, cleaning the floor, washing the kitchen utensils, bottling up the empties – we are expected to do it all. I finish too late for an omnibus and, as it is too expensive to hail a cab, I have no option but to walk to my lodgings. Luckily, Emily, a skinny blonde girl a few years older than me and who has, she says, been working the music halls for years and will show me all the tricks, is walking home in the same direction. I am fearful of robbers, but we encounter no one save for an inquisitive gentleman who asks us if we come as a pair, causing us to crease up with laughter and the gentleman to walk away bemused at the outcome of his innocent request. I resolve in future to always have enough money for a cab, and if my tips are not large enough to cover my outgoings I will have to become more proficient in my pickpocketing. I creep in through the unlocked back door and climb into my bed; I do not recall falling asleep, but I dream of an old crone in a blonde wig on stage at the Euphrosyne sitting on a swing entwined with gardenias warbling that I should keep my hand on my ha'penny. It is past midday when I wake, with a growling stomach and with a throat like glasspaper, and a banging in my head which turns out to be Mrs Bradley knocking on the door to ask if I am all right and why did I miss breakfast? I had forgotten I had not told her the hours of my employment.

Over the next two or three weeks, I get to know the regular turns. Some still have stardust in their eyes and would work for a pittance for a chance of stardom; others trudge on, knowing their time for fame has passed, but all, except the big draws, needing to rush between two or three music halls a night to make a living. Ezra has decided that in the new year there will be a change to the schedule and that there will be two performances instead of one, but with fewer acts; one performance at seven o'clock, repeated at half-past nine; at least it means some of the acts can perform twice and get a decent night's payment. For Ezra it will mean more punters to drink more ale, but for me it means more tips and the prospect of a few more pockets to pick.

Regular punters come to the Euphrosyne whatever turns are on the bill. Some come to be entertained, some to get drunk, some for the camaraderie, and some for the girls. Then there are the occasional punters, the ones who have saved all month for a good night out, scratchy in their ill-fitting suits and counting their pennies for just another beer; these are the everyday workers, not your doctors or solicitors or government officials, but factory workers, porters, welders, butchers, bakers and candlestick makers, although the latter's trade and attendance must have diminished with the advent of gas lighting. But not the very poor; Old Ezra has ensured that this is no sawdust-and-spittoon establishment: the price of admission is far too high for the very poor.

But we have our fair share of those who do not need to earn their living, too: university students, fresh from the clutches of their boarding school matrons or still with their wet nurse's milk on their top lips and all out for a laugh, out to be grown-up. Then there are the gentlemen in their top hats and tailored suits who stagger down to the music hall having been turfed out of their clubs, although they must have at least shot a waiter to warrant being expelled from one of those establishments; and those gentlemen who come here even if they have not.

'Titus was one of those gentlemen,' I say.

'I wondered who Titus was,' says Pomona.

'Yes, my very own boy up in the gallery. Well, not up in the gallery; Titus was up in one of the boxes, the gallery in the song refers to the cheaper seats, way up in the gods; the Euphrosyne had none of those. The other day I heard someone singing the song in here. Rowse perhaps, or Matron. Took me right back.'

'Now that I would like to hear.'

'You don't think Matron has ever had a lover to sing about?'

'I do not think it is my place to comment on the senior staff.'

'She must have been a good-looking woman in her day; I bet she's had her share of romantic interludes.'

'Rowse, come in, come in,' says Pomona, at the fortuitous tap at the door. 'You are a little late.'

It seems intimate relationships are not to be dissected unless they are mine. As we enter the ward, Matron is doing her afternoon rounds, and I cannot get out of my head the image of her on her lover's bed with her hands manacled to the bedposts.

That night, as we are snuggled as best we can in our beds, the lights turned off and the curtains drawn, I turn my mind away from the blackness and the snores and the whimpers and return to what I have been telling Pomona – and also what I have withheld.

Euphrosyne Music Hall, Manchester, late June 1889

'Ladies and gentlemen, and those of you who are not quite sure,' says Stan, waving his gavel in the air in a suggestive manner before continuing, 'you know who you are.' He pauses until the titters and whistles subside. 'Welcome to another night of fabulous entertainment here at the Euphrosyne. I am your host and your chairman. Tonight, the Euphrosyne presents a veritable cornucopia of outstanding acts. We have scoured the globe, and give you, having recently traversed the Channel – or should I say, La Manche – dancers from gay Paree, *ooh la la*, majestic *soubrettes* all the way from Rome with a selection of your favourite arias, and from Her dear Majesty's Empire, God save her, a delineator who has braved darkest Africa to hone his craft, from India the Jaipur Jugglers, and last but not least our home-grown comics and comic

singers from dear old Blighty.' There is more applause and shouting and down goes the gavel on to the desk and Stan holds up his
hands to restore a modicum of order. 'Now I hope you have your
victuals, but feel free to replenish your drinks at the bar or let our
lovely servers take your orders at the serving tables.'

It is my third week working at the Euphrosyne and I swear that
each week Stan's welcoming speeches have become increasingly
theatrical; but the punters seem to like them and ooh and aah at
what they deem the appropriate moments. Stan waits for the noise
to abate; there are a few coughs and snatches of conversation but
then there is a general shushing among the audience. It is mad
really: in about an hour, they will all be talking and shouting at
the turns. Below the stage, out of sight of the audience, in dressing rooms barely six by twelve, the turns are in various stages of
undress, applying make-up, pulling on costumes, going over their
lines, running to the privy. I have a quick look at a programme
that I have swiped from the foyer and a singer billed as 'The
Bolton Baby Blackbird' is to be the first into the fray. A quick introduction and the curtain is raised and out she walks, scrawny in
a black silk dress and yellow hair which has long since succumbed
to the chemist's bottle, to kick off the night's performances. The
band plays the introduction, and she launches into her first song
about losing her poor dog or some such nonsense. Poor old girl,
she been doing this for years, since she was just a fledgling, never
being placed at the end of the bill or even the other side of the
middle. She has forgone marriage and children for the chance of
being a star and now every week she packs her worldly goods into
a carpet bag and hawks herself around music halls up and down

the country. She sings three ditties about love and loss, and as the audience clap her final song she curtseys as best she can and then bows and exits the stage, and the curtains fall.

Stan bangs his gavel, but the noise in the auditorium does not subside. He bangs it again more forcefully and the room quietens a little, but despite its sumptuous interior, Old Ezra's place will always be more public house than theatre. 'Now wasn't that a wonderful hors d'oeuvres to whet your appetite?' he says, and without waiting for a reply continues, 'Now from one black turn to another. He's learnt everything he can from his stint among the natives in Africa and the cotton fields of Dixie and now has returned to our own dear shores to entertain you. May I present the very funny Mr Perfect Peruke!' A drum roll, the curtains are raised but no one walks on the stage. 'The wonderful Mr Perfect Peruke,' says Stan, a little more loudly. Another drum roll and on lollops Mr Peruke, gazing into a mirror that he holds at arm's length in front of him and curling a tendril from his wig around his finger. He is dressed like a toff, but the audience, already primed to laugh by the absurdity of his name, can immediately recognise the pretence: he will never be the gentleman he aspires to be. He wears an ill-fitting top hat, his waistcoat is vulgar canary yellow, he wears a monocle, and two watches on chains dangle around his neck. His face and hands are blackened, and his lips are exaggerated with white paint.

The Euphrosyne has had a few of these delineators in the last few weeks; they seem to be all the rage. Accompanied by a banjo and tambourine from the orchestra pit, Mr Peruke launches into a staccato dance, all flailing arms and legs and head movements like a demented chicken. He then walks towards the front of the stage and trips over a strategically placed prop tree stump, falls into the orchestra pit and is hoisted back on stage by the lead violinist. After adjusting his wig that is slightly askew, he bursts into a song lamenting living in the city and his homesickness for the cotton fields. I know Mr Peruke; his name is Archibald Tanner and the nearest he has been to a cotton field is the three years he spent in the mills before he decided to tread the boards.

Then it is the interval, and I am rushing around like an idiot trying to serve the throng before the second half starts. Sometimes I swear the ale has been doctored with salt, the amount the punters are drinking. Not that they cannot get served during the second half of the performance, but most punters like to get a few pints in to see them through to the end. The more established acts – what the punters have come for, apart from the ale and the girls – do their turn after the interval, and as we reach the end of the evening Stan is working the crowd up to the finale, the best act. Tonight it is a male comedian, who is just this side of rude, but goes down a treat with his mainly male audience. The Euphrosyne did once try to drum up trade for the quiet weekday evenings by introducing a 'Ladies' Thursday'. This was also an attempt to raise the tone of the place by dint of the perceived civilising influence of the female; ladies were encouraged to attend for 'a night of unsurpassed entertainment', accompanied by a gentleman of their choice. It was not a success, as gentlemen tended to take women who were not their wives and were definitely not ladies.

I can feel damp patches starting to form under my arms; the few ladies in the audience fan themselves with their programmes and the men mop their foreheads with grubby handkerchiefs. But it is wonderful to keep busy and try to forget the past, and not worry that I might still be a wanted woman. We do sometimes get policemen in here, and although I am still looking over my shoulder I am starting to believe that nobody is going to be looking for me. And anyway, I have changed my name three times, so that should confuse them. I'm still getting used to being called Lily Day, a name I plucked out of the air when I arrived for my first day's work at the Euphrosyne; perhaps it is a good omen. Last week I bought some pictures to decorate my room and next week I hope to buy a new rug to make it look more like my own room. It looks as though I will be staying here for a while, and I hope there will be no need to do a third moonlight flit.

CHAPTER EIGHTEEN

It is nearing the end of April and the promise of the seasonal shift from spring into summer, heralded by the profusion of flowering bulbs earlier in the month, has been fulfilled. Increasing daylight hours and the ubiquitous showers have ensured that this year, April is again the greenest of months. It is a time for growth and renewal: a time to welcome wildlife back into the garden, a time for fertilising and weeding the warming soil and, as the frosts have mostly ceased, a time for outdoor planting. Matron now allows me to stay in my garden until sunset, inevitably missing dinner and occasionally being late for our ridiculously early bedtime. But she usually turns a blind eye to my tardiness: she knows I will not jeopardise my chance of release by trying to abscond.

As the date of my potential release is growing near, my sessions with Pomona are becoming annoyingly frequent, disrupting what could otherwise be a blissful afternoon in my garden. I will not tell her of my days spent there or she will undoubtedly apply the metaphor of growth and renewal to my rehabilitation; I cannot abide such nonsense! In a few days' time, Pomona will sit opposite me, lean forward, and encourage me to divulge memories of my first meeting with Titus. I have had two weeks to prepare my story, but I needed time to brace myself for the pain those buried recollections will undoubtedly disturb.

And lo and behold at two o'clock on the last day of April, Pomona sits at our little table, drinks the dregs of her tea and places her cup down. She takes her notebook from her bag and turns to where she inserted a bookmark at our last session.

'Oh yes, tell me about Titus,' she says.

Euphrosyne Music Hall, Manchester, July 1889

It is a miserable Friday evening. The pavements have been soaked for the best part of a week and I slipped and twisted my ankle yesterday evening and it is bandaged and throbbing. It was my own vain fault, as I had taken to not wearing my hob-nail boots and am now plodding between the tables dosed up with laudanum. Punters are streaming in red-faced, their coats soaked, stamping the water from their feet, excited to be finally let in for the second performance after queuing for an hour in the rain. I am just grabbing a few minutes, having a cup of tea in the kitchen and starting to feel the effects of the laudanum wearing off, when Molly, the youngest of the servers, runs up to me all smiles and opens her hand to reveal a sixpence. I suspect the worst and frown at her, but she says, 'There's a gentleman who says can he buy you a drink? And I've got a sixpence just for asking you.'

'I've heard that before,' I say.

'No, a proper gentleman by the looks of it. Quite young. Handsome too.'

'What, is he up in the gallery?'

'We don't have a gallery,' she says in all innocence.

'Tell him he is mistaken and that I am a server,' I say, more kindly. She is only a child.

'He knows: he asked for the tall dark-haired server. That can only be you, except if he means Peggy and she's forty if she's a day. Unless he's a bit peculiar and has a thing for the old 'uns, like some of them do.'

She drags me to the middle of the auditorium and points to him. He certainly stands out: he is seated, but he towers above his companions and his hair is very blond, almost white, like that of an old man, except that the unlined face and the down above his lips give away his youth. I cannot tell if he is handsome, but he is a gentleman, or at least he dresses in the attire of one. He is in the middle of a group of gentlemen, all laughing and drinking and smoking cigars and egging each other on to lean far too far over the front of their box before being pulled back by their ankles. Just the sort from whom you can pilfer a few pennies without them even noticing the loss.

When he sees the two of us, he winks at me like a commoner and makes a motion with his hand like a tipping goblet and I mouth *thank you* back to him. He stands and shouts, 'What is your name?'

'I don't see why that is important,' I call back.

'That's a very strange name, but you are the best-looking girl here,' he shouts.

I mouth another *thank you for the drink* above the hubbub and turn to serve some punters who have been shouting for ale for the last five minutes. There is a smile on my face that really should not be there, and I admonish myself for being pleased to receive a comment that he must no doubt bestow upon every pretty serving girl he encounters.

The roses arrive the next morning. Mrs Bradley puts them in a vase on a side table in the hallway, waiting for someone to claim them, since the only clue to the intended recipient is a card with the words *For the girl with the strange name, who by any other name would smell as sweet. Titus.* It is a nice touch with the mangled Shakespeare, but I will not be won over so easily. I wonder who he bribed with a couple of shillings to divulge my address and almost certainly, although he has not used it, my name? It is bound to be one of the new girls, who get paid the least and can always use the extra money, although I expect that none will admit to it. There is much interest in the roses from the other tenants, and a few claim that they must be for them as they distinctly remember a Titus at the last concert they attended; none of your music hall attendance for these women. I have to elbow my way through the coterie and claim them and now they sit on my windowsill, filling the room with their perfume as the buds surrender themselves to the sunshine.

I am about to go out and treat myself to a coffee and iced bun at the new coffee house on the corner of Corporation Street when there is a shout from the hallway that there is a gentleman at the door wishing to speak with me. I do not know any gentleman who might call on me, and start to dither as I wonder if it might be the police. But I expect she would have said so – would have gloried in saying so. For one daft moment I then wonder if it could be my father, having tracked me down to beg me to come back. But that would be impossible, what with my change of name and moving hundreds of miles away. Perhaps I am now just starting to wish it, whereas before I would have dreaded it.

I ignore the summons and pretend I am out, but another tenant knocks on my bedroom door. 'I know you are in there,' she sings.

There seems little point in ignoring her, so I open the door six inches and ask what my caller looks like.

'Tall, blond, about twenty-five. A proper gentleman. Not your sort at all.'

'Did you ask his name? Did he give you his card?' I say, choosing to ignore the caustic comment; I expect she is jealous: roses and a gentleman caller on the same day. I will be the talk of the sitting room. She pushes the card he has given her, the details of which she has no doubt memorised, through the gap in the doorway, and I grab it from her and shut the door, nearly trapping her fingers. That will show her.

The card is of white vellum printed with the words *Titus Hurstwood* and an address that must cost ten times what I pay at Mrs Bradley's. So he is not all talk after all, as I had thought – he has sent roses – but I expect a man like that would probably have an account with a florist and a discount for his continuing patronage. I am still wearing my white shirt and black skirt, my Euphrosyne uniform which I fell into bed in last night like a sloven. I cannot be seen still wearing those, so I grab one of my own creations from my wardrobe, one of five sewn when I was at Hofstein's: a flowery dress of gold and green, but all buttoned up like a nun. I feel like running downstairs but instead walk down sedately as befits a lady, hoping he is still there. As I open the door, he is standing on the doorstep.

'Ah, my Euphrosyne girl with the strange name. I was just about to knock again after that woman shut the door in my face. I was wondering if we could take a walk together, perhaps take tea or coffee? I have a carriage waiting to whisk us off to wherever you desire,' he says.

'Without a chaperone?' I say, even though there is no one here to chaperone me whom I could trust not to run back and tell everyone my business.

He looks at me open-mouthed. I notice he has very nice teeth. He has never had to consider the possibility that in these modern times a woman of my class would insist on a chaperone. I relent. 'I'm joking,' I say. 'I would love to come with you. And you can call me Lily now.'

My stomach chooses that moment to growl, for I have not eaten since last night.

'And we could have something to eat as well, then, Lily,' he says with a laugh.

I run up the stairs to collect a coat before he has chance to see my face, which I know must have turned beetroot-red. It is just a walk round the park and a Chelsea bun. Nothing special, nothing ostentatious, and all the better for it after the extravagance of the roses; so when he says he will see me at the Euphrosyne next week I am as childish and as giddy as when that stupid twirling sealed my fate in what seems like a lifetime ago.

*

'Those roses were a very romantic gesture,' says Pomona.

'Yes, I suppose they were. Certainly the other tenants thought so,' I say.

'So you were happy to make them jealous?'

'Of course. Most of them looked down their nose at me because of my lowly job.'

'But Titus didn't?'

'No, he never did. Otherwise we wouldn't have had a relationship, would we? He was different like that. How a proper gentleman should be.'

'I am beginning to like your Titus.'

'I don't think he was ever *my* Titus. But you are right. Even then, I was beginning to like him as well.'

CHAPTER NINETEEN

I have been taken by Rowse to Matron's office and left there to await Matron's return. Not that I know when that will be, as, according to Rowse, Matron has not designated a specific time, merely morning. Nor do I know what I have done. Matron's office is the best room in the asylum: it is only ten o'clock but already the late spring sunshine is streaming through the French windows, illuminating the expensive Chinese wallpaper and the good furniture; no wonder it was chosen as the morning room. The room is unchanged since the unfortunate incident back in February, except that the aspidistra I valiantly hid behind has been replaced by a large palm.

Five minutes later, Matron rushes through the door. 'Sorry I'm late. Now would you care for a drink? Tea or coffee?' she says. She boils the kettle on a small stove and brings the teapot to her desk, where crockery for two people has been placed on a silver tray. 'And my apologies for all this cloak-and-dagger business, but there is no need to get Cook involved, is there?'

She walks to the mirror, takes off her cape and unpins her cap so that her hair falls around her shoulders; it makes her look vulnerable, naked.

'There, that's better. I look less like a matron – although you now look more like a madwoman than ever,' she says with a laugh, as I sit there open-mouthed.

The talk of daggers is unsettling. 'I don't know what I have done?' I say, wondering if so many years in the asylum have sent her a little mad.

'Done? You haven't done anything. Well, nothing wrong. I just wanted the opportunity to apologise again for what happened to Elise, and to you. You were only trying to protect Elise, and I admire that. I hope you have realised that in giving you books to read I have been trying to make amends.'

She reaches into her desk drawer, pulls out another book and hands it to me: *The Strange Case of Dr Jekyll and Mr Hyde*. I have heard of it, and it seems to me hardly the book to give to a lunatic. It is all most peculiar: first the books and now this, whatever this is.

'Do you enjoy the books I give you?'

'It's wonderful to have some new titles, instead of newspapers and the books that have been here since the house was built,' I say.

'And for me it's so nice to have someone with a shared interest in them.'

She must have a dearth of friends if she needs to find companionship with a patient, I think.

'And how is the garden going?' she asks.

'It was kind of Dr Fairchild to arrange it for me. I love being out there.'

Matron laughs. 'You think it was Dr Fairchild who arranged

that? No, she was dead set against it. When she told me of your idea, it was I who pushed the superintendent for you to have the opportunity. Dr Fairchild would have had you cooped up all year long talking about your past if she could. I, like the superintendent, am a firm believer in fresh air and action. Not that talking does not have its place. I mean, look at us now.'

Yes, look at us now. A matron and a lunatic sharing a further cup of tea. For half an hour not talking treatments, not talking asylum, not talking lunatics.

'What I propose, if you are amenable,' Matron continues, interrupting my thoughts, 'is that every month you come here – not every week, that would arouse suspicion – and we can talk about books or whatever you like, but as equals, not like the pretend equals you are with Dr Fairchild. I will have Rowse bring you, and she may assume you are being punished and wonder why, but she will not ask. And she can be relied upon to be discreet.'

I think of Rowse divulging Queenie's history to me but say nothing. She did keep O'Neill's confidence, after all.

'I realise it's an unusual situation, but it will be our secret. Neither the superintendent nor anyone else need know.' *Especially not Pomona* is implied but not spoken.

'I would like that very much,' I say, for once meaning the words and hoping she is genuine in her intentions. I knew Matron had a touch of rebellion in her beneath that austere manner and dowdy clothing.

'Have you finished?' she says as I put down my cup. 'I'll wash them myself, otherwise Cook will be most put out that I have not required her services, and most inquisitive.'

'Here, let me do that; you've done enough for me today,' I say, rolling up my sleeves and reaching for her cup and saucer. Matron looks at my arms, reddened by years in the laundry, and then at my wrists, both scarred by the manacles that have been used to hold me captive.

'Your wrists look sore. Do they still bother you?' she says.

'Yes, sometimes, but it's a reminder not to wear that jewellery again. Have you ever worn manacles?'

'No, never – why do you ask?'

'No reason,' I say, and pick up the crockery and take it to Matron's small sink.

It is the middle of May, and its namesake tree is in full bloom, wafting its sickly scent through the open French windows. The smell makes me yearn to be in the fresh air tending my garden instead of cooped up in here. But being in my garden is only a short release from this nightmare; the real release, my ticket out of here, lies within the remit of the woman sitting opposite me, and navigating that path to freedom is proving as thorny as any May tree.

'Do you wish to continue talking about Titus?' says Pomona.

'Of course,' I say, 'if you feel it may be helpful.'

The Euphrosyne Music Hall, Manchester, August 1889

Titus has not been to the Euphrosyne for three weeks; not that I have been looking out for him. It is the middle of August, and the Euphrosyne is holding a special Summer Extravaganza, one four-hour performance with some of Old Ezra's star turns from

London brought up to boost attendance. Word of mouth has made the event so popular that we have had to make it admittance by ticket only. And then there he is, slumming it in the cheap seats, ordering champagne as if it is going out of fashion, and with all the female servers snuffling around him and his friends. One of his group has bought twenty tickets and has rounded up as many of his male friends as he could muster and now they are sitting around three tables in the auditorium which they have pushed together, determined to make a night of it, singing and swearing at each other and throwing good bread at the turns, which owing to their poor aim is raining down like confetti on the other punters. One of his friends has been sick on the floor and Emily has had to clean it up. Stan has had to tell them to quieten down and would have summoned Sam and Simon to throw them out if they had not looked such gentlemen and were not spending so much money. Sam and Simon are Chinese twins employed by Stan to give some menace to the security at the Euphrosyne. Their mother was said to have been a chambermaid and to have had a liaison with a Chinese diplomat, though how much truth there is in the tale is anybody's guess; in this business everyone has their tall tales. To sound more menacing when ejecting rowdy punters, they have developed their own vaguely oriental language, but anyone born closer to the church of St Mary-le-Bow than this pair would be difficult to find.

I have been avoiding their table, not wishing to speak with him and getting the others to serve them, not that they needed any encouragement. I am working my way down the row of tables behind his party when I feel a hand grab my arm and spin me around. It is Titus, and as he attempts to put his arm around my waist he overbalances and lands head-first in the lap of his friend, who, roaring with laughter, lifts him up and shoves him back in his chair, where he slopes to his left and continues to lean there, propped up by the arm of his captain's chair. 'Ah, Lily. You are here, and you are still the best-looking girl here,' he tries to say, but the words are slow and slurred.

'And you, sir, are very drunk,' I say. 'I might venture blind drunk even.'

'Yes, I am, aren't I? But don't call me sir; I think we're past that after the last time we met. And I am not blinded by drink, just by love, and next week I shall come to your residence without any of these reprobates, and I shall be as sober as a judge.' At the mention of reprobates his friends start to shout, and he raises his voice to be heard above them. 'I'm sorry I haven't been in contact for a few weeks, but I had business to attend to.'

'And why should I care about that?'

'Because I like you, Lily, my strange-named girl, and I think you like me.'

I have seen it all before: a server or one of the turns becoming infatuated with a so-called gentleman and him leading her on before discarding her like stale beer after getting what he came to seek out without having to pay for it. I was certainly not going to be that sort of girl, and he could come next week or not, as he wished. He would no doubt soon become bored with me and move on to another girl – or boy; you could never tell with these gentlemen. 'Come if you wish. I am free Tuesday evening. Six o'clock,' I say, hoping that I sound as though I mean it, and not that I am desperate for him to turn up, and all the time mindful of the policy that we must not offend the punters or we risk getting an earful from Stan if they complain.

The following Tuesday Titus arrives at ten minutes to six. I am ready, but I make him wait in the hall so that all the others can take furtive glances and be jealous. We take a cab to the Theatre Royal where, as my stomach is doing somersaults, I say I do not wish to eat, so we have a couple of glasses of merlot in the refreshment bar before taking our seats in the dress circle. We watch the new Chinese opera *San Lin*, not because we have chosen to see it but because it is what is playing at the time; but I enjoy it nonetheless. Not that it would have mattered to me if we had seen a troop of monkeys dancing a mazurka, so long as I am near to him. The opera lasts three hours, but the hours pass like minutes; I want to stay forever sitting next to Titus in the dark, with him squeezing my hand from time to time. After the performance he hails a cab, and we sit holding hands all the way back to my lodgings. Titus walks me to the front door, takes my hand and kisses it and asks if I would like to do it all over again, saying that he will see me at the Euphrosyne next week to arrange another outing.

But he does not visit the Euphrosyne the next week. Instead, he meanders in on a quiet Friday three weeks later with a few of his cronies. It has been a hot August which had tipped over into September and folks have chosen to make the most of the sun and the daylight hours by visiting the seaside or the municipal parks and have been arriving in dribs and drabs after nine o'clock and receiving a rebuke from some of the coarser comedians for taking their seats in the middle of an act. I have been promoted to supervisor, or, as Stan likes to call me, head server. The term conjures up visions of me carrying a platter with a suckling pig stuffed with an apple or else holding one of those shrunken heads from heathen countries that you see in museums, so I prefer the former term.

I have five girls under me, and I could have sent one of them over to serve, but instead I decide to take the order myself to see if he is, as I suspected, all mouth, and had forgotten me. Taking my notepad from my apron, I say, 'What would you gentlemen like?'

'If it's not my strange-named girl. Where have you been hiding yourself?' says Titus.

'I have not been hiding anywhere. Only working here. Where else would I be?'

'Then it must be I who have been hiding.'

'No doubt from an army of pretty admirers.'

'I only have eyes for you.'

His friends shout at him to stop propositioning the bar staff, get his money out and order the ale and food before they all starve to death. I cannot imagine any of them have ever been starving.

'Four jugs of your finest ale, and bread and cheese for all of us,' he says. 'Come out with me again, Lily, and if you find that you despise my company I will never darken your door again.'

'It would have to be during the day,' I say.

'So that's not a no, then? I'm thinking of going to the races over at New Barns on the twenty-first of this month. The Lancashire Plate is being run. We could have a bit of a flutter.'

'I would need to be back in time for work.'

'I will get you back to the Euphrosyne for opening time.'

'Just before would be better.'

'Wonderful. Let's meet at the station, nine o'clock. It's the train to Salford. We will travel first class, of course. Wear something nice.'

I can feel Stan's eyes on me for fraternising just the wrong side of the correct amount of time with the punters, especially as they have already been served. I move on to the next table and as I take their order I glance over to Titus, who has turned his back and is deep in conversation with his friends.

I have no idea what is considered nice for a race meeting. It is a shame he could not have been more specific. Did he mean pretty or fashionable or smart? Whichever it was, I do not have it; apart from my black dress, my clothes are either old or handmade, or both. And I have no posh hat, which I presume must be *de rigueur* for such occasions. Back at the farm we had been to point-to-point meetings, which we had attended dressed up in our Sunday best, but because the fields were sometimes muddy or uneven we would have worn our old boots. Titus will expect to have someone elegant on his arm. I have an uneasy feeling that despite previously stepping out together, he is only inviting me for a bet or a lark; I imagine that is the sort of thing men of his class might do. I decide that at least I will look the part, and, even if his intention is to humiliate me at the races, I will make sure that I have enough money to buy my own train ticket back to Manchester. I invest in a new suit, boots and a fancy hat, and hope that the weather will continue to be mild and I will not regret my decision to forgo a new coat and sensible hat.

When I arrive at the railway station, Titus is already there with a large group of his friends; I am disappointed, as I had thought we would be travelling alone. But I put on my server's smile and he waves and runs towards me, threading his arm through mine before dragging me to the ticket office and then introducing me to the rest of the group as his 'mystery girl with a strange name'. He does not mention my job. I recognise some of the men from the Euphrosyne, but I have seen none of the women before although they are seemingly well acquainted with each other, talking about parties they had been to or are going to, and people I had never heard of who have just got engaged, and who was going down for the Season. I am very glad I have bought a new outfit. Titus pays for my ticket even though I assure him I can afford it; I am not going to have him think I can be paid for and encourage his expectations for the return on that payment. Our party takes up the whole of one of the first-class carriages, which is fortunate as the excess noise my fellow racegoers are making must be audible all the way down to third-class. I would swear some of them are drunk, but I cannot smell drink on any of them. Not that the guard is going to complain: someone has already slipped him five bob. Three-quarters of an hour later we roll into Salford and take cabs to the racecourse. As it is the day of the Lancashire Plate, we have to wait half an hour for a cab; not so the local gentry, who have travelled the short distance to the racecourse in their own carriages replete with their own luncheon and champagne.

Our day consists of eating and drinking in the grandstand and then waiting for the men to return after they have gone to the course to find their favourite bookmaker. They are placing bets on horses that cost more money than I would earn in a week, without the least qualm when they lose, which they do with regularity. The forfeit for an unplaced horse is a tumbler of whisky downed in one, and by two o'clock a few of them are a little unsteady on their feet. Titus wants me to place some bets, but I pretend that I am waiting and watching the odds and following the form. I have no idea what that means, but it was something that Stan told me I must do or face ruination; he is always a little dramatic.

'But you must have a flutter on the Lancashire Plate. Of course, this place is not Ascot or Goodwood, but it does offer the highest purse of the racing season. The other ladies are betting on the race. It's what we came for,' says Titus.

It was not what I had come for, but I say, 'Let me have a better look at the form.'

'You need to choose an outsider to make any profit.'

As he has yet to make any, I am not about to take that advice, and choose the favourite.

'You won't get much back on that horse,' he says.

'But hopefully I will get something,' I say, as I pay the bookie two bob that I can ill afford to lose.

'That horse is owned by one of Henry's friends.'

Of course one of his friends would know the odd duke; they probably all have such connections. They all know each other and go to smart occasions like this every week.

The Lancashire Plate is a flat race of only seven furlongs, so we do not have to wait long for the result, and by the last furlong I am shouting with the rest of them until Donovan romps over the line like a trooper and I receive a return of three bob and fourpence. Titus's horse hobbles in last and he is down to his last two pounds and has to borrow some money from Henry for the rest of the meeting. I do not place any further bets; Titus has shuffled off with some of his more inebriated pals, so he cannot berate me for my prudence.

I had learned from a young age to not let my face betray my feelings. It had been born out of necessity against my mother's tirades but had had the unexpected bonus of standing me in good stead for playing cheat and, later, poker, for my father liked nothing more than a good card game, unless it was a Sunday. But I must have been a bit lax today, for one of the women in our party extracts herself from the throng and indicates for me to join them, on account of my sad face and that she presumes that rat Titus has abandoned me. The girl is lumpy and red-faced and turns out not to be a girlfriend at all but the sister of one of the men, who had been forced to bring her by their parents.

'To bag myself a husband,' she says.

'I am sure you are quite capable of that on your own,' I say with as much sincerity as I can muster. After ten minutes, when she finally pauses for breath, I know her life story, and she stands there, suddenly mute, in the expectation that her divulgences will be reciprocated. But I tell her nothing of myself: I talk about the weather and the races and enquire if she has had any winners. I adhere assiduously to rural but proper diction throughout our conversation, and when she meets up again with her friends she will no doubt tell them that I am indeed not top drawer but I do not seem to be, as they had all suspected, a high-class trollop; instead more likely a refined country woman with the reticence of the rural, and one who is, as I was obviously unable to afford the best dressmaker, momentarily down on my luck.

Titus has not returned after placing his latest bet. I go off in search of him and a quarter of an hour later I find him in the grandstand, feet up on a bench, snoring. His friends have deserted him. I tug at his sleeve and say, 'I need to leave to get back for my evening shift. You said it was just for the afternoon.'

'Change of plan, darling,' he says, yawning and making a grab for my waist. 'Just don't turn up tonight. The day is still young.'

He leans towards my face for a kiss, but I step backwards and say, 'I can't just not turn up. I need my job.'

'Go in tomorrow and tell them you were ill. Or get another job.'

He is obviously in no mood or state to move.

'Thank you for today, but I need my job, and I need to leave now,' I say, and I turn my back on him and head to the exit, ignoring his protestations. It is just as well that I have brought some money with me, and have won a little more. I walk to the cab rank outside the racecourse, choose the cabbie with the niftiest-looking horse, and ride to the station. Half an hour later, slumming it in second class, I am speeding back to Manchester. I do not have time to go back to my lodgings, so I catch an omnibus from the station to the Euphrosyne and hurry through the stage door with ten minutes to spare.

'Well, don't we scrub up well,' says Stan, who has come back-stage to talk with Johnnie.

'Not really the attire for serving, is it? I can discard my jacket and put my apron on and hope I don't spill anything on it,' I say.

'Johnnie and me thought you had eloped with your gentleman,' he says, winking at the stage doorman.

'No, I did not!' I nearly shout at them. I knew I should not have trusted Stan to keep quiet about my day at the races.

As I am not forthcoming with the details of my afternoon, Stan says, 'Any winners?'

'I took your advice. Had the winner in the main race.'

'You must be rolling in it – won't be gracing us with your presence much longer, then.'

'You won't get rid of me that easily.'

'Good. I don't want to be looking for another head server of your quality.'

It is surprising how a little praise can perk you up for a long night of work, and I realise how easily I have slipped into the role of supervisor and how the girls are beginning to annoy me with their lack of sense and how easy I am finding it to discipline them. The Euphrosyne is quiet, and we are finished by midnight. Of Titus and his friends there is no sign. I expect he has slept it off in a gutter, or in the arms of another woman.

'No one has ever asked me to the races,' says Pomona.

'Did your father not approve of horse racing either?' I say, but she does not rise to the criticism.

'It was not something that I have ever thought about asking. I am not sure if I would wish to go to the races. But I think he would approve of Ascot. More upmarket than the other racecourses.'

'And what *do* you wish to do, or do you always do as you are told?'

'Of course, I wanted to go to university. But I am hampered by convention in what else I can do. You are lucky: it is so much easier for you to do as you please. Not in here, of course, but before, and when you are released.'

'Lucky?' I say, holding out my scalded arms and mangled wrists and lifting my hair to reveal a brow more furrowed than a newly ploughed field. 'You don't realise how lucky you are, with your milky hands and your flicking wrists and your money and your new clothes and your education and your opportunities.' I think I may have shouted at her, but perhaps she deserves it. Or perhaps I am more annoyed with myself, because in retelling the details of that day I have realised how badly Titus treated me. 'I believe I don't wish to continue any longer with this session,' I say.

'But Rowse is not due for another ten minutes – twenty, with her timekeeping,' she jokes, trying to lift my mood. I wonder if she thinks I might attack her.

'Then I will read, and you can scribble,' I say, and I turn my back to her and take from my apron the latest loan from Matron, which I had been saving for after tea.

'What are you reading?' she says, in another attempt to lighten the atmosphere that has arisen between us.

'Whatever I am given. I thought I had told you that.'

She falls silent, and when Rowse finally arrives to whisk me away, Pomona does not wish me goodbye but instead enquires about the pin badge that Rowse has on her apron, which she usually keeps hidden under her cape. I am already starting to regret my outburst. My anger has pushed her too far; I fear this may be the last time that I see Pomona, and will lose, along with her desertion, perhaps also my last chance of release.

CHAPTER TWENTY

But I am mistaken. Pomona is more resilient or obstinate than I had thought, and two weeks later, as May enters its final week, we are back to do battle in my little room.

'Well, Sarah Rowse is certainly an interesting girl,' says Pomona, as her opening salvo.

It seems we are to ease ourselves into my story after the debacle of our last meeting. I feel she may wish me to apologise, but there is no chance of that happening, so instead I reply with an unexpected fact. 'Sorrel,' I say. 'That's her real Christian name.'

'That's a beautiful name; I wonder why she does not use it.'

I have knocked her off her stride, but it is a Pyrrhic victory: I have divulged a secret that was not mine to dispense, and instantly I am back at the farm, haranguing Mercy for being a snitch, the worst kind of child, ratting me out to Mother about some chore I had failed to complete, and now I am equally bad and cannot retract my words.

'She's got more about her than most of the attendants,' says Pomona. 'She's a suffragist. The membership of NUWSS is high in the north. Although I am surprised that she has joined, as its aim is votes for middle-class women only.'

'Perhaps she is aiming high. She's been talking about the society for a while,' I say.

'Has she? I am not privy to your conversations.'

'Perhaps you noticed her bruises. They were not from the asylum.'

'I thought the organisation was non-violent,' says Pomona, frowning.

'It is,' I reply, 'but some of its opponents aren't.'

'Her enthusiasm makes me want to join.'

'Why don't you?'

Pomona smiles, a little sadly. 'It is all right for Rowse, for women of her class, and for strident middle-class ladies, but not for me.'

I sigh. Pomona is so hidebound by convention, it's a wonder she ever attended university. I wonder if it was just to spite her brother. 'Perhaps we had better just get on with our session,' I say.

'As you wish.'

The Euphrosyne Music Hall, Manchester, September 1889

When I arrive at work the next evening, Johnnie lets me in with a huge grin and beckons me into his little office, saying he has a surprise for me. I begin to walk away from him, saying that I am already late for my shift.

'Good Lord. Nothing untoward, I can assure you. Please, come in,' he says, holding open the door for me to enter. I can smell them before I step over the threshold: a huge bouquet of lilies of every hue and attached to them an envelope of pale pink with my name in gold letters. 'Arrived this afternoon. Go on, open it. I love a love story.'

'There is no love story,' I say, and to prove it I read the card aloud. '*To the fairest Lily of them all. I am sorry for behaving like a cad. I'll be in tonight if you want to talk.*'

'Now that's a proper apology. I would forgive that young man anything if he gave me those.'

'Johnnie, keep the flowers, or throw them away, or put them in the ladies' room, or give them to the girls, I don't care,' I say and walk to the auditorium to begin my shift.

Titus saunters in half an hour before we are due to close, weaving his way between the tables before sitting at the one next to the orchestra pit. Most of the punters have started to make their way home and so, taking advantage of the lull in the orders, I walk to his table and say, 'Been to our club, have we?'

'No, some other business. Sorry I'm late.'

'Did it involve a lamppost or a gutter?'

'Oh, this,' he says airily, touching his black eye with his fingertips. 'Yes, something like that. Did you get my flowers? My apology?'

'Oh, were they from you? I have so many admirers I wasn't sure who had sent them.'

He laughs. 'I deserve that. Come out with me next week. A meal first, then wherever you want to go. I can pick you up at six o'clock.'

'And what if I come with you and you abandon me again?'

'Give him another chance,' sings a voice from the orchestra pit.

'Claude, I'll thank you to keep your nose in your piano,' I say. But he knows I am only joking, because he is the sweetest of boys.

'Yes, give me another chance, Lily. Don't make Claude weep.'

'Claude will not weep on my account. Or any woman's account for that matter. But tell me why I should.'

'Because you know I am a different man when I am not with my friends. They bring out the worst in me.'

'So you went back out with him after he had treated you badly?' says Pomona.

'Yes, and every week after that as well. Everyone needs a second chance. I mean, look at you, still wanting to cure me, even after my outburst at our last session.'

'Yes, but I would say that you gave him a third chance.'

'For my sins, by that time I would probably have given him twenty chances.'

'And was your forgiveness merited?' says Pomona with what, at last, appears to be genuine concern.

Titus's apartment, Manchester, October 1889

It is the third time I have been to his apartment. It is, much as I suspected, far grander than anything I could ever afford, and I am for once grateful to Mrs Bradley's rules of no gentlemen in ladies' bedrooms, for it saves me from having to show my room to him. It is a Thursday afternoon, and we have just been intimate for the second time today. The wind is gently blowing the curtains through the open bedroom window, and I am lying naked in his bed like a wanton woman while he takes a bath. I must admit he is very good at congress, and I suspect he has had lots of practice, but I do not wish to dwell on how many women he has brought back here. After all, a handsome young man with money to burn is always going to attract female attention. I have, of course, had a few encounters of my own, but there was only ever desire, never any love involved. I have never been in love before, never expected to be, and certainly did not think that any marriage I might enter into would necessarily include it. But it is not like those stupid penny romances make out: not all flowers and holding hands and beating hearts; it is pain and doubt and worry that the feeling is not reciprocated. Titus has not mentioned marriage, nor have I told him that I love him; I know really it is too early for such declarations, but he only goes out with his friends at weekends now, when my working hours make it difficult for me to take time off, and I take that as an encouraging sign. Sometimes at weekends he comes alone to see me at the Euphrosyne with a face like a petulant child and will be distant and uncommunicative for hours afterwards, even though he must have known the hours that I had to work before he asked me to step out with him.

Titus is always able to take the time off work, and I am beginning to wonder if he does any work at all. When I ask him, he says that he dabbles in this and that and that he has investments and savings that pay a good amount of interest. He keeps his money in a safe in his room and he has entrusted me with the combination. I keep my little bit of money in there since I am always wary of carrying my savings around with me, but at the same time I cannot leave them in my room in case they are stolen. The amount he has in his safe dwarfs my piddling savings and I doubt he ever saved any extra money in there for a rainy day, but in truth, I expect his family's wealth ensures that he has never had to consider inclement weather.

But he is always generous with his money, especially at the beginning of the month when it is all wine and shows and flowers; by the last week of the month it will be a walk around the park and fish and chips on the way home. Yet those latter days are the days I prefer, when we are not caught up in the noise and the singing and dancing of the theatre or the music hall. Those are the days when he is himself, always eager to engage in conversation. He is not the buffoon he pretends to be among his friends; he has a first in Classics from Cambridge and is as smart as a whip. And for my part I know I have surprised him by not being the country bumpkin he had initially thought me to be.

'How long are you going to be in there?' I shout, but he is singing and does not hear. I wrap myself in the bed sheet and walk to the open bathroom door.

'Ah, Lily,' he says. 'Come in and join me, there's plenty of room.' He stands and leans over the bath, leaving little puddles of water on the floor. He tugs playfully at my sheet, but I haul it back; despite our previous intimacy, I do not want him to see my nakedness. 'A bit late for modesty, isn't it?' he says.

'I prefer to bathe alone,' I say. How can I tell him my nakedness is perfectly fine in the bedroom but in a bathroom it reminds me of how I used to feel violated, having to share a bath as a child with one of my sisters? He has never wanted for hot water and has never had to share anything.

'Let's go shopping today,' he says, stepping out of the bath and drying himself with a towel that has been warming on the radiator.

'I don't need anything,' I say.

'Oh, Lily, I do love you. I have never in my life offered to take a lady shopping and received such a reply. There must be something you would like.'

I know he does not mean he loves me, it is just a turn of phrase, but it is nice to hear it. 'I would like to have a bath, on my own, and then go back to bed.'

'And so we shall, later, but when you have finished your bath we shall go out for coffee and cake, and I will buy you something. So hurry up with your ablutions and we shall be off,' he says, walking out of the bathroom and shutting the door behind him.

Later, I find myself sitting at a table in Titus's favourite tea shop. What had started as a pleasant afternoon has now turned into a cold wet dog of a day. The windows are misted with steam, and I am staring out of the makeshift porthole that a fashionable lady at the opposite table has wiped into the window with her handkerchief, waiting for Titus to return. He has gone off in search of a present for me although I have told him again that I do not need one. Five minutes later, he bounds into the room, takes off his wet coat, hangs it on the back of the chair and hands me a pink candy-striped bag. 'For you, madam,' he says, holding up his hand to beckon the waitress.

'You didn't need to buy me anything,' I start to say again, but then I look inside the bag and my protest dries in my mouth. It has not cost much, but it is the best present I have ever had. Far better than any flowers. 'You remembered,' I say in a whisper. I take it out of its bag and hold it to my nose – the unmistakable smell of new book: *Aesop's Fables*, with the words *with love from your Titus* written on the flyleaf.

'To replace what you left behind at the farm,' he says.

The waitress comes over to our table and he orders another pot of tea and a toasted teacake, 'for my soppy sweetheart', as I wipe my eyes on a napkin.

'Oh, Titus, I do love you,' I say, taking his hand across the table.

'Well, I should bloody well think so, too,' he says with a smile.

CHAPTER TWENTY-ONE

Builders have now finished constructing the new wings of the asylum; the wings protrude from the house like tentacles, finally completing the destruction of the symmetry of a once beautiful house. The new wards have all been filled with male patients, who it seems are nowadays becoming just as hysterical as women. Not that we have been told any of this, but you always hear rumours in here, and from my garden I can see that for once they have some foundation, as in the afternoon the male airing courts are full of men milling around.

It is a Tuesday in early June, on the cusp of summer, and I am in my garden with two helpers from the tribe I like to call my 'garden girls', although they are all at least twenty years old. I am unsure which ward any of them are from, and I do not ask. They have been specifically selected by Matron to help me: strong girls who have no problem digging a trench or pushing a cartload of muck. Today it is the turn of Flossie and Jane to work with me and I certainly need the help of all my girls, as my garden size has increased threefold since March. It was Matron who sanctioned the increase, and we had to dig up some of the lawn, which did not please the gardeners, but the soil in my new patch is much more amenable to growth without the need for raised beds. We look like proper gardeners with our muscled arms and our hair pinned back, digging and planting in our shirts, trousers and boots, much more practical than our skirts and aprons.

'Got any baccie?' shout some of the new patients from the airing courts.

We ignore their requests because of course we do not have any; but also because, unlike the gardeners, these newcomers do not know we are women. I do not want to encourage them to escape from their attendants and distract my girls. But then one of them does walk down to our little garden. He is about twenty-five, tall and good-looking and he does not look mad at all. I can see a flicker of interest in Flossie's face, reciprocated in his. I need to nip this in the bud, or else those who would love to see my garden fail – and I am sure there are a few, including the male gardeners – will complain to the superintendent that we are masquerading as men and then encouraging bad behaviour with our womanly wiles. I pick up a garden fork and have a few choice words with both of them. Flossie begins to cry, and the man runs back to the airing courts, hopefully with tales of the harridan in the lower garden, and I spend the rest of the afternoon digging and wondering how long it will take for my reputation to spread around the new male wings.

Pomona declines to conduct our session outside in the shade of the trees, and, despite the French windows being flung wide open, the room is like a furnace. But she will not have the sun on her skin, even under a sun hat, for fear of turning her skin brown like a common labourer. I tell her that we are in an industrial age and that most labourers are ghostly white from being inside a factory or foundry for all the daylight hours, but she continues to confine our sessions to the asylum. We must now have our sessions on a Monday or a Friday, as the increase in the acreage of my garden has seen a blessed increase in the hours that I may spend there. But Pomona is not interested in sitting in or even seeing my garden, even though I thought she might like to see my progression, and I must resign myself to this June inferno indoors.

Hale, October 1889

It is a fine day in late October, and we are on our way to his parents' house, and I cannot chase the smile from my face at the prospect of his having no other women in his life and that I have been chosen to meet his mother and father. I have a vision of us arriving at their grand house in Hale with me on his arm and him proclaiming to his dear mama and papa that I am his great love and them declaring how wonderful it is that he has at last found someone, for they had surely lamented his behaviour. The previous week, Titus's mother had bought and posted our tickets, to ensure, she later confided, his having no excuse not to go home. We are the only two occupants of the first-class carriage and so we spread ourselves along two seats like vagrants. Titus sleeps for a short time while I eat my cake and sandwiches like a glutton: I had had no food in the larder for breakfast and had put a few slices of fruitcake in my handbag out of habit. At my feet I have my new carpet bag purchased especially for the trip, as we are to stop the weekend and I could not countenance turning up with my old tattered one. Titus carries no luggage; I presume that he has a surfeit of clothes, now newly washed, ironed and pressed by servants and hanging in his boyhood bedroom.

I have managed to wangle a weekend off by agreeing to work over Christmas, which was either a decent or foolish decision by Stan, given that in all likelihood I will have left his employ before that date. A week before our trip we had to visit a ladies' outfitter's to buy a floor-length evening gown, as Titus says we will be expected to dress for dinner. I would have declined his money, but I could not afford to buy the dress myself, although I insisted that I would pay him back every week until the debt was paid, and even bought a receipts book in which I was going to make him sign for the receipt of my monies. He had laughed at my book and said the gown was a gift and told me not to be so bourgeois, which was a bit rich considering his background.

His father has sent his carriage to meet us from the station. The coach horses, two black stallions, pull a polished oak carriage, the doors of which carry his monogram: the letters HH embracing each other in gold lettering. The driver doffs his hat to us and asks how young sir has been keeping and says that the staff are sad that they have not seen him since last Christmas. As we near the house, the driver says that the mistress is very much looking forward to our arrival. I would have thought that the mistress would have come in the carriage to greet us if she were that keen, but perhaps this is the way that the rich do things.

I should have had an inkling from the opulence of the carriage, but I had not realised that what Titus had referred to as his 'little home' would be so grand. On seeing my surprise he explains that the house had been built in the previous century when it was the home farmhouse, but subsequent owners had sold most of the land and built extensions here and there so that it was now an eight-bedroomed mansion. We enter the vestibule and Titus rings the front doorbell instead of rooting in his pocket for the key; he always likes to make an entrance. A maid opens the door, bobs, and says that the mistress is in the morning room. The entrance hall is tiled, all polished and shining, and large enough to merit the need for a fireplace. To our right, a swirling staircase leads to the upper floors. I deposit my carpet bag at the bottom of the stairs and Titus takes my hand. His hand is warm, and I am grateful for it, since mine is suddenly cold and leaden; as we walk to the morning room our footsteps echo across the vastness of the hall.

His mother is standing by the French windows, gazing out at the rear garden. She is thin, almost translucent, and I swear I can see the sunlight shining through her. When she hears our footsteps, she turns and says, 'Darling,' and Titus swaddles her with his long arms.

'This is Lily,' says Titus, extracting himself from their embrace. His mother holds out her hand to me, and when I take it in my own I know how the milkman's carthorses must feel when they deliver milk to the tradesman's entrance and spy Titus's father's black stallions striding out through the front gates.

'Lily, let me show you to your room. You must want to refresh yourself. I have put you in the room next to Titus,' she says.

'Thank you, Mrs Hurstwood,' I say.

'Please, call me Augusta.'

'Where's Father?' says Titus, interrupting our conversation.

'He has a business meeting in Leeds but will be back for dinner. He's looking forward to seeing you. When Lily is rested, why don't you two go for a walk, or take the carriage and show her the countryside?'

'Lily grew up in the countryside, I doubt she will find it much different here.'

'A walk through our gardens, then, blow away the awful smell of the train.'

'Perhaps later. I'm going over to the stables, take Duke out for a canter. I'll let you two get acquainted.'

I silently curse Titus for abandoning me yet again but nod and joke that I think this a wonderful idea as I have had enough of him today. Augusta takes my arm and we walk arm in arm to the bottom of the staircase. My carpet bag has already been spirited away to my bedroom, and we climb the staircase without encumbrance. The wall to the left of the staircase is lined with so many portraits that it would be difficult to believe there can be anything but still lifes to be found in any of the other rooms. There are portraits of Titus at every age: chubby and angelic at five; shy and awkward at thirteen; handsome and debonair at eighteen. Along the landing, portraits of Titus give way to portraits of his mother; beautiful, poised, painted when she was about eighteen years old.

'These were painted the year I came out. I was nearly the débutante of the year,' she says.

I had heard of these things and attempted to show interest. 'You should have won,' I say.

'Henry, my husband – Titus's father,' she adds in case I am in any doubt as to his parentage, 'always says I was the prettiest and most accomplished girl that Season. Of course, he is biased and was not there to see me or any of my rivals, so I suspect he says it to placate me. But I did feel cheated out of the title as it was rumoured that Eleanor, the débutante who won, had had her mother influence the judging panel. I see Eleanor sometimes in town; she waddles along and wears the dowdiest of clothes. Of course, she lives a life of luxury, because shortly after the ball she bagged herself a duke who is a rich as Croesus. But her looks have long since gone, and I hear he has a string of mistresses.' A smile plays around her lips, as if this infidelity is some satisfaction for this long-ago but not long-forgotten slight. I sense a rabbit hole opening in front of her and guess that she would somehow disappear down it for days, the way Titus sometimes did.

'But you won Titus's father's heart. That's what love does for you. That is more important,' I say, with a genuine smile.

'Yes, I suppose it is. But that was much later.'

'Are there no portraits of Mr Hurstwood?'

'That would have been impossible until he was at least thirty, and now that it is possible, even desirable, he refuses to sit for one, as he says there are not enough hours in the day to waste on a portrait. He did, however, sit for a photograph last year. It is in his study. Now, this is your room,' she says, opening the door to a wood-panelled room decorated in shades of blue. 'We usually put visitors in the guest wing, but I thought you would be happier next to Titus, and this room has been recently redecorated. Martha has lit a fire for you. I always find it cheery, and, as we are in autumn, evenings can be cool out here. I shall leave you now, as I need to check that everything is in order for our meal this evening. Is there anything that you do not eat?'

'No, there is nothing,' I say. She would find it difficult to imagine that on most days I had little choice in what I ate.

'Very well. I will see you at eight o'clock. There's a bell-pull by the fireplace if you need anything.' She closes the door behind her, and I lie on my bed, drinking in the silk coverlet and matching curtains, the Turkish rug, the hand-painted wallpaper and the fire heaped with coals with more in a scuttle, thinking that I could get used to this life. There is a knock at the door and at my command to enter, a maid comes in bearing a tea tray, saying that the mistress thought I might desire tea or coffee. She tells me that her name is Annie and that she is charged with looking after me for the next few days, and would I like her to pour? I decline, telling her to leave the tray on the side table. She is a bit put out by this change in her serving routine and is unsure if she should stay or leave, so I tell her that she may go and she toddles off and leaves me to enjoy my coffee alone. My evening gown has not travelled well and there is no iron in sight. I cannot go to dinner in a creased gown and so I reluctantly do what Augusta had instructed and ring the bell. A minute later Annie arrives, out of breath, and asks me what I require. A few years ago I would have prefaced any request with a 'would you' or a 'could you', giving the person a choice in the matter, but a few months supervising my elders at the Euphrosyne – and since I am only eighteen virtually all the waiting staff are older – has cured me of that subservience; I find it more beneficial to instruct them and then toss in a thank-you at the end. The girl must be used to taking orders, for she picks up my gown and my travelling dress at once, saying they will be back with me in an hour if that is acceptable. I tell her I will leave the door unlocked and that she is to hang them in my wardrobe. I ask her if she knows the whereabouts of young Mr Hurstwood. I nearly stumbled, nearly called him Titus, which he had warned me would never do. But, like workers in all establishments who know more of the goings-on within and without the walls than their masters, she tells me that he has just returned from his ride and that if madam wishes to walk to the stables to meet him I am to turn right at the front door and follow the path through the orchard.

I have only ever seen Titus in his smart city clothes; in his riding garb he looks even more handsome, if that is possible. The ride has put colour in his cheeks and smears of dirt on his chin, and the shirt hanging halfway out of his jodhpurs gives him a wanton appearance; I am tempted to drag him to the nearest hay-loft and to hell with their no longer containing any hay on which to lie. But the thought is fleeting as he walks towards me and takes my hand, claiming that the ride and the country air have made him exhausted and he is going to have a bath and a sleep before dinner. As we walk back to the house I wonder how, living in such a house, he could bear to go back to the noise and grime of the city, even though I will be doing the exact same thing.

Three hours later Titus's father has, as promised, returned from his business meeting, and is sitting at the head of the table with Augusta at the opposite end, waiting to be served. I can see why he was not keen on a portrait, though I assume he must have other redeeming features. We have waded through the pea soup and have just started on the beef. I can feel Augusta's eyes on me at every bite, willing me to trip up by using the incorrect cutlery or passing something the wrong way around the table, but, thanks to Nanny Day and her insistence on my father's being taught table etiquette, she is never going to catch me out like that.

Mr Hurstwood dismisses the staff from the dining room, telling them he will ring the bell when we require pudding. After taking a sip of his wine he turns to me and says, 'Now, Lily, do you work, or are you another one of Titus's flighty young people?'

Titus had told me that his father would ask what I did for a living, that he measured a person's worth by their job, and we had discussed what I should say. I would have been happy to tell him I was a supervisor in a music hall, but Titus felt we should elevate my position.

'I am a manager,' I say.

'Aren't we all? And what do you manage?' he says.

'I manage the waiting staff at a music hall in Manchester.'

'Excellent, and a proper job with prospects. You might own your own catering company one of these days. Might even be able to work until the children come along. I started with nothing, so I know that hard work and determination is important to any enterprise. I would say I pulled myself up by my bootstraps, but for a long time as a child I had no boots. Sometimes I had clogs, and sometimes when I did have boots I had to share. I only went to school on the days it was my turn for the boots.'

'Lily doesn't want to hear your rags-to-riches story, Father, and Mama and I have heard it a thousand times,' says Titus.

'On the contrary,' I say. 'What line of business are you in, Mr Hurstwood? Titus has not mentioned it.'

'I bet he hasn't, although he is happy to live off the proceeds of it.'

I begin to wonder if it was more than forgetfulness that had led Titus to not mention his father's profession. Perhaps he is a moneylender or a casino-owner or owns a string of houses of ill repute.

'Shit,' he says.

'Really, Henry, not at the table,' says Augusta.

'Well, excrement, then, or, if you prefer, manure. Lily, you know the saying "where there's muck there's brass"? Well, for me there certainly was.'

'Where I am from, we say, "where's there's muck there's money". That's what they used to say about farmers, thinking we were rolling in it. But although we were never destitute, there were lots of lean times,' I say.

Henry draws himself up proudly. 'I import bird faeces, seabird faeces – guano, it's called. Imported by the shedload from Peru. Farmers use it as fertiliser. Excellent source of phosphorus and nitrogen. They have been using it in the Americas for centuries but it's only just become popular here. I started off by buying shares in a small shipment with all the money I had saved. It was quite a gamble, but it paid for itself tenfold. Then I started importing it myself – small shipments at first, but now my company makes loads of money: all from shit.'

'Enough!' says Augusta, throwing her napkin on to the table like a second at a boxing match and ringing the bell for pudding. Henry smiles at her fondly.

'It seems my wife has brought our conversation to an end. But

I'll be in my study tomorrow morning, if you would like to know more.'

'Yes, I would,' I say, as Titus rolls his eyes at me.

After dinner, Augusta and I retire to the drawing room with coffee while the men stay in the dining room to smoke and drink. It seems a tad like a fabricated display of gentility since there are only the four of us, and we could just as easily have privacy by re-treating to the far ends of the table. Perhaps they are putting on act for the servants. I had been prepared for a grilling from Augusta but instead she talks about herself: the theatre performances she has seen with her husband, the holidays they have taken when his work schedule allows for it, the problems with finding a decent dressmaker and, finally, whether I am managing to keep Titus in order. I joke that I am but will ask for some tips from her if I have any problems. By half-past ten I deem it plausible to be tired. I feign a yawn and ask if she would mind if I retired to my bed. She says that she quite understands and that it has been a busy day and asks if I would like Annie to put a warming pan in my bed or help me to undress. I am concerned to realise that Annie has had to stay up on the off-chance of my needing her. I tell Augusta I can manage very well on my own and to let Annie know she can retire to her bed.

I have been in bed about half an hour when there is a knock at my door and a second later it is opened to reveal Titus leaning against the doorframe. I had kept the door unlocked in case he wished to join me, and draw back the eiderdown.

'I just came to say I'm going riding in the morning if you care to join me,' he says.

'I don't ride – well, not as well as you do.'

'Then come and learn.'

'Next time, if there is one. I thought that tomorrow I would speak with your father about his beloved guano.'

'You mean you weren't humouring him?'

'No. I'm interested.'

'He will love that.'

'Aren't you going to hop in?'

'No thrill of the chase, my darling. If Mama had put you down in the guest wing it would have given me a proper frisson sneaking down to your room with all those creaking floorboards. I would have been down there like a shot out of a shotgun. But not to-night. In the morning I will be out before you have had breakfast, so I shall bid you goodnight.' He kisses my forehead and then closes the door and retires to his room. Half an hour later he is snoring like a piglet. I get out of bed and lock my bedroom door; he's not getting a second chance. As I lay my head on the pillow, I think clever, clever Augusta.

Next morning, true to my word, I go to see Henry after we have had our breakfast.

'I didn't know you used to live on a farm,' says Henry, as he now insists I call him. We are seated in his study, sitting either side of his desk with between us a pot of coffee and a pile of his papers. I do not wish to pry but I can make out shipping sched-ules, bills of lading and projected crop yields. Here is a man who brings his passion home. The room is very brown: oak panels; tan leather chairs; a dark brown chaise-longue; and an oak desk. I can imagine him sitting there smoking his brown Cuban cigars and drinking his golden whisky. I expect Augusta has tried to inject a little colour with cushions and curtains, but this is his domain, and he would have had no truck with her meddling. He insists that I sit with my back to the fireplace, more, I think, so that I will not feel compelled to look at the famous photograph that hangs above the mantelpiece, in which he looks embarrassed at the fuss of it all, than out of concern for my comfort. He is not a man you would have thought could ever have been handsome, or even presentable. The ravages of time have not inflicted damage to his face but merely accentuated the features with which he was born, and it is a miracle that he and Augusta have produced such a handsome son.

'I lived on a farm in Shropshire until I was seventeen years old,' I say.

'Then you know all about the necessity of good fertilisers,' says Henry.

'We farmed both livestock and arable. But we did make use of the cow muck on the fields and cottage garden. And my father always had an interest in innovations that might improve yields.'

'Guano certainly improves yields. And long may it continue, so that I can keep my wife and son in the manner to which they have become accustomed. One day some scientist will invent an alternative and I will be out of business. Tell me, do your family still farm?'

I wonder if he is a little tipsy, divulging such private family matters to a stranger, although it is a little early in the day. Or perhaps I have one of those faces that invite confidences but retell none. The women at the Euphrosyne say that I do.

'I don't know if they do,' I say, and he is wise enough not to press me further.

'None of Titus's other young ladies have shown any interest in my line of work.'

I wonder how many Titus has brought home but dare not ask, and instead say, 'I expect none of them grew up on a farm.'

'Some did. Doubt they ever got their hands dirty working, though, unless they were mucking out their horses. Fathers were gentleman farmers. It would be useful to have a wife such as you if Titus ever comes into the business.'

He must have seen me blush. Even though Henry had mentioned children at dinner, it is the first mention of my being more than a girlfriend. I doubt Augusta will be so keen.

'Does he not already work for you?' I say.

'No. He gets an allowance at the beginning of the month to pursue his own business interests. But don't tell him I told you.'

No wonder Titus is so blasé with his money; and that is why there is usually a lack of it towards the end of each month.

'Of course not; it will be our secret,' I say.

'I think I hear the bell for luncheon. I expect Titus is back from his ride. Shall we?' he says.

Titus and his mother are already seated at the dining room table. She does not look up to greet us, but Titus gets up and makes a show of pulling out my chair. Luncheon is less formal than dinner but still comprises a superfluous number of dishes. When we have been served and the staff dismissed, Henry turns to his wife and son and says, 'What have you two been up to this morning?'

'We haven't been up to anything. Why do you ask?' says Augusta.

'The fact that your head has nearly been in your soup for most of the meal and Titus is as jumpy as a flea.'

'Just lively from my ride, and Mama has one of her heads. Isn't that right, Mama?' says Titus.

'Yes. I did not want to be absent for the last meal before you young people go back to Manchester, but now I feel it has conquered me and if you will all excuse me, particularly you, Lily, I will retire to my bedroom.' She walks over to me and holds out her hand. She is pale and her hand when I take it is cold, like a dead thing. She barely squeezes my fingers, and I wonder if she does indeed have the headache she claims. She steps towards Titus, who is already standing pending her departure, hugs him and whispers, 'I'll see what I can do.' Augusta has her back to her husband, and he does not hear or see this exchange; had I not learnt to lip-read over the hubbub at the Euphrosyne, the words would not have reached my ears either.

On our departure that afternoon, Titus barely speaks in the carriage, and on the train journey back to Manchester he turns his head to the window and will not be distracted from the devil that is riding him. I know not if he sleeps or if it is pretence, but I know to leave him alone when he is in such a mood; when we reach his apartment he can drink himself to sleep and wake in the morning refreshed and full of apologies for his behaviour. But the next morning he has gone before I awake, leaving a note saying he has left a spare key on his desk and that I should lock the door when I leave.

*

'Did you always have to placate this man?' says Pomona.

'Don't all women?' I say.

'You were hardly a woman at the time. Just eighteen. What was he, twenty-five, thirty years old?'

'Twenty-seven when we met. But maturity cannot be attributed to a number.'

'But still, there was quite an age difference.'

'On the contrary. Men are usually much older than their wives. They must establish themselves, in order to be able to provide for a wife and child.'

'And did you believe Titus would be able to provide for you?'

'I believe anything is possible, with a little encouragement.'

CHAPTER TWENTY-TWO

It is my birthday and to celebrate we are to have a Victoria sandwich with our afternoon tea. Pomona declines a slice, saying that she does not intend to be a fat fiancée, but I eat two slices, as it is unimportant if my waistline spreads. After five minutes there is a knock at the door, and we are joined by Matron.

'I've just dropped in for a few minutes,' she says.

'Cake?' I say.

'Of course. We need to celebrate your progress as well as your birthday, and, to mark both, I have a present for you.' She hands me a wrapped parcel; it is another book, but there is not much else she could give me that would not be either confiscated or stolen.

'I'll give you chapter and verse when I have finished,' I say.

'I've already read a copy of it, but I would be interested in your thoughts,' she says with a smile, and eats her cake, remarking that she will give our compliments to Cook.

'Well, Matron,' says Pomona, 'now that your cake is finished, perhaps I may be allowed to continue with my work alone with my client? And is it the asylum's policy to show favouritism to a patient?'

'I do not consider a gift to acknowledge achievement an act of favouritism,' says Matron, and she puts her tea plate on the table and walks out of the room without a backward glance.

I wonder if Pomona is jealous of the passion for reading that Matron and I share; it is a good thing she does not know about our regular secret meetings. Turning to her, I say, 'You gave me a gift at Christmas.'

'But I do not run the asylum. And now shall we continue?'

Manchester, November 1889

When I return from work on Sunday night, a week after our visit to his parents, Titus is waiting for me on the front doorstep.

'I've been waiting for over an hour,' he grumbles. 'Had to decline the attention of two ladies of the night and the enquiries of a policeman wanting to move me on.'

'You do look a little sinister under that streetlight, and we ladies are all a little jumpy with all that Jack the Ripper business last year. I know it was in London, but he would only need to hop on a train, or someone else decide to copy those atrocities . . . But why didn't you come to the Euphrosyne?'

'Didn't have the stomach for it. Can I come in? I could do with a drink.'

The back door is open as usual, and we sneak in and I give him the key and the directions to my room, hoping he will not think it a hovel, and tell him to creep up the stairs while I waylay a drunken Florrie, who instead of going to bed has fallen asleep on a sitting room chair and has been roused by our return. I cannot have her reporting me to Mrs Bradley, who always tries to keep up the pretence of a well-ordered house. But the menacing appearance of Titus and the conversation about the Ripper has set me thinking that I need to get a key cut for the back door rather than having it left open. I will need to make it worth Florrie's while to get one cut for me, and to keep her mouth shut about it.

Titus is sitting on my bed, whisky in hand, shivering, with my eiderdown wrapped around him. He gets up from the bed, dragging the covers with him like a cloak, and helps himself to another.

'I'm in trouble, Lily,' he says.

'What on earth is the matter?' I say.

'It's freezing in here. Can you light a fire?'

'It's a bit late, but I can burn a few sticks of kindling for you.' I take yesterday's newspaper, tear off a few strips and place them beneath the kindling. When I put a match to the paper, the kindling sparks into life, and, as Titus is still shivering, I add a few lumps of coal that I can ill afford.

When he has warmed a little, he unwraps himself from my eiderdown and lifts his shirt and vest to reveal a multitude of bruises.

'Next time it will be my face,' he says. 'You saw what they did the other month.'

'Oh, you mean the lamppost. How could you be so stupid? But who did this to you? You should go to the police,' I say.

'No, no police. I have been rather silly and owe some not very nice moneylenders rather a lot of money. Been losing a lot at cards lately, but I'm sure I will be winning again soon.'

I am no fan of the police, especially with my little sideline. Not that I have needed to return to it for a while, on account of my promotion, but you never know what circumstances might befall you. 'Why don't you stick to horse-racing?' I say. 'I thought you liked it.'

'Not as much as poker.'

'But you have loads of money, Titus. I expect that every month you get more than I earn in three.'

'It's not enough. I've been paying them off in dribs and drabs, but they want it all back.'

'Couldn't you talk to your parents?'

'Not my father; he already thinks so little of me. Mama usually helps me out by telling Father she needs money for a new dress or something. Sometimes she gives me bits of her jewellery and trinkets from the house to pawn, but she has nothing left she can give me without Father noticing. Last month he remarked that a few things had gone missing from the house and rounded up the staff and accused them of stealing! Mama says a few of the housemaids were in tears. Couldn't prove anything, of course, but he keeps a watchful eye on them now. Poor Mama had to stay silent.'

'I know how that feels, to be accused. Is that what last weekend was about – just you squeezing your mother for more money? Augusta's "see what I can do"? Nothing to do with introducing me to your parents?'

'You heard that? You mustn't think that was all it was. I wanted to kill two birds with one stone. And you were a hit with Father. Never seen him so animated.'

'Does your mother not have money of her own that she can give you? I thought she was an Honourable or something when she married your father.'

'She has a title and was born into old money, but by the time she came of age there wasn't any left. And even if there had been, any she had would have gone to Father. Grandfather didn't have the money to set up a trust to give her a little independence; he was up to his eyeballs in debt. He would have lost the family estate if Father hadn't agreed to pay off his debts. Mother was the auction lot sold to the highest bidder. Bit like those impoverished British aristocrats who marry American heiresses, those rich Yankee businessmen's daughters we seem to hear about every month. At least those women get a title for their troubles. I suppose Father just got a trophy wife and the prestige he craved. Pour me another whisky, will you?'

'But he seems so devoted to her – to love her,' I say, filling his glass and handing it to him.

'I believe he does love her. Mama accepts her position, and she has done her duty and produced an heir for him. But he would have preferred someone more like you, even if that was a daughter.'

'That's not true. I think he just wants you to do well in your business ventures.'

'Did he tell you that?'

'Not in so many words. But perhaps you could ask him for business advice. I think he would appreciate it.'

'Advice about what exactly? There are no business ventures.'

For the second time I must have lost my poker face, for suddenly he is wrapping his long arms around me, telling me not to be so shocked. His face, flushed with the whisky and the fire, has lost its pallor and is warm against my cheek.

'I know you have some money saved,' he says. 'Could I use it to tide me over? With your money and mine I could offer a three-month payment plan which might buy me some time. I'll pay you back as soon as I have it, and I promise I will buckle down to work. With your encouragement I can't fail,' he adds, with a smile.

'But that's all I have in the world. Can't you ask any of your other relations? Does your mother not have brothers? If your father saved the family silver, I presume they are not destitute.'

'And let everyone know my business? I couldn't have that. Word would soon get around to my friends. They wouldn't want to be with someone who is penniless.' He disengages himself from our embrace and throws some more coal on to the fire; I will have none left for morning at this rate. I wonder if he is going to sit there and stew all night, but instead he turns and says, 'But you are right. It was wrong to ask you for money. I'm sure I'll sort it out somehow. However, I am a little shaken. Can I stay here tonight? I'll be up and out the back door before Florrie has even prised open her eyelids, the state she was in.'

We laugh together as we used to, and all is well in the world, and I say of course he can stay.

Ten days and nights pass after that, without a single sign of Titus. I am increasingly worried: I realise that it was out of character for him to turn up on my doorstep at midnight and I should have been more concerned. What if something has happened to him? What if he is angry with me for refusing to help him? Last night I saw some of his friends at the Euphrosyne. I asked them if they had seen Titus and they said that like me they had not seen him and they laughed and joked that he was probably off with another of his girls. I laughed with them, as they were, I hope, only teasing me, and know nothing of his debts.

I can wait no longer, and, on the pretext of returning his key, I go to his lodgings. I ring the bell and the concierge – who remembers me, which at least gives me some assurance that I am not one of many – lets me into the lobby. He says he has not seen Titus for a while but then again he is not the nosy sort, and says I can go up and knock on his door. The knock is not answered and so I say his name, a whisper at first and then more boldly, but as there is no reply from within, I try the handle. The door is locked, and the frame shows no outward signs of having been forced, which reassures me a little. I unlock the door, turn the handle and slowly step inside his apartment, nervous of what I might find.

Titus is not there, and has not been for some time, as the smell of his Trumper's lime cologne always lingers in a room long after he has left it. The whole apartment is cold, as if there has been no gas heating or even a coal fire lit for some time. I feel the radiators; they are stone cold, and, in the fire grate, ashes lie grey and papery. I agitate them with the poker, but even at their heart no warmth remains. There are no items of clothing in the wardrobes and nothing in the drawers; and in the kitchen, which never housed much more than wine, the cupboards are bare.

My thoughts turn to his safe, which is housed at the back of the drinks cabinet, and, glancing over, I see that the cabinet is still intact, probably because the glass frontage shows there to be no bottles within it. When I try the handle, it is locked. Titus keeps the key to the cabinet under one of the loose floorboards beneath it – the first place anybody would look, I often told him. I lift the board, pick up the key, unlock the cabinet and press the combination of the safe. There is, as I had suspected, none of his cash in the safe, only my black and red metal tin. Titus must have taken his money and his belongings and fled, perhaps to his parents to beg some money from his father, leaving mine secure in the safe for when, he must have surmised, I would eventually turn up to collect it. But when I pick up my tin it does not rattle. The insignificant lock has been forced and all my savings – there must have been at least twenty pounds in there – have gone.

Yet for all the cursing I do – and I call Titus all sorts of names that a lady should not use – I cannot be sure something awful has not befallen him: his creditors could have taken the money he had offered them, done away with him, and taken anything portable of value from his apartment.

The following Saturday morning, I know I must do something, so I catch the early train to Altrincham that just three weeks ago we had both climbed aboard with such merriment and high hopes for our future. His father is not at home, but his mother tells the maid to show me into the morning room and to bring tea. I wonder if this is the pattern of their lives, week after week, punctuated only occasionally by the arrival of their errant son. I envy Titus this life, the obvious love and care of his mother and father, and long to be part of this world. Augusta Hurstwood seems unperturbed by my arrival, as if there has been a procession of young girls who have at one time knocked on her front door, their eyes red and swollen, seeking the whereabouts of her son. She says she has not seen him since he last came home with me in tow, but that she had flowers and a lovely thank-you note from him only a week ago. This does not sound like Titus at all, since his grand gestures are usually reserved for the beginning of the chase and I know he was scraping money together for his creditors. I wonder if she is lying, but without betraying Titus's position I cannot divulge my fears. She assures me that he often goes away for weeks, even months at a time, and will turn up when he so desires. I swear I see relief in her eyes: she thinks her son has finally seen sense and is avoiding me. I write my address on one of her lavender notelets and she says she will contact me if she hears from him. As I turn to leave, I see her scrunch the notelet in her tiny pale hand.

I return to Titus's flat, just in case. But there are still no clothes, no fire, no cologne. I am tempted to go out and buy a bottle of the stuff and slosh it around like a heroine pining for her love in a bad melodrama, but I am not one of those girls, and, besides, it would be way too expensive. I know Titus has paid his rent at least until the end of the month and, as his apartment is vastly more comfortable than my room, I decide to stay. For a price, the concierge has agreed to turn a blind eye, and if his creditors plan to return then they must do as they must; there is nothing left to take, unless they want the furniture. I fetch food and clothes from my room, clear the ashes in his sitting room grate, light a fire, and wait.

Titus returns after three days. Just after midnight I am roused from my sleep by the unlocking of the apartment door, and, cursing myself for forgetting to draw across the bolt, I hear the door creak open. I jump from the bed and feel my way along the wall to the sitting room, reasoning my intruder will be at a disadvantage and unaccustomed to the sudden change in light from the gaslit hallway. In the sitting room I thrust out my hand and fumble among the companion set, hoping to find the poker but only managing to grab the sooty end of the coal tongs, which I pick up and hold above my head, ready to strike.

'I'm armed,' I say. 'Don't take another step.'

'I'm glad to hear it, Lily,' says Titus.

As he steps into the dwindling firelight, I can see he is unshaven, and his clothes are unkempt. He heaves himself into the fireside chair and says, 'God, I'm cold. Put a few more coals on the fire and make me some tea, will you? And a few biscuits?'

'The state of you! I would offer you something stronger if there were anything here.'

'Sorry about that.'

When I come back with the tea, he has fallen asleep in the chair; the questions will have to wait until morning. I wrap a blanket around him and sit in the chair opposite, drinking my tea and eating his biscuits, watching him sleep. He reminds me of Honesty's baby Elijah with his blond hair and whistling breath, and I can see how a mother could dote on him and forgive him anything. I leave him in the chair and retire to his bed, and when I awake I can hear him singing and splashing water in the bathroom.

'Let's take a train somewhere today; the fresh air will do us good,' he says, breezing into the bedroom naked and newly shaven.

'Don't you need to rest?' I say. But he does not take the hint.

'Why would I want to rest? I know I looked a mess last night and I know the money is gone and I can see you are eager to know what has happened. We will take a trip, go for a walk and perhaps have something to eat at a tea room, and I will explain it all. And there's something I want to ask you. Now get dressed like a good girl and we will be off.'

'What about the seaside? I could do with some salty air.'

'Maybe next week, although it might be a bit choppy by the coast. We shall have salty air and saltier fish and chips in one of those little shelters. How does that sound? Today I want some country air, blow away the stench of the city.'

'Then let me go back to my place to pick up my old boots. I can't walk in these lady's shoes, can I? Meet you at the station in an hour?'

As I leave my lodgings it starts to spit with rain; by the time I reach the station it looks as though the downpour has set in for the day. Titus is already on the edge of the platform, hiding under a huge black umbrella and beckoning me to join him underneath its manly canopy. I am afraid that we will have to avail ourselves of it all day, but as we steam away from the city the clouds part in our wake like a stage curtain. We reach Windermere station around eleven o'clock and are greeted by the promised sunshine even though we are well into November. We alight and hail a cab and ask the driver to take us to the most picturesque walking place. He must have good local knowledge, for he drops us in a spot with scaleable hills; nestled in the crook of two of those hills we spot a tea room, empty until we arrive, and order tea and pikelets and four bottles of ale to take with us. We must look the most novice of walkers, me with my carpet bag and Titus with his city umbrella. We walk for about an hour, with Titus lagging way behind; since his childhood he has been more used to riding on a horse than travelling by Shanks's pony. But at least he has fashioned his umbrella into a makeshift walking stick, whereas I must lug my superfluous bag, wishing I had a little knapsack for our ale. I goad him for being unfit and say that despite my accoutrements I will race him to the top. I reach the summit five minutes before him, wait for him to catch up and then, laughing, we collapse under a wind-battered rowan and drink our ale, shaded by the tree's crop of ripened orange berries that still cling to its ancient branches. Below us the hillside falls away, not smoothly but with outcrops that are jagged and gnarly, and, below, a gash of deep blue. I beg Titus to stay away from the edge, as I had seen a childhood friend disappear over Wenlock Edge while we played a game of tag. The child had survived, caught in the cradle of some holly bushes, and the men had lowered themselves down on ropes to rescue the scratched but otherwise unhurt girl. But no such benign bushes lie beneath this drop.

Titus lies on his back, basking in the early afternoon sunshine like a grass snake. I lie down beside him with my head on his chest without thought of being seen: it is a weekday, and we are the only people walking to the summit today. The ground is hard and a little damp, with only tiny patches of grass to soften our slumber, but Titus can fall asleep anywhere at any time, and if he were ever on his uppers he would have no trouble sleeping propped over a line in a doss house like some poor souls have to.

I am desperate to ask him where he has been, and cannot wait for him to wake up again if he drops off, and so I blurt out, 'What happened, Titus? I presume you were beaten up and robbed. I was robbed as well. Was it the moneylenders?'

'Who says I was beaten up and robbed?' he says.

'The little matter of all the money being gone, your apartment empty and you being away for weeks without contacting anyone, plus the state you were in when you returned.'

He moves my head from his chest, sits up, and takes a swig of his ale. 'I wasn't robbed. I cleared out my stuff in case the money-lenders turned up, and then went to see Father.'

I remain lying on the ground, eyes closed, letting him ramble. 'Your mother said she had not seen you,' I say. It is surprising what you can say when you do not have to look directly at someone.

'You went to see them, did you? I thought you might. I saw Father in his office. Mama does not know anything about it, unless he has told her. I was desperate for the money to pay off the debt, desperate enough to plead with Father, what with Mama not giving me another sou, though I suspect she has some squirrelled away somewhere.'

'But you took my money as well! Did your father refuse to give you as much as you needed?'

'I took your money just in case. But when I explained my pre-dicament he was very understanding and gave me the money, plus a little extra.'

My small knowledge of his father makes me think this an un-likely scenario, but I hold my tongue and instead say, 'Wonderful. It's a shame you didn't go to him first. So, you have my money with you?'

'Ah, well . . . I'm sure you will find this a hoot. After I had paid off my debt – and you will be pleased to know I got a receipt, although with it being from a moneylender I don't suppose it's worth the paper it's written on – I decided to go to just one more card game. Harry and James had found this club just off Park Road, all high class and respectable with tables in the back room. We were there a few days, drinking, sleeping and gambling, we lost track of time, and we all looked a right dog's dinner when we finally left. It was good fun. I lost my remaining money, and yours as well. But I stopped playing after the money was gone, Lily – I didn't even ask for credit.'

I can feel the tears stinging my eyes and my fists curling up in balls so that my nails start to dig into my palms. He takes my silence as my approval of his good behaviour and continues, 'Now that that's out of the way . . . I brought you up here to ask you something.'

That can only mean one thing, but this is not how I have im-agined a proposal. I saw us perhaps on a punt on a river on a lazy summer Sunday afternoon, Titus steering the punt to the shore so he did not overbalance as he knelt; or snuggled on a sofa in front of a roaring fire in his apartment on a winter's night with Christmas fast approaching and snow falling softly against the window-pane. Not lying in the dirt on top of a windy hill, red-faced and snotty-nosed, with a sheep inspecting my ankles and without two ha'pennies to rub together.

'The thing is, Lily, we have known each other for quite a time, and you know you can trust me.'

I am not sure of that at all, but if we are to be married I must learn to trust him, and I will have to convince myself that his at least not incurring further debt is a sign he can change.

'When Father gave me the money, there was a condition. He said he will continue to pay for my lodgings, and I can stay in my present place even though he considers the price inflated, but he will be cutting my allowance by two-thirds, and I must go out and make some money by myself. Prostitute myself to the mighty pound. So, I wish to ask you if I can pay you back a little every month – well, in the months when I have any excess. It might take a few years.'

If I were a child, I would have beaten his chest with my childish fists and then run away into a corner and sulked. I am not a child, and there are no corners, but, as I cannot trust myself not to let out a childish rant, I tell him I need to go for a little walk. I expect he thinks I need to relieve myself, so he turns his back, and I walk along the rocky edge for about a quarter of a mile, not looking back until I find a shady place to rest.

When I return to the top of the hill Titus has gone. Had he walked in the same direction as me, we would have passed each other on the path. I shout out his name, but there is no reply, and the wind carries my voice out over the hills like a whisper. I start to panic and worry that he has gone over the edge, either by choice, which seems unlikely, or by misadventure or even malice. I sidle to the edge and lie flat on my stomach and peer over the precipice. None of the soil has been disturbed, no stones or grass lie below the edge, and I cannot see him, unless he has fallen to the bottom and been subsumed by the water. I shuffle back from the edge. My bag lies undisturbed under the rowan tree, along with his umbrella and our empty ale bottles, but of Titus there is no sign.

On an impulse I look in my bag, where I had kept our return train tickets; Titus is adept at losing things like that. His ticket is missing. I cannot believe he has gone again. Why bring me all the way up here if his intention was to abandon me on a hillside and abscond again – and did he even mean to repay me?

By the time I stomp back down the hill it is late afternoon, and the sun is already starting to set. The waitress at the café tells me the carriages have ended for the afternoon, expecting there to be no further trade, it being out of season, and I must walk to the station in the gathering gloom. When I finally arrive back in Manchester my mood is as black as the sky. I buy a quarter-bottle of gin and a large bag of chips and eat them in my room, not caring that the smell might be reported to Mrs Bradley.

There is no alternative but to go to the police to accuse Titus of robbery. Not that I have much hope that the police might find him, but perhaps his parents, if interviewed, might feel guilty enough for their son's misdemeanours to pay me back what he has stolen; they can certainly afford it. I go the very next morning and the police take my statement but seem more intent on refuting my accusation than in searching for him. They ask why a man of such means and from a good family would steal from a poor waitress, and I toy with the idea of telling them about his gambling debts but relent; I suppose I am still in love with him. They ask why I had not reported the theft straight away but instead gone on a jaunt with the supposed villain. They propose that I am just a jealous fishwife maligning a young man of unblemished character.

I expect the report will be filed away as soon as the ink has dried on it.

I return a week later to enquire if any progress has been made, but they say that they have been unable to find him, or any evidence that a crime had occurred. I expect that they have not even looked for him. I swear at them then, accusing them of not doing their duty, and am threatened with arrest, and then I cry into my silk handkerchief and they usher me out, glad to be rid of me.

That's it, then: no money except what is in my pocket, and all my savings gone. It is a good job I have paid a month in advance for rent and can eat at the Euphrosyne for free; it will give me a chance to save a little of my wages and to pick a few pockets before the next rent becomes due.

'That's awful,' say Pomona, once again forgetting her professional disinterest. 'Was there never any word from him? How did you cope?'

I am surprised she has swallowed such twaddle. I thought I had given her enough clues, diced with her finding out the truth, like a game of dare. I mean, how many times could I say the word 'edge' before she noticed? I did go to the police, had to show my concern at his disappearance, gambling that they would not believe Titus had stolen from me and absconded. I did not tell them about our visit to the lakes, although I did mention the moneylenders, but they scoffed at that idea as well. By the time his parents or friends had started to wonder what had become of him, no one would remember two travellers on a train to Windermere.

'No, no word, and I had no choice but to cope. That's what we do,' I say.

'We?'

'People who have no safety net except the workhouse or the street; and I would rather jump in the cut than take either of those options.'

'You are far too clever for either option.'

'For people like me, cleverness does not fill your belly. Sometimes it pays to be stupid.'

'You undersell yourself. I hope that your time here has assured you that you will get a less menial job than supervisor. Governess, perhaps. I would certainly give you a reference, despite your admission of pickpocketing, as would Matron.'

'You have more faith in others' charity than I do.'

'A good Christian family would see that you have paid the price for your actions and deserve a second chance.'

'Amen to that,' I say.

Windermere, November 1889

Titus is shouting my name, but I am halfway down the hill, and I will not look back at him. I need to get away, but I'm hampered by my bag and every minute he is gaining on me. 'Lily wait, what have I done?' he shouts, and I genuinely think he does not know. To him money is a thing to receive, to borrow, to pay back, to gamble, to fritter – a means to an end, not an end in itself. And he had not ever implied that he would propose marriage; I alone had constructed the idea, on the weakest of foundations, like a house of cards. I did get a proposal of sorts, but not the one I wanted: I, who was once so against becoming a bride, am now distraught that the man I love proposes, not marriage, but how he might pay me back for the money he has stolen from me without a hint of remorse.

It was the visit to his parents that did it: it made me dare to dream. I had allowed myself to think of a future with Titus – that with my encouragement he would beat the demon of his gambling and find himself a job and by Christmas we would be engaged and snug in his apartment, or cradled in the bosom of his family, implored by his parents to celebrate Christmas and the New Year with them. I could see it all. We would arrive on Christmas Eve, met by his father's carriage, the driver resplendent in a new livery for the season and the horses with red garlands around their necks. When we arrived at the house, Augusta would drag me away as we stepped over the threshold and say there had been a catastrophe with tree decorations and they had guests arriving and I could I possibly put it right? I would avert the imagined catastrophe by redecorating a Douglas fir that took up a third of the hallway and the guests arriving for a Christmas Eve supper would compliment Augusta on her decorating skills and I would smile but stay mute. Christmas Day would start with a church service and then a family luncheon and in the afternoon we would all go for a stroll, and Titus and I, reverting to childhood, would throw snowballs and build a snowman while Augusta and Henry would look on, reliving their own youthful indulgencies. On Boxing Day there would be a hunt and Titus would be all dressed up and looking more dashing than ever in his pinks and me begging him not to go, thinking of the poor fox, and him questioning whether

I really was a country girl, and did I not know that foxes were nothing but vermin? He would come back after the hunt, and we would not speak, for I would be annoyed at least until dinnertime. In the hiatus between Boxing Day and New Year's Eve we would muddle along doing this and that and visiting aged aunts, but always together, agitating for the end of the year, and his father would take the opportunity of our indolence to invite me to his study to discuss the latest guano markets and whether he should expand his business further than Britain. We would have only family on New Year's Eve, and I would be the first-footer since, although a woman, I would be the only dark-haired person among us. Clutching a piece of coal, I would run out into the cold, but not feeling any of it since I would be buoyed with drink and high spirits, and Titus would lock the back door and pretend to not let me in. Then he would unlock it, all apologetic, saying he thought it was open, and smother me with kisses and blankets while his parents avert their eyes. By the second of January Titus would have itchy feet, whereas I would crave to stop a few more days, and we would say our goodbyes and catch an early train back to Manchester where the streets are not Christmas-card white but dirty brown, and icy with trampled snow.

It will not happen now, and perhaps it never would have. I expect Augusta would have trampled on the idea of our marriage with her pretty little privileged foot and Titus's father, despite his talk of marriage and children, would, blinded by his love for her, follow her lead.

I am at the lake now, wet with sweat despite the mid-afternoon temperature dropping like a stone. The place is deserted: it is too late in the year for sensible tourists. The lake is cool, dark and silent; today no noisy paddle-steamers disturb its depths. I need to rest after my exertions and so I drop my bag on the gravel path and walk out along the longest of the wooden jetties that jut out into the lake. I am standing at the end of it, looking out at the water, when Titus shouts, 'Lily, I'm sorry. Don't do it!'

Finally, some sort of apology. Too late, of course, and it is only because he thinks that I am going to jump in. I take a step nearer to the edge, only the heels of my boots now on the jetty. I can hear his footsteps, slow and cautious at first for fear he might precipitate my demise. Then he is running up to me and putting his arms around my waist and hauling me backwards with such force that we both end up supine on the jetty with my head on his chest and with him kissing my hair.

'I see no ships, only hardships,' I say, not turning to him but sitting up and continuing to stare out into the lake like a madwoman. If he thinks I am delirious I might as well go the whole way.

'What are you talking about?' he says. His words would hardly be comforting to a jumper; perhaps he is in a state of shock.

Then we are standing up and he is trying to hug me, and the jetty is slippery and, as I turn from him, he reaches for me again. I do not see it happen but there is a splash, and he starts shouting for help and tries to swim back to the jetty, but he is weighed down by his thick clothing. I scream for help although I know it is a vain hope as I passed no one on my descent. It would be foolhardy to jump in fully clothed as my dress will become waterlogged and we will both be drowned, so I start to tear at its buttons. But there is no time for even that, as he is floating away from the jetty despite his attempts to swim. I will have to find something to reach him – a branch might do it, but I would never reach the bank in time. My scarf – yes, my scarf might work, and I start to unravel it until I spy something sturdier: his umbrella, which he has left halfway along the jetty. I sprint along the jetty, pick it up and lean out as far as I can, holding it out to him. He manages to grab it and for a few seconds I am hauling him in, inch by inch, until he is a few feet from the jetty and I can nearly touch him. If I can manage to pull him out of the water I will be a heroine, his saviour. But who will I be saving him for? Not for myself, as he has already shown no compunction about robbing me and there is no hint of a proposal, not even an 'I love you' – well, not a proper declaration. Perhaps he will marry me out of gratitude – but how long will that last? After a few years we will drift apart and he will marry a more suitable woman and when their children are old enough to understand, they will hear the tale of when their Papa almost drowned and was saved by his first wife, a music hall waitress. They will be shocked by it all, but mostly at the revelation of the lowliness of their father's first wife as they will be too young to question the snobbishness they have absorbed at their mother's and grandmother's knee. Titus will tell them it was all a long time ago, but his wife will continue to fret about the smile that lingers on his face every time the story is retold.

The umbrella handle is slippery in my frozen hands and I cannot grasp it for much longer. Another few seconds pass before I have to let it go – have to let him go. At first neither of us makes a sound and then Titus shouts my name, and flounders a little longer before being carried away and down. The umbrella, re-leased from his grasp, floats back to me like a raft on a calm sea.

CHAPTER TWENTY-THREE

July is well under way, and I am soon to have the use of my very own glasshouse, and will no longer have to beg the gardeners for space for my seedlings in the one attached to the asylum. Last week my girls and I started work on cleaning the original glasshouse, built when Sunnyside was a family home. When the new glasshouse for the asylum was built, the exterior of the original was covered in wooden boards to dissuade any vandals or vagrants who might have the temerity to scale the railings, but it is much superior, being twice as large and positioned to receive glorious sunshine for most of the day. Matron was dubious of the merit of any enterprise that would bring her charges into contact with so much glass and metal, but as none of my girls is deemed to be at risk of taking her own life, we were allowed to plough on with the cleaning. The glasshouse was covered in moss and mould, but once the boards had been removed the structure was found to be sound, with only two panes of glass having to be replaced. With a good bit of elbow grease, and gallons of Jeyes Fluid, we have made it usable again.

I have made plans for my glasshouse for this year and the next, although I am hopeful that I will not be here to see them through and that it will be one of my garden girls who will bring next year's plans to fruition. I want to produce more than the asylum staples of cabbages, carrots and cauliflower. I know of the recent penchant for growing orchids and other such exotic flowers, and I am sure they would flourish in my glasshouse; I could grow enough to brighten up the asylum reception for the whole of the year – but my glasshouse will be useful rather than ornamental, and will supply the asylum with produce throughout the year. In the winter months, while the other gardeners restrict their activities to the cleaning of the asylum glasshouse, in mine, herbs, kale and endives will flourish. Matron has given me free rein to choose what I grow, as long as it is not vetoed by Superintendent Sharp.

The mercury has been in the eighties for a week or more, and working outside is a making us all as brown as berries. Although Pomona still refuses to visit my garden, for the past month, I *have* had a visitor: instead of our secret morning meetings, on a Thursday afternoon, as it is her half-day off, Matron walks over to see how my garden is progressing. Today she brings lemonade in a vacuum flask, and we survey my many vegetable patches. She asks about what other vegetables I hope to grow; she has obviously been studying the topic. We sit under the shade of the largest oak tree and sip the cool lemonade. Today she does not talk about books, or my progress, or my garden, or even how pleased she is with the progress of my garden girls, but for the first time about herself and her childhood in Kent.

I had imagined her being the product of a dour mother and an overbearing father, birthed into an autocratic household somewhere north of the Midlands. She laughs at this suggestion and says, 'Is that how you see me? Then I have hidden my Kentish accent very well. But it was not like that all. We were what later came to be classed as bohemian. There were ten of us children, always barefoot in summer, refusing to do our lessons and running through the fields and the orchards like urchins, even though my father was a well-respected lawyer. He was away at work for days at a time and our upbringing was left to my mother, barely a child herself, who let us do whatever we wanted to do. She was loving but totally impractical, and unsuited to the role of educator, and would be holed up for days either painting or writing, or goodness knows what else; there were always other men in the house. I was not the eldest but always the most pragmatic, and ended up looking after my brothers and sisters and handling the household accounts when I was eleven years old.'

'Is that why you became a matron?'

'I never thought of such a profession when I was a girl. I think I wanted to be an actress or an artist – such a ridiculous idea – but I married young and was widowed during the first year of our marriage and I didn't want to run back home. Not that they would not have welcomed me, but my husband had not left me destitute, and I wanted to make my own way in the world. There were no children to support and so I threw myself into what I knew best: organising and nursing.'

I had never thought of Matron as having been married. I had expected there to be lovers, but not a husband; there was no ring, not even an indent. 'You have never thought of remarrying?' I say.

'I was not asked, but I would have refused. There was only ever George.'

'Memories do not keep you warm at night.'

'I have a hot water bottle for that. And a tot of rum.' Matron looks at her watch, sighs and then rises, patting down her mufti clothes that have become creased and damp from the only part of the lawn that has remained shaded. 'I fear the sun has made me loose-tongued,' she says.

'All your secrets are safe with me. Besides, who would believe me?'

We are in the middle of a heatwave. In my little room there is not the sniff of a breeze, but I have resigned myself to the continuation of our indoor sessions. Pomona's face is bright red, even though she has only walked up the driveway, and for one moment I think she might discard her previous anxieties and agree to sit in the shade of the trees. But instead she divests herself of her wide-brimmed hat and summer coat, pours herself a lemonade, fans herself with her notebook, which is the only item she carries, and sits in her chair. 'Where were we?' she says. 'Ah, yes, Titus had just disappeared and left you penniless. Are you happy to carry on?'

'One has to carry on, whether one is happy to or not.'

'Quite so,' she says.

The Euphrosyne Music Hall, Manchester, December 1889

It is Christmas, and I have painted on a smile for the revellers at the Euphrosyne. Titus has not returned and so to keep myself from fretting I have worked extra hours in addition to those I had promised Stan, way back in October, when the fulfilment of that promise had seemed improbable. I have only allowed myself a whisky or two when I am back at my lodgings slumped in a chair with a fire lit and a blanket around me, bone-tired after a shift, sniffling a few self-pitying tears, for becoming maudlin at the Euphrosyne is not an option. Many a chanteuse will sing one of those sentimental songs that seem to be popular at this time of year and will elicit a tear from the crowd for five minutes, relieved that they are not in her predicament, but mainly they come to forget their miseries for a few hours, not to have my sour face compound them.

Christmas somehow drags itself into New Year and I make a resolution to swear off men. The servers are in the kitchen of the Euphrosyne, before the evening rush, discussing our resolutions. There are the usual resolutions: find a husband; find a *rich* husband; make more money in the absence of the rich husband; find better lodgings. Stan has eavesdropped on his 'girls' and he says he will marry any of us, or even all of us if he could, and all our resolutions will be fulfilled. We laugh and say why not because we know he is already married with two children and another one on the way. When he leaves the kitchen, the women crowd around me and tell me not to let one relationship sour my view of life, that I am far too young to swear off men as I am barely a woman myself; and they add, with a laugh, that they give it two months.

Working at the Euphrosyne, I have had many romantic offers from gentlemen, which can be seen as an annoyance or a perk, depending on your point of view. A polite no sometimes does not suffice, and I must resort to a stare or the removal of the gentleman's hands from my waist. If this fails to curtail his ardour, I can always get Stan to have a word with him. Stan will inform them that Tilly has made it clear she is not interested, and any further shenanigans will see him barred from the establishment. There is no malice in Stan's insistence on calling me by the wrong name; he knows it well enough, but he says it suits me better, and in the end it has turned out to be useful, because if any gentleman asks the other girls where Tilly lives, they can say in all truthfulness that no one called Tilly works at the Euphrosyne.

To fulfil my resolution, I decide to forgo trips to the theatre and afternoon walks in the park in favour of, in the early morning, long walks by the cut. The cut is a poor substitute for a river – even with the best imagination a person cannot imagine kingfishers diving or salmon jumping in its murky depths – but it suits my purposes, as everyone is about their own business with no regard for a passing stranger bundled up in a coat and headscarf like an old hag. There are fewer and fewer narrowboats plying their trade; their heyday is a distant memory, their livelihood overtaken by the speed and power of steam. Whole families must live and work on the water now, not just the breadwinner, since earnings have been cut to a pittance. River gypsies, they call them, all blackened from the coal they carry to the factories; now they must live and die on the water. I often wave to the children, but they are engrossed in their labours and never wave back.

From mid-January onwards, every afternoon I walk to the free library, which is situated on King Street and is an impressive building, Grecian in style with a colonnaded façade; it was formerly the Town Hall. I had stumbled upon it when searching for a coffee house after my morning walk. It houses an impressive number of books and even eighteen donated by Prince Albert when it was first opened in '52; I have yet to find which books were donated and wonder if they were gifts from our dear Queen and there might be a saucy inscription somewhere, perhaps hidden, from his *Gutes Frauchen*, as she is rumoured to have called herself in his presence.

It is a long, bitter winter, but one day in early March, as I select a new book, for the first time spring sunshine is inching its way through the library windows, and I walk with a little bounce in my step to the reading room, book in hand, to read the daily newspapers. As usual I cause quite a stir, for newspapers are still considered the domain of men, and women in other libraries must content themselves with a magazine room. But I see the same old faces – mainly aged, since by afternoon most of the young working men are at their labours – and after a while the regulars have desisted from tutting, and instead ignore me. I have taken to reading *The Times* and the *Financial Times*, and spread them out in front of me like tablecloths to while away a couple of hours. The *Financial Times* is always the less well-thumbed of the pair, but since my encounter with Titus's father I have started to think of my future with purpose and it has become my favourite: I devour the business news and always see how stocks, especially in fertiliser, are performing. I take a pencil from my pocket and make a few pencil marks in the newspaper's columns, and circle stocks or news of interest to me so that, as the library keeps all its newspapers, I can look back on them at my next visit to see how my chosen stocks have fared. I know that I could always buy my own copy of the

Financial Times and read it at my lodgings, but the library affords a warm, quiet environment which might, I reason, be useful in saving a bit of coal. So far the library staff have not noticed my pencil marks, but if they do they may decide to ban the defacer of their newspapers. They are real sticklers for rules. Sometimes the more popular newspapers will go missing and a wordy notice will be posted that a newspaper has been 'abstracted' and they 'earnestly solicit' the readers to find the culprit; they must feel a compunction to educate the masses even as they scold us. I always wonder what the thief has used the newspaper for, if not to read it.

It was two weeks ago when comments in ink next to my pencil scribblings started to appear in the *Financial Times*. It cannot be the library staff, who would recoil at the idea of defacing news-papers with ink and would anyway have just erased my pencil marks, so I assume it must be one of the old boys who come in the afternoon to read, or more likely to keep warm and snooze under a newspaper after I have left. The writer asked why I had chosen a particular stock, or commented that one I had chosen was potentially a good idea, or said with two exclamation marks that he suspected I must be bankrupt by now. Last week I decided to play the game. I admit I had been a tad bored of late, and I rea-soned it would at least give me some entertainment and give my correspondent a shock when my identity was discovered. We have corresponded for another week, with him – I assume without any foundation that it must be a man – always replying to my com-ments, but never submitting any ideas of his own. I assume that my correspondent comes to the library every day as, whatever day I go, there is always a reply.

Three days ago, I replaced the newspaper in the rack and stayed in the reading room with my novel, looking over the rim of it like a detective; to get into character I was reading *A Study in Scarlet*. My newspaper was removed three times: first by a youth of about sixteen, who read the headlines, looked at the clock, muttered something unintelligible and left; the second two were older gentlemen who read it for about an hour but neither wrote in it. There was a moment when one of them dived into his pocket, but it was to retrieve a dirty handkerchief, blow his nose, and carry on reading; I made a note to check for droplets on future newspapers. It seemed that my respondent had tired of our little game, but two days ago there were more comments, and so I decided, like the best detective, that I needed to flush him out. I wrote *Let's meet to discuss our stock preferences*, not really expecting a reply; he was probably a youth, and I would have scared him off. However, yesterday there was a note saying *Tomorrow at one o'clock in the foyer*. I am not sure if I should turn up; half the library could have read that note and it could be an axe murderer waiting in the foyer for me; but here I am waiting, for, since I was a child, curiosity has always got the better of me – and I have survived until now with my nine lives intact.

It has been raining all morning, and the colonnade in front of the library is awash with people shaking their coats and umbrellas before entering. I stand under the colonnade until ten past one, take off my coat, and step into the foyer. Inside, there are two women, whom I discount, and a gentleman in the corner reading the notices. Titus, I think, and nearly say his name. He turns away from the notices, and I wonder if I have actually shouted out Titus's name. He walks up to me and says, 'There you are.'

From the front he is nothing like Titus. He is the same height, and has the same blond hair, but his is shorter and far neater than Titus's unruly crop, and his face, although now wreathed in smiles, has the potential to be serious, whereas Titus always had a glint in his eye and the potential to be up to no good. This man would never be a rake.

'How did you know it was me?' I say. 'There are two other ladies here.'

'Ah, that's where I have you at a disadvantage. I have always known it was you. Does that make me sound like a cad? I saw you two weeks ago when I was choosing a new book. You did not notice me; you had your head down and were charging through the door like a tornado. I saw you go to the reading room and rile up all the old boys and I thought, that's an unusual woman. I didn't know you were writing down your ideas until the next lunchtime when I looked at the previous day's *Financial Times*; it's something I do as well, the looking that is, although not, previously, the commenting.' He blushes as if he were admitting to a sexual peccadillo. 'It could have been one of the others in the reading room, but nothing had ever appeared in the newspaper before. Afterwards I sort of looked forward to it, although I only ever commented on your choices. I would never have written any of my own predictions; you might have thought me an expert and gambled all your money, and I could not have that.'

'Why did you not just speak with me?' I say. 'It would have been much simpler than all this subterfuge.'

'That would have been too forward of me. I had to wait and rely on your curiosity.'

'Lily,' I say, holding out my right hand.

'Arthur,' he says. 'Arthur Smith.' He takes my hand in his and shakes it, revealing the cuff of his suit which, although immaculate, is not Savile Row. 'Perhaps I may be permitted to see you again, Lily?'

'I will think about it,' I say, and walk out of the library away down King Street without a backward glance, although I fancy I can feel his eyes on me, and that under his breath he is probably cursing me for playing a kittenish trick on him when I, in all innocence, had only sought some mild amusement.

I do not write in the *Financial Times* for the following three weeks, since I do not wish to encourage him; it seems cruel, as nothing can come of it; and when we pass each other in the library foyer we are like the sunshine and rain characters in a weather house: I nod to him and feign lack of time to talk and walk in the opposite direction, even if I have not changed my books. I have started to go to the library much later in the afternoon, when I know his lunch hour will be finished.

But now, on a Saturday night in the last week of March, he is sitting in the auditorium of the Euphrosyne with what I presume from their attire to be his work colleagues. He is all straight shoulders and unsmiling, only sipping his ale, as if it is spoiled, talking to no one, while his colleagues are swaying backwards and forwards and singing loudly enough that they risk prompting some complaints if they are not careful. Stan asks me to go over and tell them to tone it down a bit and, being the supervisor, I can find no reasonable excuse why I should not, despite the feeling of *déjà vu* that is bubbling in my stomach.

'Excuse me, gentleman. Can you turn down the volume, or else Stan over there might have you thrown out,' I say.

One of the louder singers is making repeated grabs for my waist until Arthur says, 'Come on, Charlie, take your hands off the waiting staff.' It takes him a few seconds to realise that the skittish woman at the library is the waiting staff. 'Sorry for Charlie's behaviour, Lily,' he adds.

'Lily, is it, Arty?' said Charlie, and the others join in the ribbing by whistling and banging their fists on the table and chanting, 'Lily, Lily, Lily.'

Arthur attempts to clamp his hands over their mouths. 'I apologise for my so-called colleagues. They do not normally behave like savages. I fear they have been let loose tonight and are making merry after too much studying and a hard week's graft.'

'We are in the business of making merry here, but not at the expense of other customers or of drowning out the turns. See if you can keep them under control,' I say, and turn to walk away.

'You are not going? Now that I have found you again, can you not sit for a while?'

'I must work. But it was nice to see you again.'

'It was not nice. It was fate. Kismet. Call it what you will. Fate brought me here when I had originally declined Charlie's invitation.'

It was the drink talking, but I had been trained not to be rude to customers. 'It was coincidence, then, Arthur.'

'Oh, Lily: the face of an angel and the heart of a sceptic.'

'I prefer pragmatist, and hardly angelic. You should see our Honesty.'

'Then I too shall be pragmatic and honest, and order gallons of ale so that you will have to serve me and pass the time of day, or night, whatever.'

'And I shall send over Sally or Milly in my stead, and you will have a table groaning under the weight of your unsupped ale.'

'You cut me to the quick,' he says, with his head hanging down and his right hand clasped to his breast.

I turn from him and trot back to the kitchen with a smile playing on my lips, unsure if I am running away from him or myself.

Three weeks pass and then it is another Saturday night, and we have a couple of decent comedians, brought up from London by Old Ezra, who is trying to establish a more comedic slant to our weekends since he has denuded us of our best singers. Arthur is here again, alone, for the third time, looking at his pocket watch every few minutes and tearing bits of his bread and cheese supper like a condemned man who has been served the wrong final meal. He is hardly going to make Old Ezra rich with the two pints of ale he has mulled over all night. On his previous visits I had sent one of the other women to serve him, but now I relent and go over to his table.

'I presume you have come to see me, as you look like a fish out of water here,' I say.

'*Au contraire, ma chérie*, I come for the turns. I am particularly fond of your Parisian ballet dancers, who must have crossed the Channel, got lost in Lambeth and danced at the Canterbury Music Hall for the past two years before finding their way here. And your Norwegian Nightingale, almost as good as the real thing would now sound, considering the real thing died over two years ago.'

That is a little cruel, but it makes me laugh out loud, and I realise I have not done that for a long time. 'You do not like the ballet?' I say.

'I am not saying they are not good dancers, merely that they are falsely advertised. And as for your Norwegian Nightingale, she is falsely advertised on both counts, but with those feathers barely covering her modesty I suppose no one is listening to her voice.'

'You should come here on Friday night.'

'And why is that?'

'Amateur night.'

'Lord save us from amateurs.' Then, looking up at me, he says, 'Come out with me, Lily. An evening in the week if you cannot manage a weekend. With a chaperone if you wish. All above board.'

It seems only good manners to accept, so I say, 'Shall we say Wednesday? I'm not scheduled to work.'

'Where would you like to go?'

'Anywhere that is not above board.'

He laughs, asks for my address, and says he will sort out something special for our first assignation.

On Wednesday evening, he arrives ten minutes early. I spy him from my bedroom window walking up and down the street looking at his watch before knocking at the front door at the appointed time. Apart from the first time we stepped out or when we had to catch a train, Titus had a tenuous relationship with punctuality, and I used to tell him he would be late for his own funeral. I let one of the other tenants open the front door and make him wait in the hallway; it has been a while since I have had a gentleman caller and I want to give the other women something to talk about; besides, it does not do to appear too eager. I do not know what depravity to expect and am hoping he realises that I spoke in jest, and as he steps into the street and hails a carriage I wonder if we are going to an opium den or one of those seedy clubs you hear about. Then, like a magician, out of his tailcoat he extracts two tickets for *The Gondoliers* at the Theatre Royal.

'Those tickets are like hen's teeth,' I say. 'How did you manage to get hold of them?'

'You are not the only one with thespian connections. But sorry to disappoint you – these are for June. I have something else planned for tonight and the next few weeks.'

I raise my eyebrows. 'That is a bit presumptuous. We might hate each other by the end of the evening, never mind in a few months.'

'And presumptuous of you to think I wish to take you to see *The Gondoliers*. I might just be showing off.' But he doesn't sound sincere in his casual riposte and I smile: if he had ever chosen to gamble at cards – and from our short acquaintance I would hazard a guess he never would – he would make a useless poker player. He knows it too. 'But of course you are correct, I would like us to go, but tonight I thought we could go for a meal. You haven't eaten, have you?'

'No, I am clammed,' I say. I could not tell him that the only decent evening meal I ever ate was when I was working at the Euphrosyne.

'I do not like to just turn up at a venue and take pot luck as to what is on the bill. I looked at all the theatres today and did not like the look of anything that was on, so I thought a meal would be a good alternative. So where would madam like to dine?'

'Anywhere you like. But not fish and chips by the cut,' I say, when in truth I would not have complained at all, if that was all he could afford.

'I hope I could do better than that for any lady I would ask out,' he says, as we get into the cab. 'I took the liberty of reserving a table at the Grand Hotel. I hope that is acceptable?'

'Very acceptable,' I say, but as we sit down to eat our meal I cannot get away from the feeling he is testing me just as Augusta had. When we return to my lodgings, he walks me to the door but does not try to kiss my cheek or even my hand, merely thanks me for a lovely evening, and wishes me goodnight before getting into the waiting cab.

The next day, I receive a letter from Arthur asking if I fancy a trip to the seaside. No bunch of flowers, though, which I had somehow expected, but perhaps I was just used to Titus's extravagance. So a week later we travel in a second-class carriage on the train to Southport. Arthur has our day all mapped out and has it written in a notebook: a visit to the pier to take the sea air followed by a trip to a café for a modest luncheon, then a paddle in the sea and back home by five o'clock and then out for dinner to anywhere I choose. It is because he is a solicitor, I suppose: he must plan, not trust to luck, not take life spontaneously like Titus. And perhaps, after all the turmoil in my past, I need some order in my life.

As it always does, April warms its way into May, and Arthur arranges a trip to the Lakes. I try to dissuade him but cannot think of a decent excuse, so before I know it we are on the same train that I took with Titus just six months ago.

'It's wonderful to be getting some fresh air, isn't it?' he says.

'It would have been nicer to travel first class,' I say, like a spoilt child. 'And it's too hot to be walking today.'

'I really don't understand you sometimes, Lily. I thought you liked the countryside.'

I cannot yet tell him about my bad memories of this place so instead I am silent for the whole of the journey, and make him suffer with my bad temper for something he knows nothing about. But when we arrive there are no vestiges of the time I spent here with Titus, or, if there are, they are overshadowed by the beauty of the place, and I am pleased that it has not been blighted by his desertion. We walk and talk and even visit the same café that Titus and I visited. The waitress does not remember me; why should she? When we walk back to the station, Arthur takes my hand when no one is looking. I want him to take my hand when someone *is* looking, but that is wanton and he is very proper, and I knew that from the start, so I can hardly complain now.

On the journey home I say that next week I will arrange something for us to do, but he will not hear of it. I know I should make a stand, but somehow, with the extra responsibility of being a supervisor, it is quite pleasant to have someone make decisions for me. Last week, buoyed by wine and a good meal, he kissed my cheek in the foyer of the Grand Hotel when he was certain no one was looking, but otherwise he continues to be the gentleman, not even a kiss outside my lodgings on our return or a tentative hand on my knee in the darkness of the cab journey back there. But despite little outward sign of affection he continues to want to see me, and I him, and now, at the end of May, without even noticing it, I have grown accustomed to our arrangement, and all my New Year resolutions, so earnestly made back then, have melted away like winter snow once spring has arrived.

'It seems that you had finally found a man with whom you could plan a future,' says Pomona.

'Yes, I thought I had. Arthur was a real tonic: hardworking, staid and reliable. Being with him was the antitheses of the hurly-burly of life with Titus, and at a certain age a person must stop having fun and think of the future,' I say.

'You make married life sound like a custodial sentence.'

'A woman in my position has to consider her future. I had had my fingers burnt with Titus. I wasn't ever again going to let myself become involved with someone so feckless; even for love.'

Pomona glances down at her hands, turning her engagement ring round and round on her finger. After a few seconds she looks up and asks, 'Shall we continue with your story?'

'Of course,' I reply, and continue with sordid tale . . .

Manchester, June 1890

It is the first time I have been to Arthur's lodgings. I had asked to see where he lived a couple of times, and he'd said he was so busy he hadn't had time to tidy up, but I had got the impression that by asking to be invited back to his lodgings I had fallen in his estimation. So it was a surprise when he asked me back there for a late supper after the promised trip to see *The Gondoliers*.

His flat is what an advertisement would describe as being in a 'good neighbourhood', but is nowhere near as grand as Titus's apartment. But then Arthur does not have a rich father, or, if he does, he must have decided to eschew family money and make his own way in the world, which warms my heart towards him. The flat boasts three rooms: a sitting room, recently painted and wall-papered, with space for a settee and a small dining table and chairs which is taken up instead by a bureau and a huge chaise-longue; a kitchen in which you could not swing a cat but which has, as compensation, modern gas appliances; and a bedroom, of which I have only seen a glimpse through a half-opened door. It does not have the luxury of a bathroom; this is at the end of the landing and has to be shared by the occupants of three flats. Arthur is in the kitchen whistling as he prepares our sandwiches and tea and will not accept my offer of help. I sit on the chaise like a waxwork, wondering where he is going to put the tea tray. The mystery is solved when from his bedroom he produces a small coffee table, sets it in front of the chaise, places the tray on it and belatedly asks me if I like cheese and pickle. We sit side by side on the chaise, drinking our tea and eating our sandwiches without so much as a kiss or a hand held. I have begun to think that he does not like me, not in that way, or that perhaps he is peculiar; or maybe he has not done it before and is holding out until he is married. It has been over two months since we started stepping out, and I wonder how I can initiate something without looking like a whore. I put my hand to his face and place butterfly kisses on his nose and his lips. At last, he kisses me back, and I try to stick my tongue into his mouth to ensure he knows what I mean. 'Are you sure?' he says, and, when I nod, he says, 'Not here on the chaise,' taking my hand and pulling me towards the bedroom with my trollop's mind screaming, 'Yes, yes, on the chaise.'

It is serviceable, no fireworks, but after a drought a thirsty person will take serviceable, and there will be plenty of time for improvement and the piquancy of the chaise-longue.

By the end of July I have stayed overnight three times, and one morning Arthur brings me breakfast in bed. He has placed on the tray a single rose in a vase, coffee, for he knows I prefer it in the morning, and some of those Frenchie croissants that you can only get at the pâtisserie on Queen Street.

'What's the occasion?' I say.

'No occasion.'

'You are an awful liar.'

'You say that as if that is a crime rather than an attribute. But you are right. There is something.' From the pocket of his dressing gown, he takes out a small box. 'I have been told the correct protocol is left knee on the floor and right hand outstretched. So here I go. Lily Day,' he says, kneeling so that we are eye to eye and thrusting the opened box towards me, 'will you do me the honour of becoming my wife?'

I do not reply, and he says, 'I can see you think it is an awful idea.'

'On the contrary, it is a wonderful idea. Of course, I will marry you. It was just unexpected.'

I hold out my left hand and he slips the ring on to my finger and in that moment, I feel the safest I have for a very long time.

'Do you think the feeling of safety is a reasonable basis for marriage?' says Pomona.

'As good as any other and a lot better than some,' I say.

'Do you think you viewed this man as being merely a safe bet and nothing more, and ignored his other attributes such as kindness, punctuality and loyalty, because of your relationship with Titus? Titus had sparked something within you and then let you down, tainting your attitude towards any future relationships?' asks Pomona.

'I thought it was not for me to speculate on my decisions but for you to form an opinion on their effect on my life,' I say.

'You are right, of course. Forgive me,' she says, and I swear there is a tear in her eye as she hurries from the room and locks the door, leaving me to wait alone for Rowse's return.

CHAPTER TWENTY-FOUR

It is a sunny afternoon in late September and Pomona has just scuttled in through the French windows, which she continues to use even though, being a regular visitor, she could easily use the front door and walk through the asylum; but she likes to be clandestine in her endeavours. I have not seen her since the middle of July. She wears a grey linen dress and jacket, her hair is newly coiffed, her stubby nails have been manicured, and she has a new hat to complete the ensemble. Whatever problems caused her unkempt appearance back in the spring, and her parting sadness at our previous session, have obviously been addressed. I miss the old gauche Pomona with her mannish clothes and unruly tumbling hair.

'Shall I pour?' I say, as Pomona has long since dispensed with the rule of Cook only bringing our tea when we are both present. I am already on my second cup. She nods her head and pushes some stray hair behind her ears. I pour her tea, which is stewed, but she drinks it anyway as penance for her lateness. Then she takes a deep breath and looks up.

'I am nearing the end of my allotted time with you, Lily, and I suspect you are nearing the end of your story—'

'I hope I have a few years of my story to go,' I say.

'As do I,' she says, not rising to the sarcasm. 'Shall we begin?'

Manchester, Late August 1890

I have no idea how it has happened. I have never engaged in intimacy during the middle days between my monthlies, and in the past this has always served me well; and besides, Arthur and I have only been intimate a few times. Over the past few weeks, I have vomited every morning, but Old Ezra has engaged a new cook, and she is rumoured to be none too particular and a few of the waiting staff have gone down with the runs and so I thought it possible that I too had fallen foul of her slovenliness. But in truth I have been pretty sure after I had missed the first month, and after six weeks there is no doubt that, by next spring, I will be a mother. Had it happened two months ago, and in the absence of being able to gather the necessary herbs, I would have hot-footed it down to the chemist's shop for a packet of Dodd's Female Pills. But now, with Arthur's ring sparkling on my finger, none of those remedies will be necessary, and I am eager to tell him of our upcoming addition.

Arthur has invited me to his flat for a late supper. He says he will pick up some bits from the delicatessen on his way home and I am hoping there will not be too much spicy food, as he has had a penchant for the stuff since his childhood, when his father had returned from the Punjab with a gammy leg and a permanently changed palate. If I have to run off to be sick it might give away the surprise before I have chance to tell him the good news.

We are having a hot, humid summer, and his rooms are unbearably warm despite the windows being flung open; he picks up a newspaper to swat a fly that has been enticed by the food. He makes a pot of tea and we eat our supper as if it were any other evening. He starts to tell me about his day and some tale of the peculiarities of his clients. That makes me laugh, and he says that I must not repeat what he has said but it is worth his indiscretions to see me smile, as I have looked a little distracted of late. I take his hand in mine and say that there is something that I need to tell him.

'What is it, my darling. Are you ill?' he says, clasping my hand in his.

'Not ill. In fact, in rude health. I didn't know at first but now I am sure,' I say.

'Sure of what? Tell me – you're worrying me.'

I take his hand and place it on my stomach. 'We are going to have a baby,' I say.

He detaches his hand from mine as if he has picked up a hot coal and goes over to the window, lifting the nets and staring out to the street below. He must have stood there for a minute, silent, motionless, and all the time the sound from outside seeping into the airless room: children's footsteps, running, heavy in their clogs; a couple of drunks arguing over something or nothing; a woman chastising her child for stepping into the road without looking for traffic. Finally, he turns and says, 'How has this happened?'

'I presume in the usual way. There has been no immaculate

conception,' I say, and laugh a weird high-pitched laugh, afraid of where the conversation is heading.

'Is it mine?'

'Of course he or she is yours. What do you take me for?'

He starts to stride around the room, wringing his hands and sighing, and then he says he has to go out for a walk for ten minutes to think. I can feel my eyes starting to sting, and tell him to go and that I will wait for him to return.

I have two cups of tea to quell the soreness that is starting to form in the back of my throat. He is in shock, I tell myself; he needs a while to get used to the idea of being a father, and he will return with a bunch of flowers from a street seller and sweep me into his arms, putting his face against my belly and swearing it has already become rounded and that we shall be married immediately. His parents, who I have not met, will travel down from the Orkneys for our happy day.

He is away for an hour, and when he walks in I can smell whisky on his breath.

'You cannot have a baby,' he says at last.

'I think our present conversation proves that I can.'

'I mean you cannot have one *now*. I am so near to being qualified, but I have exams still to complete. I cannot support a wife and baby.'

'So you still wish to marry me when the time is right, but not now?'

'Of course I will – are we not betrothed? But not now – later, when I am more established, making more money. You can have another child then, ten of them if you wish.'

'But we could have this one, move from here, take cheaper lodg-ings. I could take in sewing.'

He looks at me as if I have suggested that I wish to set myself up as a procuress. 'No wife of mine will take in sewing,' he says. 'How would it look for newly qualified solicitor, not being able to support his wife and child?'

'It would show his wife was enterprising and not just a decora-tive skivvy.'

'It is a moot point, because you need to get rid of it. How far along are you? You may yet lose it spontaneously. My cousin had two early miscarriages, and she has five children now.'

I shrink back. 'I am appalled you think a miscarriage might be a good thing for us. I am going back to my lodgings now and I think we should meet up in a few days, in the park perhaps, not here, nor at my place where everyone will be listening to our busi-ness, or one of us may say something we may regret.'

After a week he has not changed his mind, and in the inter-vening days has made enquiries into how an abortion could be accomplished. He is right of course, it is not the ideal time, but that is my head talking; my heart is saying *keep the baby*. But if I choose to keep the child, the most that Arthur could be compelled to pay me in support is five bob a week.

'Now I don't want you taking any of those quack medicines,' he is saying, 'or poisoning yourself with pennyroyal or arsenic. I have a client, a doctor out Oldham way, a real doctor, a general practitioner, not one of those quacks, and he has been known to perform the requisite surgery.'

'You know he could be struck off for that?' I say.

'He has helped some high-class ladies. All hush-hush, as you must be. But should he be questioned, he will deny any accusations and say he was treating a woman after the consequences of a back-street abortion, and all his colleagues would rally round. Don't worry, he takes great care, and his instruments are all sterilised, so it is safe.'

'Nothing is ever completely safe.'

'Safe as can be, then. I realise there is always a chance of a problem.'

'And if I refuse?'

'You have that right, and I would provide for the baby, but I would feel coerced, and it will divide us. Is that what you want?'

It is blackmail really: he is saying it is me or the baby, but not both. It's not what I want – I want both. I already love this tiny speck growing inside me, but I have worked so hard since Titus left me to become financially stable, and, even with Arthur supporting his bastard child, I might still end up in the workhouse or on the street, and that is no place for a baby. That cannot be allowed to happen. My head tells me I can always have another baby but if I lose Arthur I lose him forever, and I cannot lose another person. So the next day I tell him that I agree to the abortion.

Monday evening of the following week is the sort of balmy evening where you would take a walk to a park and have an ice cream under the trees, and I am wishing I were there or anywhere instead of sitting in the doctor's waiting room long after his receptionist has departed. Arthur has taken the afternoon off and is sitting by my side, holding my hand, his face paler than mine, and I hope for a moment that he has changed his mind, that he will drag me out of here and insist we keep our baby. But then the smiling doctor comes out of his consulting room and ushers me inside and Arthur says he will be outside in case I need him. I want to run away but my feet are leaden and in a few minutes I am up on a bed with my leaden feet up in stirrups, and a man I have known only five minutes is furtling away inside me. After ten minutes it is all over and the gubbins of my baby lie in a kidney dish on a side cabinet until, realising his error, the doctor covers the dish with a towel. He helps me off the bed and I dress behind the screen and wobble to a chair in front of his desk, a little woozy from the chloroform, with blood still sticky between my thighs.

'You were about seven weeks pregnant. The procedure went well. You may experience some bleeding, but it should not be excessive. But come back if it is. I advise you to buy some laudanum,' he says. On he drones, my brain only retaining half of what he is advising: I should not be intimate for at least a month; would I like some advice on not getting pregnant; am I able to walk? He takes my arm and helps me into the waiting room and I hobble over to Arthur. I am glad I have worn a dark blue dress.

When we get back to Arthur's flat I lie on top of a blanket on his chaise and he makes me cups of tea, which are all I can stomach. I drift off to sleep, and when I awake he has bought laudanum from the all-hours chemist. After three hours I insist I want to go back to my own lodgings, where I sneak in through the back door and inch myself up the stairs to my room. I stay for four days without seeing anyone, until on the Friday evening I go back to work and tell everyone of my wonderful few days in Blackpool.

*

'That was an awful situation to be in,' says Pomona. 'I do not know what I would do in such a situation.'

'It was, and I am confident you will not include it in that paper of yours,' I say.

'Even if it is pertinent to the discussion of your case?'

'I thought my "case" was merely to establish if am cured, and that you could be selective in your decision as to what precipitated my condition. All three of us who participated in the removal of my baby risk ending up in jail for two to three years for doing what we did. But I suppose no one would be prosecuted now, and the other two would deny it. There is, after all, no proof, and I would plead insanity: that I did not know what I was talking about. That tends to work. Or I would say that the revelation was fabricated by you, and I never said such a thing. But I am asking you to not mention it because it is something I do not wish to be dissected by your cronies. It was a private matter.'

Pomona considers. 'Well, as I said, I must consider all information that may be relevant to your condition. But yes, I will leave it out, since you have entrusted me with the knowledge of that painful incident. It is still painful to you?'

'Physically not; I healed well and am hopefully not damaged inside. But I still think about the baby sometimes, although Arthur and I never discussed it afterwards. Least said, soonest mended.'

'I do not believe that to be true. Feelings tend to fester if they are not talked about.'

'I think you might be correct,' I say, and for the first time I feel a little closer to Pomona.

CHAPTER TWENTY-FIVE

Queenie has never returned to Sunnyside. We have had no news of her, not that we expected to receive any, and unless she has passed away I hope that she is happy and will be able to spend the autumn of her years with her sister. I would not be able to forgive any sister of mine for not writing or visiting me for thirty-five years, but perhaps Queenie has decided not to hold it against May, to block it out; or maybe she does not even remember the loss of those years. September has turned to October now and there is a new woman, Hester, in Queenie's old bed; she has taken up the mantle of resolutely stopping there. Opposite her, in Maggie's old bed is the same girl who replaced her last year. Poor thing, she is still cradling her imaginary baby, and has been in and out of here more times than either she or I can remember.

In the ward we are now all squeezed together like canned sardines with barely a foot between our beds; there are sixty beds now where there used to be fifty, with no prospect of new wings being built to house the increase in female patients. But at night, despite the warmth and the noise generated by extra bodies, we all sleep surprisingly well, and I suspect that Queenie's ramblings about poisoned cocoa may have come to pass and we are being sedated by some form of narcotic to subdue us through the night. Nowadays I am never awake before the first bell.

There are just too many of us now, for the recent Victorian interest in the science of caring for the mad has heralded an on-slaught of new admissions, both those newly diagnosed and those removed from the lunatic wings of prisons and workhouses. There are lots of new asylums being built, modelled on the structure of prisons, where a person must feel like an inmate rather than a pa-tient. But, at Sunnyside, the success of the more humane methods favoured by Superintendent Sharp and other like-minded superin-tendents that have been used in the last two decades have been an instrument of their own demise: the increase in numbers admitted to Sunnyside means that the staff are having to revert to the meth-ods of a century ago to control us. More patients are shackled to their beds at night and the seclusion and padded cells, once only used for extreme cases, are now in constant use.

Superintendent Sharp visits the female wards every week now; before, he used to leave the management of all the female patients to Matron. I expect he thinks she cannot cope with the influx, but Matron is made of sterner stuff than he imagines. Not that the treatment of patients will be my problem much longer, as I expect I will soon be released, but I doubt that if my treatment were to start today I would be afforded individual sessions with a visiting psychiatrist, nor my own garden plot to cultivate unsupervised. It is the garden and the books that are keeping me sane in here, and for that I am indebted to Matron – and begrudgingly to the superintendent, who, for all his overtly religious zeal, has allowed me the chance to escape this place once, and definitely, for all.

'Arthur Smith is the sort of name a person might invent as an alias, a nondescript, forgettable name, not a real person at all,' says Pomona as we settle in my sitting room.

'Believe me, Arthur Smith is most definitely flesh and blood,' I say.

We sit by a roaring fire sipping Pomona's choice of hot choco-late made from a bar of Belgian chocolate she has brought with her and which she gave to Cook to prepare, and I expect Cook has kept a few shavings for herself. The hot chocolate has given Pomona a brown moustache and I am tempted to say nothing, to send her back to her residence looking like a man, but when I relent and tell her, she wipes it away and remarks that she should really start to be more ladylike and carry her hand mirror with her. She takes another sip of the chocolate and says, 'Do you feel ready to tell me about what happened after the loss of your child?'

'I believe I need to, if, as you say, we are nearly at the end of our time together,' I say.

'We can have one more session after this. I do not wish to push you.'

'Sometimes a person needs a push, wouldn't you say?'

Manchester, October and November 1890

September has meandered into October, and in the city autumn has begun in earnest: in the parks the leaves are starting to turn

273

and fall from the trees, and the early morning air is a wintry por-
tent of the coming season. Arthur too has been cold towards me,
as if not trusting himself to heed the doctor's advice of refraining
from intimacy for a month. But now, even after that time has
elapsed, he says that he will only come near me on the first few
days after I have finished my monthlies, when there is no chance
whatsoever of my getting with child. I suspect the loss of his child
has affected him more than he envisaged, and that he has fretted
about me and does not wish to risk either of us going through that
anguish again; I am grateful for that concern. Since the middle
of October he has been working late and studying for his final
exams, which are looming at the end of November. I will not
complain; I know we need time apart for him to do the best he
can, and that come December we will be together again like in
the old days.

More weeks pass in this unsatisfactory manner, until, on the
morning of the twenty-fifth of November, Arthur comes to my
lodgings all breathless as if he has been running and asks me if I
would like to go for an evening meal and that he has something
important to tell me. I reply that a meal is a lovely idea, and that
I will choose my best dress for the occasion. He smiles a lopsided
smile and tells me not to go to too much trouble, but I know he is
joking for he always likes me to look my best.

I have an inkling what it must be: his exams have finished
and now I should be preparing myself for a wedding, perhaps in
the spring – or even Christmas. Yes, that must be what he plans.
After all, for all his measured and conservative ways, in matters
of the heart he is as impulsive as a puppy; did he not spring the

engagement on me after only three and a half months? And now, barely seven months after meeting, we are to be married. As church weddings are known to be popular at this time of year – for we are all romantics at heart and have embraced Prince Albert's vision of Christmas – I know that if a Christmas wedding is in the offing he must have already booked the church, for this will be no register office occasion. There will be enough time to read the banns though; he is meticulous like that.

After the meal we take a cab back to his flat and sit on the chaise drinking wine. He puts his glass on the coffee table and the base makes a red stain like a pustule on the white oak.

'I don't know where to begin,' he says.

It seems a strange start to a wedding discussion, but I let him find his own words.

'We have been engaged for some months now . . .'

'Wonderful months,' I say, ignoring the fact that he convinced me to abort our child and wishing he would get on with it.

'Quite. But I have to say that . . . I cannot marry you.'

I frown, puzzled. 'Do you mean you have to study further? Is it a matter of money?'

He holds my face in his hands and says, 'Sweet Lily, if only it were. No. I cannot marry you because I am in love with another, and we are soon to be betrothed.'

I pull my face away from his touch. 'What? But you are betrothed to me! You took me out for a meal and brought me back here just to tell me this? I thought we were going to set a wedding date. I *love* you.'

'And I thought I loved you. I *do* love you, and that's why I

275

wanted to soften the blow of what I must tell you by taking you out for a meal. And I brought you back here to explain – much better than in public. It's simple really. Someone else has come along, and I love her more than I love you. Real love. You are within your rights to sue for breach of promise. I could give you the names of some good solicitors, if you can afford them. Or we could settle out of court and save ourselves both time and money.'

'How long?' I say.

'How long what?'

'How long has this been going on?'

Arthur looks away, then down at his hands. 'A few weeks. Estella and I are to be married in the new year.'

So, Estella is the name of his trollop. Not that I know she is a trollop, or if she even knows about me, but it feels better to call her by that name.

'So, you made me have an abortion knowing that you were going to leave me?'

'No, I had not decided that yet. But I felt trapped, pressured to get married to you. It had all happened so quickly between us.'

'But it was you who proposed to me! Didn't you feel trapped and pressured with your new fiancée, with whom it has happened even more quickly?'

'Soon-to-be fiancée. No, with her I am glad to be trapped. I would marry her tomorrow if I could.'

I have to get out of his flat, I have to run and scream and rant, but instead I walk back to my little room and throw myself on to my bed and weep for what should have been.

*

'That is enough sorrow to make anyone turn hysterical,' says Pomona. 'There are words for men like that.'

'He was just weak,' I say.

'He treated you appallingly.'

'Do not we all get treated the way we expect to be?'

'I do not believe that.'

'As a psychiatrist, or as a woman? Just because you do not believe it, that does not make it untrue.'

'Now who is doing the analysing?'

'I leave that up to you. After all, I am just a hysteric.'

CHAPTER TWENTY-SIX

I shall miss this little room. In a few weeks it will be mine no longer and some other sad case will have his or her life dissected within its pleasant walls. I wonder if I should steal a pencil and write my name in an unobtrusive place on the wall, or take a piece of paper and feed it between the cracks in the floorboards so that in a hundred years from now a builder may find my scrap of paper and ponder what fate befell Lily Day.

Pomona has arrived but is disinclined to talk, even though for once I try to instigate conversation. I pour her a cup of tea and she takes it from my hand without a word. It is the end of October and the end of our sessions; I think she, too, is aware of the fleeting nature of our remaining time together, and of the responsibility she owes me to ensure she has sufficient time to hear my whole sordid tale. I do not wait for her to ask if we should begin, but dive into it head-first.

Manchester, December 1890

I do not remove my ring as I am keen to avoid any questions at work: the red eyes I put down as being due to the beginnings of a cold, but I am not sure if any of the women are fooled. I have decided that in a few weeks, when I am stronger, I will take the ring to the pawn shop down King Street, but for now it will remain defiantly on my finger. After all, I was not the one to break the contract.

I know I should not have done it, but I had to see his trollop for myself, and yesterday I was unable to resist the compulsion. At first I was unsure it was her: she had been waiting outside his office for at least twenty minutes and my feet and legs, squashed between a large oak tree and a fence, were starting to get pins and needles. Arthur had always been punctual with his luncheon breaks, but not with his evening departure from work; his workload meant that he could roll up at his lodgings at any hour. Finally he emerged from his office, banged shut the door and ran to her, slightly out of breath and replete with apologies. He was wearing a suit I had not seen before, well cut, emphasising the broadness of his shoulders. At first, she turned away from him, her indignation unmasked by a smile, and he, playing along, stepped away. Then, moving towards her, he gave her a quick kiss on the cheek, as one might greet a sister, nothing ostentatious, but then he laid his hand on her arm and then her waist in the proprietorial manner of a fiancé. As they turned to walk arm in arm down the street to their lunchtime assignation, a squally wind whipped the sides of her unbuttoned coat into the air to reveal a neat mound, but a mound none the less: she was at least four months with child.

I wanted to run to them, to tell her of his dishonesty, of the abortion, to rant at him in the street like a madwoman. But what good would it have done? If she knows about me, he has obviously told her some tale, and if she does not, was I going to condemn another poor child to be fatherless?

Arthur has sent a letter asking me to share a final meal, which he is going to cook, and we are to discuss the payment he will make to me. He had learnt to cook at his father's knee: his father, whose injuries made him unable to sustain any job that entailed standing for long periods, and unwilling to lower himself to office work, had decided to live off his army pension and had turned his hand to cooking, fuelled by the love of spices he had gained from living in the Punjab. Ultimately, he had opened a shop to cater for the changing British tastes the Raj had inspired; this was before their move to the Orkneys. Arthur is a very good cook; it was one of the perks of our relationship that I was not expected to cook all our meals.

It has been foggy today, dense, rank, a fog that emanates from the cut and hangs in the air like a shroud. I walk to his flat, talking to myself, going over and over what I am going to say to him, and I am sure some of those I pass think me mad. I reach his residence and unlock the outside door with the key he had cut for me months ago. I walk through the hallway without impediment, for I do not have to run the gauntlet of a nosy concierge, as I had to whenever I visited Titus's apartment. I can already smell delicious aromas wafting from Arthur's flat as I mount the stairs.

I stand outside his door and almost turn around, almost march back down the stairs, but instead I knock, already a stranger, even though in my hand I hold his door key.

'Come in, it's open. I'm about ready to serve,' he says.

I walk in, place the redundant keys on the chest of drawers in his bedroom, and walk back to the chaise. He comes from the kitchen, red in the face and with his shirt stuck to his chest and his hair in spikes where he has run his hands through it. I have worn his favourite dress and brushed my hair until it shines; I have to make sure he knows what he has given up by taking up with his bit on the side.

'You look nice. Please sit down,' he says, and rolls down his sleeves and disappears back into the kitchen to emerge seconds later with two plates of steaming food. 'Drink?'

'To celebrate?' I say with an edge to my voice.

'No, because a good red goes nicely with this meal.' He fetches a bottle without waiting for my answer. He has cooked something spicy, lamb I think; it is difficult to tell with so much sauce. We sit side by side on the chaise, although not scrunched up together with our knees touching as in the old days. He talks about work and asks after mine and I wonder how he can behave as though nothing has changed between us. I suppose he has had enough practice in the past few months when he was holding on to a lie.

'Of course, I do not want the ring back,' he says.

'How gracious of you,' I say, and he grimaces as if he is annoyed that I have not been softened by this perceived favour. 'You don't wish to give it to Estella? No, I suppose not; I expect you have already given her a much more expensive one.'

The meal is a mistake: I eat like a mouse, cutting up pieces of meat and then scraping them to the side of my plate. Arthur shovels in one mouthful after the other like a starving man, clearly wishing now for the meal to be over even though he had been the instigator of it. The whole pantomime is performed in silence until he asks me if I have finished and, when I nod, he picks up the plates to take them to the kitchen. I say I will help him with the washing-up as it is the least I can do after such a lovely meal. He thanks me and says it will be our last domestic task together, which I say will be tragically romantic; he never could detect sarcasm. We labour side by side, him washing and passing me the plates and me drying and putting them in their rack as we have done so many times before, until he turns to me and says, 'I could offer you fifty pounds for breach of promise.'

'Surely I am worth more than that?' I say. 'That's barely seven pounds per month for my services.'

'I could at most offer you seventy-five pounds, but it would be a stretch. I might have to ask my father for a loan. We must consider what exactly it is that you have lost. I think you have done quite well out of me, what with meals out and everything else, and you will soon find someone else. Admittedly you will be damaged goods, but there is not much I can do about that.'

He goes over to the chopping board to pick up a knife that lies on it; the knife is bloody and has scraps of lamb sinew attached to its blade. He drops the knife into the sink and goes over to the stove to get some boiling water to scald it and I am thinking, why is he not scalding the chopping board as well? I go to the sink, grab the knife and stab him with it as he faces the stove. He falls to the floor, and I stab him again in the back and the shoulders until there is no hope to be had and I leave him in a pool of his own blood on the kitchen floor. I grab my coat, put the knife in my pocket and jettison it in the cut as I run, as a woman running hell for leather through the fog with a bloody knife in her hand like a ne'er-do-well in a Gothic novel would have caused a commotion even in the back streets of Manchester. When I reach my lodgings, I throw myself on my bed and burrow beneath the covers like a child to try to combat the shivering and fear with which I have suddenly become afflicted. After a few minutes I get up and lock the door against the inevitable arrival of the police, a laughable action, as that small door lock and slide bolt would not have kept out a petty thief let alone a determined police officer, but a person's mind is disturbed after a murder.

Once I am thinking clearly again I know I must go to the police; even if I was not seen, I cannot live with the guilt of taking a life. I determine that I will give myself up in the morning, and have already started to pack a bag when there is a hammering at the front door. I am praying no one else is in the house, but they continue to knock and eventually someone goes down to let them in and shows them to my door. I do not resist. I am dragged from my room by two policemen and shoved into the back of a Black Maria, where I cover my face with my shawl against the gawping pedestrians as we drive through the streets to the police station. I have to give my details to the sergeant and then they put me into a cell, where I have to wait two hours before an officer comes in to question me. And that is when they tell me what I have done, piece it together from the evidence, because in all honesty I do not remember the stabbing, only the aftermath of Arthur's bloody body on the kitchen floor.

'We meet again, Miss Day,' says the officer. 'I see you have been in here before: you made an accusation of theft against a gentleman only last year. This is another level, though, is it not?

Attempted murder of a Mr Arthur Smith, a man known to you for several months.'

'You mean he is not dead?'

'You do not deny the stabbing, then?'

'What is the point of denying it? I would have come in tomorrow to confess, had I not been manhandled and dragged here this evening.'

'He is not dead but is in a very bad state in hospital, so it could yet be murder.' The officer makes an unpleasant gesture of putting his hands around his neck and says, 'You were seen leaving his premises and, as you have confessed to the act, you will be remanded in prison until your trial.'

Two weeks later and I am up before the beak. A fortnight sharing a cell with rats and a slop bucket and no chance of bail for such an offence, even if anyone could put up the money. Arthur has not died, but he remains in hospital and is deemed by his doctor to be too weak to attend court. The courtroom is ice-cold, and the judge seems to want to get through his caseload as quickly as possible to get back to his wife and his own fireside. I am indicted for attempted murder and a secondary charge of wounding with intent to do grievous bodily harm. I plead guilty to the second charge, which is accepted by the jury and as the prosecution offers no further evidence for the murder charge there is no need for a trial, which has disappointed those ghouls wishing to revel in the gory details. The beak goes off to consider my sentence and warm his frozen fingers, and I am led back down to the cells. Two hours later I am dragged back up to the dock and made to stand for his decision. The beak must have eaten the equivalent to the convict's prerogative of a hearty breakfast, or else have been on a Christmas promise, as he sentences me to eight years but not with hard labour as I had feared. Not that I will not have to graft in prison, but I tell myself that eight years is not that long, and there is always a chance to be sent to a refuge or out on licence before the end of the sentence, and if I keep my head down I will still be a young woman when I come out.

The folly of youth! The women with whom I am incarcerated are real killers – not the pickpockets or prostitutes who might get a few months in a local prison and with whom you could have a laugh and a joke, but women who would slit your throat for fun as soon as look at you, especially if you looked at them or spoke to them in the wrong way. But I soon learn not to; it is just like being back at the farm really.

'So tell me how you ended up here in Sunnyside,' says Pomona.

'I'd been in prison just over a year when they sent me here. I was hauled out of my cell one day, I still don't know why, but I expect a mentally ill woman does not recognise her own symptoms. Doctors say that all women in prison are susceptible to destructive behaviours and suicidal thoughts. They tell me that when I arrived at Sunnyside I was sedated and rammed into a straitjacket for two weeks in a padded cell before they would let me on to the ward, so I must have been in a pretty bad way. But I don't remember any of it.'

'I have read the details of your plea before I took your case. I am interested in why you refused counsel and would not plead "not guilty", introducing mitigating circumstances such as provocation,' says Pomona.

'I couldn't afford a lawyer, and was not told that there is a fund for the poor to obtain representation. But either way it was irrelevant, as I was intent on pleading guilty for my wrongs.' I need to pile on the Christian guilt, and she seems to accept it. 'As for the mitigating circumstances – the abortion, or the broken engagement? One is illegal and I would have been prosecuted for it, and the other is hardly a reason to butcher one's fiancé,' I say.

'I would still say you were provoked. I have read of trials when provocation was a defence, and the defendant was acquitted.'

'I'm sure a woman of your standing could plead not guilty and get a fair trial, compassion even. I couldn't take the risk of pleading not guilty and being convicted of attempted murder. Besides, I *was* guilty. It was no one else's fault. I was the one who picked up the knife, I was the one who stabbed Arthur, and I was prepared to accept the consequences of my actions without implicating anyone else.'

Pomona looks at me consideringly for a moment, then takes her pen and puts it into her bag. 'This concludes our last session,' she says. 'Thank you for your persistence in this endeavour. I hope that you have found our time together helpful. I will soon be making my report to the superiors of this establishment. Whatever happens, I wish you well.'

'Thank you,' I say, holding out my hand. She puts on her gloves and shakes my hand, takes the key from her coat pocket and deposits it on the table, opens the French windows and walks through them for the last time.

'Well, that's it,' I say to Rowse as I lock the French windows and give her the key. 'Pomona holds all the cards. Let's see how she chooses to deal them.'

All the cards indeed! What Pomona does not know is that she has been dealt cards from a stacked deck, and I still hold all the aces.

Poor Arthur – it was my hubris that did for me, and for him as well. I could not let him get away with having another woman, another child, another life, all the things we could have had if he had chosen to stay with me; and I was so confident of my plan that I did not envisage it could fail.

I cannot solely blame him for the abortion. I should have insisted on keeping the child, insisted that he marry me or at least provide for the child; but I had been forced to rely on no one save myself for so long that dependence was an anathema to me. It is a pity my child could not rely on me, but that is water under the bridge now. And I was too careless to pay any attention to the possible consequences; I had heard some horror stories of girls bleeding to death or else so mangled inside that they would never again be whole. I do not know if I will ever bear children, but if I do, after the initial necessity, I may decide that it will be without a husband.

Arthur may reason with himself that it was a crime of passion. He is wrong. I was never that passionate about him, not like with Titus. It was a wonder I did not fall many a time with Titus, but I never did, and then a few times with Arthur and Fanny's your auntie. But I really did love Arthur, once upon a time.

Manchester, December 1890

I have not seen Arthur for two weeks, but today I am to pick up the money he has agreed to give me for breach of promise without the faff of any legal proceedings. A friend or relative might have advised that I demand more than he has offered, since it would reflect badly on his moral integrity should it all come out, but in respect of the happy times we had shared, and the dearth of any friends or relatives, I am prepared to accept the seventy-five pounds he has offered. I had wanted to tell him where he could stick his compensation, but the money will set me up well for the future, and luckily my bravado had not descended to the depths of throwing my engagement ring at him like a ranting actress. It is certainly worth a pretty penny and will sell well on the second-hand market; Arthur Smith would never be seen to be scrimping on his fiancée's engagement ring.

He pulls the notes from his wallet, nineteen in all; he must have been to his bank as they are all crisp and smell new and are secured with a paper band. He counts them out in front of me like a client paying a whore. He wants me to sign a receipt for the money, but I am having none of it; if he wishes to avoid a legal case, he will have to dance to my tune.

'It's all there,' he says, pushing the notes towards me and checking his watch for the fourth time. It is the one I had stolen for him as a present for his last birthday.

'Somewhere to be?' I say.

'Work.'

'On a Saturday afternoon?'

'I am very busy,' he says with the practised ease he has recently perfected that will stand him in good stead in his future career. I wonder why I have not noticed it before. He is not dressed for work; he always wears morning coats for the office. I had chosen them for him when we were young and carefree. He said I had an eye for design and he was merely cock-eyed, and we had laughed together because it was true. But today he is dressed in a lounge suit in dark blue. Too casual for work, it is a suit for a saunter through a park followed by an afternoon tea; a suit chosen by a lover.

'A final meal, for old times' sake?' I say, knowing he is a bit of sentimentalist, and there had been good times. He is about to shake his head, but some instinct makes him agree to it.

'Next Friday, I might be able to get away from work a little earlier,' he says.

'Friday it is. It will be our last supper together.'

I take on extra hours all week so that I can have the whole day free for our assignation. I cannot stomach any breakfast and spend the hours before noon drinking copious cups of tea and flitting between dresses, eventually choosing the blue dress that he always said brings out my eyes. After luncheon, when I have only managed a small piece of bread and butter, I walk to the butcher's and greengrocer's to pick up the ingredients for our final meal. I let myself into his rooms; what is it about men and their willingness to dish out keys to anyone? I start to prepare our dinner: I have chosen lamb, his favourite.

When Arthur breezes through the door the lamb is resting, and the vegetables are simmering on the stove. I am by the sink chopping mint for the sauce. Chop, chop, chop, in with the sugar, in with the vinegar. Back in summer this would have been a normal evening for us. He would waltz in and chat about his day and we would eat and then if I was not working, we would perhaps go out to the theatre or music hall if I could persuade him, and then come back to his flat and fall into bed. It was on such days that I was relieved I had no family to insist we be chaperoned. But nothing had ever been normal; it was a charade. We were a couple with a double life to which only one of us was privy. His Estella should be careful lest she ends up discarded like me.

'You look nice in that blue dress and it's a good idea to wear a heavy apron over it, especially if the lamb were to spit. Would you like some wine?' he says, taking a bottle of Bordeaux from the safe and holding it aloft and taking two glasses from the cabinet.

'A cup of tea will suffice. I don't feel like celebrating. But you may have one if you wish.'

He replaces the wine and glasses and starts on the business of boiling the water and reaching to the high shelf for the caddy. 'Tea for me too, then,' he says.

A paring knife is the most accomplished of knives, incorporating versatility and precision in one small implement: good for chopping hard vegetables and mincing herbs. We had many herbs growing in the herb garden on the farm, but it would be the mint that would break out of the confines of the garden, tunnelling underground and popping up between the slabs up to the front door, enticing visitors with its refreshing aroma. According to one of Uncle Herbert's books, mint is named after a home-wrecking nymph; they knew a few things, those Greeks. A final stir and the sauce is ready.

I have to reach up to stab him, even though I am tall for a woman, or so they say. I doubt if he knows what has happened until the pain hits him. But my aim must have been true, as he falls against the cupboard and then face down on the floor, which is fortunate as, if he had fallen on to his back, looking up at me, I might not have been able to continue. He does not cry out; he does not say anything at all. For a moment I am back in my bedroom at Little Meadows and another man is lying on the floor, his blond hair matted with blood. But this is no case of self-defence – well, not in the way any jury would understand. I stab Arthur a few more times in the neck and in both shoulders until the blood starts to flow, bursting through his shirt and dripping underneath his body to form pools on the linoleum beneath. He must be healthy, as the blood is very dark red and has a not-unpleasant odour of mint and metal.

I turn off the gas – I do not want the building to burn down – and leave the keys in his bureau. I do not want to be found in possession of them and if I am interrogated about his attack, I will sob and tell the police I left them with him at our last meeting, and certainly not the day he was assaulted so grievously. I take off my apron, bundle it into my bag, wrap a scarf around my head and tiptoe out. I need not have worried; there is no one around. I don't know who will find him; probably they will miss him at work on Monday and send out a junior to enquire, or perhaps Estella will come round for one of their trysts; I expect she has a key as well. But it matters little for him. I have a spot of blood on my shoe but otherwise my clothes are untouched. I do not go back to my room but walk about a mile and throw the apron into the cut and wait until it sinks beneath the filthy water. The police will not think I have done it: I had bought the ingredients for the meal some miles away, and there is no evidence of blood on any of my clothes.

But the police soon come a-knocking. Two of them, rapping on my door and the neighbours all peeking through their lace curtains. I give them a wave, and wail and weep as befits a broken-hearted fiancée, but the policemen still take me down to the station. I had not bargained for Jimmy, Arthur's nosy neighbour, going round within minutes to investigate the noise of Arthur's fall, and having a rush of blood to the head and taking a hammer to break down Arthur's door when he received no reply. I had not bargained for them being on such friendly terms as for Arthur to have told him that we were to have a last supper; I would have thought he would have wanted to keep that private. They cannot prove I have been at Arthur's flat, and it is Jimmy's word against mine. But why would an assailant turn the gas off? they say; look at your record, they say; why did you take the day off? they say; we can make it stick, they say. It is all circumstantial evidence, but I do not want them digging up everything else and fabricating the rest, so when I go to court I will plead guilty to grievous bodily harm, as I have heard a whisper that the prosecution will then drop the murder charge. Perhaps the authorities have been toying with me all along. But, since the transportations have stopped, a prison sentence is still preferable to losing your life.

Leeds, 5 November 1898

F.A.O. Superintendent Sharp, Doctors and Trustees of Sunnyside Asylum, Leeds

Dear Sirs,

Re: Miss Lily Day, hysteric, due for release
15 December 1898

On the instructions of Superintendent Sharp, I have spent the past eighteen months treating the patient Miss Lily Day. Miss Day was transferred from Strangeways Prison in February of eighteen ninety-two, one year and two months into an eight-year sentence for grievous bodily harm, with a diagnosis of hysteria. I have been assigned the task of not only treating Miss Day for her hysteria but ascertaining if, at the end of the treatment period, she is suitably cured and a candidate for release at the end of her prison term.

When I first encountered Miss Day, I found her to be truculent and unco-operative, but not displaying the usual symptoms attributed to hysteria that she had displayed in prison and in the weeks after her initial admission into this asylum. I wondered at first if her current symptoms were more in keeping with another malady, perhaps melancholia. However, as Miss Day had been diagnosed with hysteria, and not all symptoms manifest in all cases, I have followed Freudian ideas for the treatment of hysteria, now commonly known as 'the talking therapy', rooted in the idea that hysteria is not intrinsic to the female condition but is a consequence of an undiagnosed trauma that must be discovered.

Upon starting her therapy, it became apparent that there have been major traumas in Miss Day's life: she had a strong and I think perhaps unnatural attachment with her father that was severed when she ran away from home at seventeen years old; she had, and continues to have, attachment issues with both her mother and her sisters which I believe stem from jealousy and competition on all sides; her first love interest robbed her and left her destitute; and her second love, who became her fiancé and who was the recipient of her attack, left her for another woman who was carrying his child. It is unclear if her symptoms appeared before this attack and may have contributed to it, or surfaced while she was in prison, there being no mention of hysteria or any other mental abnormality at her trial.

I believe that considerable progress was being made until an incident in February of this year, when Miss Day attacked Matron and had to be restrained. I was prevented from continuing with her therapy for two weeks, but I became aware that the incident had occurred because of Miss Day's reaction to the maltreatment of a fellow patient, a young and exceptionally childlike woman named Elise, and this made me more convinced of the diagnosis of hysteria. Freud proposes that hysteria has a particular trigger, and I believe that the maltreatment of

Elise was a trigger that aroused, perhaps subconsciously, thoughts of a previous trauma in Miss Day. When treatment recommenced, I began to see Miss Day on a more regular basis, and was reassured to see that even when the unfortunate patient Elise passed away, there was no recurrence of the previous reaction. I felt vindicated in my approach to Miss Day's treatment and over the subsequent months she has continued with the talking therapy. She has shown no further symptoms of any nervous condition, nor have there been any further outbursts, and I believe that whatever memory has ailed Miss Day, it no longer holds her in its thrall. Matron reports that Miss Day has been an exemplary worker both in the sewing room and in the gardens, where she now carries out work previously assigned to male patients.

In conclusion, it is my professional opinion that Miss Lily Day has suffered from a classic case of hysteria from which she is now fully recovered. She is extremely unlikely to regress and therefore should be released at the end of her prison term, where she will without doubt reintegrate as a productive member of society.

Yours sincerely,

Pomona Fairchild

CHAPTER TWENTY-SEVEN

It is a bright, frosty afternoon in late November. The frost is a welcome relief from the last few days of warm murkiness that has clung to our clothes and played havoc with the breathing of those in the isolation wards. I am sitting in my little room with Pomona and Matron, who has requested my presence even though my sessions with Pomona are over. There is a knock at the door and Cook trudges in with a trolley on which sits a pot of tea and a pot of coffee and two plates of biscuits: shortbread and, beloved of tall Jones, flapjacks.

When Cook returns to her kitchen, Matron gets up from the table and warms her back and legs on the fire like an uncouth gentleman, remarking on the cosiness of my room. When she re-takes her seat at the table, Pomona pours the coffee. Matron takes a letter from her pocket and places it on the table. The letter is addressed for her attention, but she has not yet opened it. After she has finished her coffee Matron closes one of the curtains to shut out a sliver of sunshine that is obscuring her vision. She picks up the letter and hands it to Pomona.

'It's addressed to you. You should read it first,' says Pomona.

'But you have done the hard graft with Miss Day,' says Matron. 'Shall I open it at my desk and report back to you?'

My arms and legs are all gooseflesh, as Matron's presence and the letter's contents must concern me; I am tempted to grab it from them and open it myself instead of watching them playing this annoying game of Pass the Parcel.

'I think it best if we all know the contents at once,' says Matron.

'As you wish.' Pomona takes a bone-handled paper knife from her carpet bag and slices open the top of the envelope. She extracts the two typewritten pages and begins to read, and as she reads, she shakes her head and says, 'I don't believe it,' before handing it back to Matron. Matron reads the letter, replaces it in its envelope, jerks her head towards the fireplace and the two of them shuffle over to the warmth, where they speak in whispers.

Returning to the table, Pomona says, 'I'm sorry, Lily. That was a letter from the board of the asylum. The gist of the letter is that, despite my recommendations, the board does not think that you are well enough to be released.'

'It's absolutely ridiculous,' says Matron. 'Miss Day – Lily – is a changed woman, and as for the mention of past instances of her unruliness and aggression, she has progressed in leaps and bounds since the beginning of the year. Look what she has achieved in the sewing room and garden and glasshouse.'

'Certainly, and my report said so,' says Pomona, as if she is being accused by Matron of not including all relevant details. 'I am astounded that they rejected my conclusions. In the past, Lily was obviously triggered by certain events, but now she is quite clearly cured of her hysteria.'

'What does all that mean for me?' I say, just to ensure that they know I am still present. I know what it means; I just need to hear the words from one of them.

'I'm afraid it means that you will not be released in December at the end of your jail term. You must stay here until they deem you fit to be released,' says Pomona.

Pomona has misled me, or perhaps she was misled herself. Her opinion of my sanity is just that – a recommendation, not a definitive decision. All that work I did to enable Pomona to reach that decision has been for nothing. But the consequences for her will be merely a blot on her professional record; for me they will be dire.

'But Queenie was released after a trial run at home,' I protest.

'She had been here for decades and was deemed of no harm to anyone.'

'*I* am of no harm to anyone! Will I really be here forever?'

Perhaps after all I do have the gift of foresight and those monochrome days I envisaged all those months ago will come to pass: the only colour in my days will be my garden. If I am not mad now, I have no doubt I will be after a few years, and when once I had stared out of this very window and wanted to stay forever, now I want to smash the glass and burst through it.

'I will not have it!' says Matron, banging her fist on the table and making the cups jump out of their saucers. 'I'm going to find out what on earth those old duffers are talking about.' She stands in front of me, puts her hands on my shoulders, and lifts her face to mine as if in supplication. 'Lily,' she says, 'you must be patient. Do not react to this news and confirm their decision.'

Matron says she will ensure that my work for today is cancelled and walks me back to the ward. Pomona follows us through the asylum and disappears without a backward glance.

I do not see Pomona after that meeting and I miss our talks, even if all that soul-bearing and hand-wringing was futile in the end. I expect she has no further use for me since the end of her assignment here, and that she is out there somewhere raising the hopes of some other idiot. Over the next few days, Matron too avoids eye contact with me as she makes her daily rounds. For all their indignation, neither acts to overturn the board's decision, and my own polite daily requests to see the superintendent fall on deaf ears.

CHAPTER TWENTY-EIGHT

It being the second Sunday of advent, Superintendent Sharp is treating us to a sermon on the peace to be found in the grace of God. He speaks more slowly of late, slurring his words and repeating the same sentence so that each week we are forced to sit on the cold pews for a progressively longer stretch of time. There will be two more of these services in the run-up to the big day, each with its own advent message, but most patients do not mind the services as they are a forerunner to a period of good food, days off work and the eagerly anticipated Christmas meal. I am fidgeting in my seat, eager to return to my garden, my own place of peace in this madhouse, and Flossie glances across and taps her left wrist as if looking at a watch. I mouth 'I know' to her: there are myriad tasks to complete before winter arrives. At eleven o'clock we are released and march across the lawns to set about our work for the day. Most days we are left undisturbed; the gardeners, both workmen and patients, keep to their own parts of the grounds, and the attendants rarely make the journey across the gardens to check up on us.

At one o'clock I summon the girls with a bell, and we gather for tea and sandwiches and to discuss our morning's progress. It is about a third of a mile back to the asylum, and a few weeks ago, what with having to change our muddy boots and clothes before going to the refectory, Matron suggested we take sandwiches with us for luncheon. Cook continues to complain about having to make sandwiches in the morning and so sometimes she gives us scrag-ends of meat on day-old bread, but with a few cups of tea brewed on the recently installed pot-bellied stove, if you close your eyes it is like having a winter picnic. The stove is my favourite addition to the glasshouse; it stands in the corner rumbling away, boiling water and taking the chill out of the air even on the coldest of days.

We are rightly proud of our efforts. In our newly excavated outdoor beds we have grown asparagus and broccoli, including the purple sprouting kind. In the glasshouse, as well as the summer staples of tomatoes and peppers we have sown herbs which flourish all year round; there will be plenty of sage and rosemary for Cook's Christmas stuffing. The season also sees us busy raising winter lettuce in trays on wooden shelves, and we have sown onions and beans for spring planting. In a line along the back wall, the warmest part of the glasshouse, are orange and lemon trees covered in gauze against the frost, which I have managed to grow from pips planted in summer. I have been unable to coax grapes to grow, but the citruses should be in flower next year and one day we might even have fruit.

I am not prone to self-reflection for no good can come of it, but I acknowledge that I have come full circle, that my wanting to escape from the confines of a forced marriage has been replaced by raising vegetables within the confines of twenty gated acres. But there is at least a little of the peace that the superintendent has preached, and a certain amount of autonomy, which is, for now, all that I can cling to.

But there is a setback to our gardening schedule: next week I am to be sent back to the sewing room for two whole weeks to oversee the sewing of silk runners for the Christmas tables at the Grand Hotel, as they were so impressed with our last consignment of napkins. They have given the order to the asylum in the spirit of the season and the board members have been invited for a Christmas Day meal to receive their grateful thanks. I argued that there was still so much work to do outside, but it seems there was no one suitable to take my place; I will give my girls instructions for the weeks I am absent and appoint Flossie supervisor in my stead.

These winter days are short, and we always work up a sweat trying to get the work done before sunset. As the light fades, I send the girls back to the asylum and am packing away my tools when a figure clad in black walks through the mist towards me like a phantom. It is a good thing the girls are not here: they are young and silly enough to imagine that, as we are near to the asylum cemetery, it is the ghost of a poor tormented soul out to wreak revenge on whoever caused their demise. I am not a believer in all that, but I grip the handle of my fork just in case, until out of the mire steps Matron.

'Lily, may we talk?' she says.

'About the silk runners? I know, I have been told,' I say.

'You think I came all the way out here to discuss silk runners? No, I have some news about the board's decision, and I thought I would tell you in private.' She looks out into the garden, but none of my girls is to be seen.

'They will be back in the asylum now,' I say, 'as should I, but if you wish to talk we could go to the glasshouse. We have no lights installed there yet, but it is warm, and I can light a candle.'

'Perfect. Let's sit and talk.'

Inside the glasshouse Matron sits and unwraps herself from her ghoulish shawl, only to put it back on moments later.

'Tea?' I say. 'Warm you up.'

'No, but thank you. I had better just tell you what has transpired in the past two days. Two nights ago, I had a night off and I went for a meal with Dr Dreyfus, a member of the board and an old, old friend of mine. I know you think I am wedded to this place and perhaps I am, but I do escape from time to time.'

'I said the very same thing to Pomona – Dr Fairchild,' I say.

'I have news of Dr Fairchild also, but first your news. Now I know of old that Thomas Dreyfus cannot hold his liquor, so after he had had his port and another and another – you know how these doctors like their drink – I told him that I did not agree with the board's decision on your case and asked him if he had agreed with it. Of course, he couldn't remember you, so I reminded him of your details. He laughed and said he did now recall your case, and he had not agreed with the board's conclusions but had been outvoted. I think he was trying to get into my good books.'

'I'm sure he was trying to get into somewhere,' I say.

'Well, yes, anyway, I asked how they had come to the decision, because I believed you had improved in leaps and bounds since you came to us. He leaned on my shoulder – he was pretty far gone by then – put his finger to his lips and whispered that I must not tell anyone, but the reason they did not release you was not that you were not cured, but that, with your expertise and supervisory skills, you are too much of an unpaid asset to be released.'

I let out a laugh, or a cackle – whatever it is, it sounds mad. The very thing I tried to do to display my sanity has instead got me incarcerated for even longer. Talk about being hoist by your own petard!

Matron, through years of practice, ignores my laugh and says, 'I couldn't believe it, wouldn't believe such a thing, but he swore it was true. I thanked him for the meal and took my leave of him; the state he was in, I have no idea how he got home. That night I couldn't think what to do, as who would believe me? But by morning I had hatched a plan to call their bluff. Yesterday I went to the superintendent, who said he knew nothing of the real reason for the board's decision. I told him that if he did not talk to the board, I have a friend who is a journalist who would be very interested in your story.'

I am impressed, and moved by her efforts on my behalf. 'And what happened?'

'They reviewed your case pretty damn quickly after that, and you, my dear, are to be released! I don't know whether I will still be employed come the new year, but the truth had to come out.'

I was right about her having a streak of deviousness. I want to hug her, and I think she feels the same way, but we keep our distance, and I stick out my right hand, which she shakes vigorously while I continue to thank her. I lock the door of the glasshouse, and we walk in the twilight back to the asylum.

'About Miss Fairchild,' says Matron, 'or should I say Mrs McCloud . . .'

'She is married so soon?'

'I was as shocked as you, but perhaps her husband wanted a short engagement; they do say that people begin to talk if the engagement is too long. She came to see me last week, newly married and off on a skiing honeymoon to St Moritz. She wished you well and said to tell you that she was sorry she could not procure your release. I did ask if she would like to speak with you, but she said that she believed you would not wish to see her. She is taking a break from her career, perhaps starting a family, as she knows it is what her parents and husband desire.'

'She always said she hated the cold,' I say. 'I think she hated the heat as well.'

'I expect love is keeping her warm,' says Matron, and we laugh together at the improbability of it all.

When we reach the asylum, Matron unlocks the front door and holds it open for me and we walk to the ward side by side. 'Tomorrow morning,' she says, 'come to see me in my office. I'm sure you can remember the way. I am so pleased that we can finalise your release details.'

CHAPTER TWENTY-NINE

Last night I saw every hour of the clock pass. After breakfast I walk to Matron's office, and we complete my release paperwork and have our final cup of coffee. Superintendent Sharp is nowhere to be seen. I am to be released after luncheon and, as I have no family, the asylum will delve into their coffers and provide me with a bag of coppers for my omnibus or train fare and one week's lodgings. Whether I will end up in the workhouse by the end of the month is not their concern.

I have only the clothes I brought in with me; no doubt the garments will hang off me, even if the moths have not eaten them. I loiter on the ward, since I have no work to do, and start to read the novel that Matron has given me this morning. It is *Dracula*; her book choices do veer towards the macabre.

The ward clock has surely malfunctioned, as it is taking an eternity to reach lunchtime. I cannot sit and wait, and as Matron has allowed me to wander where I wish within the asylum grounds I decide to visit my garden for the last time. There is not much growing outside now save for some sprouts and broccoli, but there is still muck to be dug in, so that by spring it will be thriving again. I shall be sad to leave it, but I have at least left a legacy, something to mark my almost seven years of incarceration here. I have no friends on the ward since Elise's demise and Queenie's departure, but I say my goodbyes to my garden girls, who vouch to continue my good work and will no doubt fight among themselves as to who will take charge of my glasshouse and garden. I wonder if Matron will let them carry on without me, but that is not my problem now.

I return to the asylum and sit at the end of my bed. Rowse walks over; she is herself leaving next month to take up a clerical job in Manchester. I knew she would not last long here. O'Neill, my lost lamb, has never returned.

'What happened to Agnes's baby?' I say, giving her the dignity of a first name.

'I didn't realise you knew about that,' says Rowse.

I should be offended that she finds me incapable of listening or observing, but that is the opinion that the staff have of patients throughout the asylum, and so I cannot fault her for her beliefs. 'I see more than you know,' I say.

'I don't know what happened to the baby. All I know is, Agnes went back to Cork. Hopefully not to "the Mad, the Bad, and the Sad" that she talked about.'

'God forbid. Perhaps her mother welcomed her and the baby with open arms.' I do not hold out much hope of this, but say it as a comfort to Rowse.

It is two o'clock when Matron arrives in the ward, carrying two hessian bags for my possessions. I have very few: five books, underclothes, headscarves and my special scarf from Pomona. Matron brings me the clothes that I took with me to prison, which were then transferred to the asylum and which, owing to their near pristine state, survived the usual institutional incineration for fear of lice; they now reek of mothballs; but at least they are well preserved, and over the next week a few sachets of lavender will take away the smell. My black dress is there, and a couple of the dresses I sewed at Hofstein's, but of my posh carpet bag and evening gown purchased all those years ago, there is no sign; I expect one of the prison warders took a fancy to them. I go to the bathroom with my bags, change into one of my hand-sewn dresses and kick my asylum uniform around the wet floor. My belongings now fill a solitary bag. I return to Matron, and we walk together down the ward, with all eyes upon us. As we reach the door to the hall I turn around and wave to a sea of faces all wishing that they too could escape, before I open the hall door and disappear from their view forever.

As we approach the asylum foyer, the smell of pine wafts towards us, for this morning a Christmas tree has been decorated for the coming season. Matron says I can take a few of the edible items off the tree if I wish, so I pull a few gingerbread men and candy canes off the branches and put them into my bag.

As we step out of the front door it begins to snow, slowly at first and then with more determination; by the time we reach the front gate, the drive and trees are already covered in a powdery white veneer.

'Looks like we will have a white Christmas after all,' says Matron.

I turn to look at the asylum; even that looks welcoming with a sprinkling of snow.

'Here,' says Matron, handing me a large paper parcel, which is already sodden and starting to fall apart. Inside is a new coat, woollen, with a fake fur collar. I haul it out and put it on, buttoning it up to my chin. 'Had to guess your size. Don't want you catching your death, do we?' she says.

As no one is looking, I hug her; she does not resist.

'Don't lose yourself in your job,' I say. 'You are not old. Take some time off, see the world.'

'I may do that, as I probably have no job to go back to.'

'The asylum couldn't survive without you. And please make sure my garden girls keep up the good work in my garden and glasshouse.'

'I have all the plans you have left and will give the girls strict instructions to follow them to the letter.'

So she is going to let them carry on gardening. I am relieved my work will not go to ruin.

'I have no doubt that next year they will grow that pineapple you always wanted, and it will sit centre stage at the Grand Hotel Winter Ball,' she says. We laugh and she adds, 'You will be all right, won't you? Do you really have no family?'

'I will be perfectly fine. Tough as old boots.'

'Come back to see me some time.'

'Yes, of course,' I say, although we both know I never will.

She unlocks the front gate, and I step out into the street. The snow has already covered our footsteps. We shake a final goodbye and Matron closes and locks the gate, and through the wrought-iron filigree I watch her diminutive figure with its small, rapid steps until she disappears under a blanket of snowflakes.

I am the sole inhabitant of the street until a lamplighter rounds the corner and starts his daily work, despite its being barely half-past two. I skip past him and shout, 'Merry Christmas!' in my loudest voice, even though there are weeks to go. He does not reply but stares at me spinning round and round with my arms outstretched and my head upturned to the sky as the flakes land on my face, in my open mouth and in my hair; perhaps he thinks I have just escaped. I pull my headscarf out of my bag and wrap it around my head, as my hair is fairly soaked by now and it is a mile into the city centre. I could wait for a tram – it would be a new experience, since they were installed when I was incarcerated, and impending darkness should dictate that I do – but I have decided to flout prudence and walk, because now I can walk anywhere that I please.

The city lies before me, clothed in a cloak of snow. It is dark now and the streetlights are lit and the shop windows blaze with colour. But, today being Monday, the streets are quiet except for a beggar huddled in a doorway with one eye open for the police, and schoolchildren tumbling out of school and grubbing around in the snow, gathering it in their cold red hands to build snowmen or to shape into snowballs to chase each other down the street. I give the beggar a few pennies and he shuffles away, and then I retreat to the safety of a cul-de-sac off the High Street. I find a tea shop and order a pot of breakfast tea and a slice of chocolate cake. The tea shop is empty save for me and one old-timer who is taking hours over one cup of coffee. The waitress must be bored because she is intent on engaging me in conversation about my occupation, and whether I have been Christmas shopping, and have I seen a turn I have never heard of at the Grand Theatre? I am tempted to say I have just been released after years of incarceration, but instead I ask her about reasonably priced hotels in the vicinity. She tears a sheet off the back of her order pad and writes down the names of and directions to four establishments she considers 'clean, reasonably priced, and discreet', whatever that means. I pay the bill and leave the waitress a threepenny bit and go in search of her discreet hotels. At least I can afford one for a few weeks – months if need be – because in the inside breast pocket of my new coat is a five-pound note and a handwritten note attached with the words: *To help you find your new life. M.*

CHAPTER THIRTY

Strangeways Prison, Manchester, January 1892

My new cellmate is snoring like an old boar. I should not have a cellmate at all, but the prison is overcrowded, and the one-inmate-per-cell rule must be broken. Now two of us are crammed into this tiny whitewashed cell with our regulatory prison essentials: a tin bowl; a bible; and a board to lie on. But at least we have a pot to piss in, one each, and both are half-full, their nightly contents mellowing; the sight makes me wish for the time I had the choice of fumbling my way down the garden in the dark when I needed to go. I lean over and poke her twice in the ribs. She turns over, quietens for a few minutes and starts snoring again. My previous cellmate, a tiny red-haired girl from Eccles with impeccable sleeping manners, has been carted off to the seclusion cells and shackled for whittling a knife from laundry tongs and attacking one of the guards, who it is rumoured will be off work for a few months. So, it's out with the old lag and in with the new.

I have progressed past the seclusion stage of my sentence to the silent isolation stage, which means I am allowed to work with the other inmates but cannot talk with any of them. When women are first imprisoned, being locked away and with no human contact save for the guards and the priest is alien to many who since childhood have never slept alone. But solitude has never bothered me much; if I am ever redeemed and called to the faith I will have no problem adapting to a cloistered life. Instead, it is the ever-present menace from the other prisoners that wears you down. And the boredom, that wearies you as well. And the incessant workload.

But now I have a reprieve from work: the prison doctor has declared me unfit for work as I have cracked my ribs when I fell from my bed. It took a few attempts at falling off the board bed but I managed to crack them well enough and now they are bandaged and hurt like hell. But I have now been noticed by the doctors, so when, yesterday morning, I had to be threatened with a straitjacket for kicking the iron door of my cell at four in the morning and waking not only my cellmate but the whole block, it is all noted in my prison record.

It is six o'clock in the morning and the prison is stirring: the landing lights are lit, the warning bell sounds, and the inmates rise from their beds and relieve themselves in their chamber pots ready for the slopping out, awaiting the rising bell that tells them to dress. I have taken my uniform and wrapped it around the bars of the cell window, blocking the little natural light that manages to sneak its way though. Now that the exterior lights are on, I take off my nightwear, rip it as best I can and tie it to the bars, where it dangles like a white flag. I sit on my board in my chemise and drawers even though it's mid-January, waiting for the right time. I have already tipped my cellmate's gazunder over her bed when she was asleep and now the contents are seeping through her blanket, and she has woken and, touching the blanket and sniffing her wet fingers, has realised what befoulment has befallen it, and is swearing at me and calling for the guards. I take my own gazunder and throw the contents at her; this time she screams.

From under my bed, I take the glass that I have eased out of the years-old loose lead of the cell window. I have been teasing the glass out for weeks, bit by bit, in the small hours when my cellmate was asleep, in case she told on me. You cannot rely on honour among thieves any more. This is the difficult bit, the untidy jagged bit over which I have no control: the risk that may see me bleed to death on the floor of my cell, before I am spirited away. My veins are bulging, and the glass is sharp; two determined slices and the deed is done. When the guards barge their way into the cell, my cellmate is still screaming and I am parading down an imaginary avenue with cherry trees in blossom, my arms aloft, blood dripping off my elbows, singing the best rendition of 'Where Did You Get That Hat?' that anyone has ever heard. The last thing I remember as I fall to the floor is one of the guards saying that there is no need for a straitjacket.

I wake in the infirmary, with shackles around my bandaged wrists. I cannot be too damaged if they think I am able to run amok among the patients. I must wait an hour before the doctor makes his rounds. A nurse sticks a thermometer in my mouth and unwraps the bandages on my wrists, tearing off some of the loose skin, ready for the doctor's inspection. The doctor is rough, curt; he is suspicious of my cracked ribs, and the cuts are superficial, and I am ill of my own making, too well for the infirmary, and must be moved to an isolation cell in a straitjacket so that I do not attempt to finish the job. Ten minutes later two guards arrive to envelop me in a straitjacket and take me to the cells; I do not resist. The cell is not padded, a wonderful oversight, and when the guards leave I start to bang my head against the brick wall until the plaster starts to flake and become speckled with red. I am wailing and shouting and wondering how long I will have to keep doing this, hoping that in a few weeks, if my late lamented red-haired cellmate is to be believed, my plan will have worked, and I will have acted mad enough for the prison governor to request that I be sent to an asylum.

EPILOGUE

Nine months later

I have some sympathy for Pomona: all that knowledge and potential and yet compelled to follow her family's wishes, to be tied to her marital home, ankle-deep in children. It will be a comfortable cage, a posh house in Harrogate or Leeds' Roundhay Park, with servants and a nanny and a garden that requires the services of a gardener, but a cage nonetheless. Perhaps when she and her husband are old and grey, and the children have fledged, she might throw off the yoke of her family's expectations, pawn her jewellery, steal away to the Southern States, and take a steamship down the Mississippi with a lover.

I have no expectations and no ties that bind; I can go anywhere, further afield than my smallholding of Welsh scrubland, purchased three weeks after my release from the asylum, which can support only sheep and heather. At the time it was all that I could afford, but it has allowed me to follow my dream of sheep-farming, even during that first winter, when the streams froze and the snow lay four feet thick and my nascent flock had to be dug out of the drifts, and which has turned out to be both as wonderful and remote as I had imagined. Next year I might go to the Antipodes, far away from the cold and the rain, where sheep outnumber people and where a person might feel at home among the convicts.

I am surprised people swallowed my rubbish, but I suppose people will believe what they want to believe. Even right back to when I pretended to have hysteria in prison. Had I known it would turn out to be such a costly gamble I might not have done it; if not for Pomona I might still be in the asylum with my sheep, instead of holed up with my real flocks. If the truth of my supposed recovery ever seeps out, Superintendent Sharp, now fully ensconced in his retirement villa on the coast, will rouse himself from his bath chair and distance himself from the débâcle by claiming he was remiss in giving such an opportunity to an unproven psychiatrist, and to a woman.

I do not think of Arthur and expect he does not think of me, or at least he does his best to forget; we are both scarred by our relationship. But I still think of Titus, poor drowned Titus. It was quite romantic in a doomed, poetic sort of way, his beautiful face disappearing beneath the water, never to grow old, preserved in my memory for posterity the way he was that day. There will be only bones now; the fish will have eaten his flesh. I saw a notice in *The Times* earlier this year, his mother asking for any information on his whereabouts. I wonder if Henry has passed away. They had not started looking for Titus until the new year; I got a visit from the police but there was never anything to connect me to his disappearance, and besides, had I not been the one to report him missing? Augusta says she has never given up hope of finding her only son. Poor Augusta; perhaps I should write and tell her where his body lies. Anonymously, of course.

I have a new friend, John, a farmer, and a widower of some twelve years. We met at chapel, which is the only form of amusement around here. We have known each other barely four months so I cannot say if anything will blossom, or even if I wish it to, but he has helped me with my lambing, and I have cooked him a few dinners. He is two inches shorter than me and has a ruddy complexion and the beginnings of a stoop and possesses that curious mixture of rigid stoicism and weatherworn arthritic bones that could snap like a twig under the slightest pressure; but I have grown bored of tall, handsome men. I have not told him of my past and he has not asked. Nor have I asked about his; it's better that way for both of us. His home is a fine five-bedroomed farmhouse of sturdy Welsh stone, but he has only sons, all with their own homes and families, and it is lacking a woman's touch, or that is what he tells me.

Next year will herald the beginning of a new century and Britons will venture forth into the unknown as Edwardians, for our current sovereign is on her last legs and can surely only reign for a few years more. I choose to look forward to the twentieth century with hope for my future rather than with the pessimism of the *fin-de-siècle* doom-mongers, despite the books that Matron has drip-fed me. I have not been back to see her. I have a ridiculous feeling that I would be grabbed and sucked back into the asylum and that this time she would be unable to save me. In the end, Matron turned out to be the best friend I could have wished for. I had no qualms about duping Pomona, but I feel guilty about deceiving Matron; our friendship was true, truer than the friendship of my unfaithful sisters, even if I will never know her real name.

Two weeks ago John and I went to the Shrewsbury Flower Show, which was a bit of a trek to Aberystwyth and then a couple of hours on the train, but it promised to be a good day out; it's one of the highlights of the farming year, attracting crowds from Shropshire, Wales and beyond. The previous week I had been to Aberystwyth and begrudgingly bought myself a new outfit and to complement it had chosen a hat with a very large veil, for I still live in fear of being recognised, even though it is almost eleven years ago. We travelled first class both ways; only the best for me, says John. There was always a chance that I might see my sisters, but I convinced myself that, with my disguise and the large crowds that were expected, we could easily lose ourselves in the throng.

I saw Honesty first. She had put on a bit of weight but that was to be expected with the five young children she was trying and failing to stop running in and out of the stalls. Another child, older, as tall and blonde as her, hung by her side. I should have realised she would remarry; she was always the marrying sort. Next to her was Prudence, hanging on to Fred's arm as if he might run away. Then, walking up to them with two glasses of cider between the fingers of each hand was a man whom I presumed to be Honesty's new husband. But when he turned to dole out the glasses, I was shocked to discover it was Percy. Not dead, not scarred, not all lopsided and slurring his speech, but the same old Percy, holding forth, gesticulating, dominating the conversation. I thought I saw Fred look the other way in amusement; but Fred can't help but look the other way. I had been carrying the dread of detection for years, moved cities because of it, and all for nothing.

John asked if I would like his jacket and for him to find me a chair, as I had turned white and was shivering despite the August sunshine. I thought then about telling him, admitting that these people were my long-lost family, even though, by omission, I have given him the impression that I have none. I would introduce him to them and they, of course, would ask after children and I in turn would ask if our parents and the rest of our sisters were still with us. There might have been a moment of confusion with my change of name, but I would brush it off with an excuse about wanting a new start; I expect they would all have believed it. But the moment had gone; they must have moved into one of the tents. It was probably for the best; if I had made myself known to them, I could still have faced a charge of assault or worse. Or perhaps they would have forgiven me and, having gagged Percy with the promise of some of my father's better fields, would have rushed to throw their arms around me, brimming with questions, grateful that I was not dead. I couldn't take the chance. I had done without them for almost eleven years, and they had done without me. It was better to let it rest and to feign being overcome with the heat and request if we could catch an earlier train; John, itchy in his best suit, was only too grateful to get back to his flock.

John is coming over for a meal tonight when he has finished seeing to his sheep. It's beginning to be a weekly occurrence and tonight I am cooking his favourite: steak and kidney pie with field mushrooms, nature's bounty, foraged from the fields at daybreak, although you have to know which fungi to pick. He has been bilious of late and is looking gaunt and green around the gills; and so, this month I have been trying to feed him up. Last week he ceded me four of his fields, saying that I would need them more than he did if I intended to increase my flock. I had protested, asking what his sons would think, but he said that if his sons were that worried they should visit him more often. Despite our short acquaintance, I expect a proposal will be coming soon and I will have my Christmas wedding after all. It will be a quiet affair as neither of us is in the first flush of youth and I will wear a simple white dress which in the run-up to the ceremony will take pride of place in my wardrobe. In the very back of the wardrobe is a black dress, a remnant of my flight of all those years ago, which will no doubt be called into use early in the new century.

ACKNOWLEDGEMENTS

I would like to express my deepest gratitude to my sons Edward and Oliver for their unwavering support during the writing of this book.

Special thanks my agent, Hannah, for her guidance and belief in my abilities, and to the editing team at Sphere for their judicious feedback and perseverance in the shaping of this manuscript. Thanks also to Elizabeth Wakou for a wonderful cover design that has brought the character of Lily to life.

Sincere thanks to Chelmarsh Book Club for their monthly support and interest in my progress, and to Joanna, who had the dubious pleasure of reading the first unfiltered chapters.

Finally, to my readers – I hope you had as much pleasure wondering where Lily's journey would take her as I did.

RAISING READERS
Books Build Bright Futures

Dear Reader,

We'd love your attention for one more page to tell you about the crisis in children's reading, and what we can all do.

Studies have shown that reading for fun is the **single biggest predictor of a child's future life chances** – more than family circumstance, parents' educational background or income. It improves academic results, mental health, wealth, communication skills, ambition and happiness.[1]

The number of children reading for fun is in rapid decline. Young people have a lot of competition for their time. In 2024, 1 in 10 children and young people in the UK aged 5 to 18 did not own a single book at home.[2]

Hachette works extensively with schools, libraries and literacy charities, but here are some ways we can all raise more readers:

- Reading to children for just 10 minutes a day makes a difference
- Don't give up if children aren't regular readers – there will be books for them!
- Visit bookshops and libraries to get recommendations
- Encourage them to listen to audiobooks
- Support school libraries
- Give books as gifts

There's a lot more information about how to encourage children to read on our website: **www.RaisingReaders.co.uk**

Thank you for reading.

hachette UK

---

[1] National Literacy Trust, Book Ownership in 2024, November 2024
https://nlt.cdn.ngo/media/documents/Book_ownership_in_2024

[2] OECD. 2021. 21st-century readers: developing literacy skills in a digital world. Paris, France: OECD Publishing.
https://www.oecd.org/en/publications/21st-century-readers_a83d84cb-en.html